NANOTIME

"Fast, authoritative, street-savvy,
and altogether too plausible—this is
a power read for the next millennium."
Gregory Benford, Nebula Award-winning
author of *COSM*

"*Nanotime* locks you in cyberspace and never
slows down. You'll never look at computers, war,
or even the future the same way again."
Richard Herman, author of *Power Curve*

"An exciting near-future thriller . . . a terrific
piece of futurist extrapolation .·. . chock full
of ideas about the social and technological
implications of oil, population, philosophy
and artificial intelligence."
SFREVU (on-line)

"Life on earth as we know it (only much, much
cooler) . . . Kosko spices up his novel with a
gaudy array of new technologies, from artificial
wombs that can tailor a fetus's genes
at its parents' whim to miniature computers
able to replace a human brain."
Publishers Weekly

"Bart Kosko is a wonderful futurist
with a polymathic combination of talents."
Professor Marvin Minsky, M.I.T.

NANOTiMe

BART KOSKO

AVON BOOKS  NEW YORK

AVON BOOKS, INC.
1350 Avenue of the Americas
New York, New York 10019

Copyright © 1997 by Bart Kosko
Inside cover author photo by David Floray
Map by Hilda R. Muinos
Visit our website at http://www.AvonBooks.com
Library of Congress Catalog Card Number: 97-5665
ISBN: 0-380-79147-1

First Avon Books Paperback Printing: September 1998
First Avon Books Hardcover Printing: November 1997

AVON TRADEMARK REG. U.S. PAT. OFF. AND IN OTHER COUNTRIES, MARCA REGISTRADA, HECHO EN U.S.A.

Printed in the U.S.A.

WCD 10 9 8 7 6 5 4 3 2 1

For the whirling dervishes
and their ecstatic search for the light

*Between the mirror and the heart
is this single difference:
the heart conceals secrets
while the mirror does not.*

Jalāl-ud-Dīn ar-Rūmi
(1207–1273)

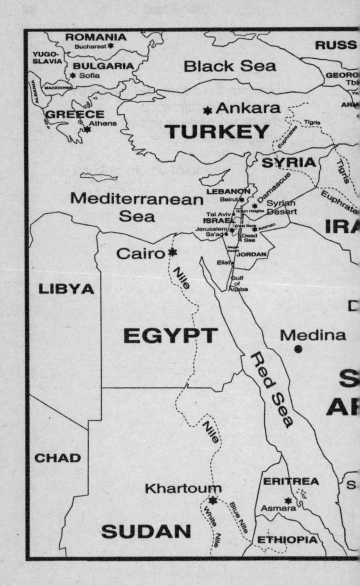

NANOTiMe

*T*he year is 2030. There are 10 billion people on earth. In 1990 there were a trillion barrels of oil left in the ground and the world burned 24 billion barrels of it a year. Now there are fewer than 100 billion barrels left. Much of that oil will be gone in five years and will require massive deep-earth and offshore drilling. Countries in the Middle East now own about 85% of the world's oil reserves.

Oil profits have reached new highs even as oil efficiency has reached new levels. Gas is $20 a gallon in 1990 dollars but gas cars can get 100 miles to the gallon. Most cars in Europe and Japan run on superconducting batteries. Most of the world's electricity still comes from ever scarcer fossil fuels and uranium. And most Western governments have long since defaulted on their national debts.

The amount of information in the world has doubled every year or two since the late 1990s. One second of computing time on the linked computer nets of 2030 involves more CPU cycles than all the CPU cycles in all the computers running in the year 2000. These vast machines compute with electrons and pho-

tons and plasma but still need power to run. Oil provides most of that power.

The oil can run out but the factories and information machines must not stop. The search for alternate fuels is the gold rush of the age. And the age is the End of Oil.

CHAPTER 1

Dhahran
Saudi Arabia

The sun set red on the dusty oil fields of Dhahran. The young man walked from the fleet of oil tankers floating in the oily green waters of the Persian Gulf. He walked next to the fresh black asphalt road and then took a dust path up the rocky hillside and into the red Saudi sunset. Adu wore blue jeans and a black tank top and a white head wrap stained with sweat. Over his back he carried an old woven bag. Adu looked straight at the red sun and did not squint.

The dust trail led to the control station. Adu had walked this trail hundreds of times to bring his father oranges and figs and outlawed plum brandy. He liked to sit with the old man and seek his counsel on Allah and women and hear his tales of the old ways and the old wars with Iraq and Egypt.

The pump station was a large mirrored box in the forest of steel oil derricks. A lone satellite dish sat on its black-pebble roof and now the dish too shined red in the sunset. The eye could miss the mirrored box in the day. The Saudis hoped the mirrors would also fool the fine eye of a smart cruise missile.

Adu stood before the seamless plastic door. His fa-

3

ther had told him as a boy to say "open sesame"
three times to himself and the door would open. He
stood still now and waited and once more the door
slid open. He felt the cool air spill out and heard the
wild rhythms of the synthesized Arabic rock music.

Adu walked in and nodded to the two guards behind the black security desk and heard the music
change. The guards had tuned the music to match
their moods. The music slowed and softened when
they looked up at Adu. Then the music returned to its
former volume and driving rhythm.

The two guards nodded to him.

He walked past the guards and could see their
hands fondle a flat gray panel. A small nude blond
Playmate danced and screamed in the air above the
panel. She was a blue-laser holograph from the new
issue of *Playboy*. Adu smiled at their mischief as he
stood at the next door and punched in the prime-
number code on the cipher lock.

Adu found his father in the silent control room. The
old man watched the green display panels that showed
each oil drill cutting through clay and bedrock. Brown
panels showed the oil volume of the capped wells and
their current market value in dollars and marks and
yen. The old man held his left eye in a tight squint
and still wore the khaki pants that Adu had bought
for him last year on his weekend vacation in Abu
Dhabi.

The old man stood when he saw his son. Adu
bowed slightly and gave him the woven bag. The old
man smiled and reached in the bag and pulled out the
largest of the three oranges. He held the large orange
under his nose and rolled it in his fingers. Then he
squinted both eyes closed to savor its citrus smell.

Adu spun and struck the old man with a perfect backfist.

Adu's first two knuckles crushed the old man's right temple and ruptured his brain. The old man died on impact with his eyes still closed. His corpse slammed against the brown display panel and bounced to the floor.

Adu turned to the computer console and tore off his white head wrap. His scalp was bald and criss-crossed with fresh thin pink scars. Adu closed his eyes and bowed his bald head to the console.

Hundreds of wireless signals filled his mind's eye. They were the same signals that the antenna dish on the roof saw. The first signals appeared as snow or static spread over wide bands of frequencies. The snow bands passed through one another in complex schemes of multiplexing.

Adu willed his own wireless commands to access the computer and use its bank of decoders to despread and filter the signals. Then the snowstorm gave way to a parallel montage of sound and images: news broadcasts of sex scandals and plane crashes and African famines. Interactive lottery drawings and bouts of casino gambling. Nature programs of ocean poisonings and new deserts. Sports programs from soccer to group bungee jumping and killer kick-boxing. Televangelists who preached modern versions of the Semitic religions. Soft-core and hard-core porn among all the races. Old movies and videos from the 20th century. Weather and smog maps of the Middle East. Hundreds of pie charts and poll results from hundreds of millions of on-line voters in the Middle East and around the world.

The montage thinned to a single news broadcast in Arabic from Riyadh.

Adu touched the HELP button on the new computer console. A small infrared light flashed on the console. It flooded Adu's mind with a fresh montage: dish and satellite schematic diagrams. Equations of orbital mechanics and telemetry and computer data flow. Circuit diagrams and help files on how the control room worked.

Adu solved the equations to find the angle to the geosynchronous Saudi satellite that carried the news broadcast. His fingers moved over the satellite-dish panel faster than the human eye could follow.

The parabolic antenna dish on the roof moved to point its center wave-guide stalk at the Saudi satellite in orbit over 22,000 miles above it. The government workers had programmed the antenna to receive signals from over 100 satellites. Now its smart control logic damped down the overshoot and undershoot in its movements and zeroed in on the new target.

The slight motion tripped a motion sensor on the roof. An alarm shrieked at the front desk and a video image of the moving dish flashed on the wall behind the two guards. The music stopped when they jumped to their feet. The nude Playmate still danced before them.

Adu stood straight and closed his eyes and went to nanotime.

The guards slowed to a stop as they ran for the door of the control room. The alarm slowed to chirps. The dancing Playmate slowed to a sequence of still holographs. Adu checked the settings once more and then counted down from three to one.

Three.

The guards had frozen fully in neural time. Only the small energy pulses of 1s and 0s moved through the air and through fiber-optic cables and through chips made of sand and light and solid geometry.

Now came the test of thousands of man-hours of planning and stealing and building and the final crushing with diamond anvils. All would depend on how well the real world matched the average of millions of software simulations.

Two.

Adu's chip brain flashed in tiny pulses of blue light. The blue pulses grew in brightness and defined a fractal code. The green wax in Adu's thin gold skull moved and then melted to form a bubbling liquid. Its atoms of francium and uranium thawed and mixed. The green bubbles were the last thing the chip sensed.

One.

The unstable francium atoms that surrounded Adu's melting chip brain gave up a great deal of their energy and set off the neutron chain reaction. The smart nanobomb had reached its own small critical mass.

A nuclear blast lit the Dhahran evening.

The blast liquefied the main Dhahran oil field that then froze as a small crater in the desert. The pressure wave smashed the oil tankers and knocked them far out to sea in large orange plumes of burning oil. The pressure wave also leveled the nearby slums and stores that the fireball had not melted. Uncapped oil wells burned along with the twisted remains of the oil refinery and its large cylindrical storage tanks. Oil spray burned on the desert sand and rocks and on the surface of the Persian Gulf. Processed oil burned in the asphalt of the new network of roads.

The antenna dish on the roof sent one great white impulse of energy as it blew apart. In less than a second the energy impulse had hit the Saudi satellite in high-earth orbit. The onboard signal-processing chips could not cancel impulsive noise of this magnitude.

Much of the fine nanocircuitry overloaded and burned as if a gust of raw solar wind had swept through it. The satellite shook in fine elastic vibrations and then tumbled slowly in chaotic instability.

Dhahran blinked on and then off as a small white light on the blue sphere of the earth.

::::■ CHAPTER 2

The Hoover Dam
Boulder City
Nevada

John Grant bit down on a gingersnap as he walked across the border to his Jeep. The dry brown cookie had no sugar or fat or calories. Its spicy taste masked the enzymes that killed the bacteria on his teeth and gums. John did not like fake junk food but he liked to chew something after he gave a talk. The hard brown disks of fiber were the only kind of cookies the government sold at the Hoover Dam.

"Why did you park on the Arizona side?" Ramachandra said. "I thought you disliked Arizona."

"Not at all," John said. "I love the land but not the taxes. I still don't know why those old boomers want to go there to cash in what's left of their nest eggs and then die. They would net more on the Nevada side of the border. Shit. Both sides have the same housing tracts and golf courses and burial plots."

"I confess that my wife and I chose to live on the Nevada side because Nevada has no state income tax."

"Ram. It's all right. You don't have to confess.

You can just say you don't want to pay a state income tax. No one will record it.''

"Are you sure?'' Ramachandra said with just a trace of a British accent.

Both young men laughed at that. They knew what they said here in public would be on file for at least two years. Their images would stay on tape for at least a year.

They walked over to the lake side of the nearly 100-year-old dam and stopped at the guardrail.

John preferred the lake side of the dam to the river side. He always felt an animal fear of falling when he walked on the river side and looked down or even glanced down out the corner of his eye. The dam's steep sweeping wall of concrete converged in perspective like a pair of railroad tracks and ended in the violent white waters of the Colorado River. The lake side was calm and made him feel as if he flew over a virtual image of a still turquoise lake with bare desert mountain walls made of scooped chocolate ice cream.

John fought these feelings and tried to see the lake as just a vast store of energy.

The wind blew John's short black hair over his forehead and blew Ramachandra's red tie back around his high white collar. Ramachandra was thin and a year younger than John and much darker from the desert sun. The two men stood still and watched the tiny specks move on the lake and in the distant parking lots.

A loud chopping sound cut the air.

The morning's sun's glare on the blue water made John squint when he looked up at the two silver tour helicopters from Las Vegas and the faces that looked down at the lake and at him through the smoked glass.

The helicopters hovered and then crossed the dam to follow the Colorado River down the other side.

John also looked down at the bright blue water of Lake Mead in front of him and at the tiny white frothing swirls of the jet-skiers and water-skiers and the paddle-wheel boats. He had to squint again to make out the antlike family members in orange vests who climbed out of their jumbo tour raft well above the Nevada spillway.

"Smell that oil," John said.

"Yes. Americans still drink it like beer."

"Let 'em drink. The faster we burn up the oil the more I like it. That's true here of these sun seekers. And it's true of the humble folks and their new cars and refrigerators and air conditioners in your home town of Madras."

"Bangalore."

"Really?" John said. "Then my agent is not as smart as he thinks he is. I thought he had your Indian resume on file."

"Please give him my regards."

"You just did."

John pulled one of the brown gingersnaps from its stack in the tight paper roll. He started to bite the dry cookie but then flicked his wrist and spun the gingersnap out over the dam. They saw the brown disk curve out in the wind toward the water. They did not see it fall back against the dam and bounce down into the water.

"John. Please. They've got that on tape. I'll tell them you were feeding the gulls."

John shook his head and smiled and turned halfway to the two large intake towers on his left. The two towers seemed to rise from the lake floor. Franklin D. Roosevelt's workers had long ago blasted out their bases from the steep sides of Black Canyon.

"Stop worrying," he said. "And forget the seagulls. Just tell them to pay me on time for once. You bastards hear me? Check that on your records. You might also tell them to stock a better gingersnap. How hard can that be? They spend hundreds of millions of dollars on this security system to analyze our speech and make sure no one spits in the water. Christ. How can you work here with no privacy?"

"It is easy to get used to what you have never had. And do not worry. For next week's demo we will fly in gingersnaps for you from London."

"Ram. Bless you. You're a model civil servant. I just hope the live demo works this time."

"I have every confidence in you and Richard."

"Bless you again," John said as he pulled a spiky green rubber ball from his pants pocket. "Someday soon I hope to retire from this work and become a true gentleman of fortune. When I do, be sure to remind me to hire you away from the feds."

"You are very gracious. But I hope you are not going to throw that rubber model into the water as well."

John tossed and caught the green ball in his right hand and squeezed it.

"If only it were that easy," he said. "Just throw this green seed in that big goddamn puddle and let the sunlight put it to work. Then watch all that cold sky-blue water turn to liquid gold. Just think what you could do with something like that. And think what these happy boaters and tourists would be willing to do to get it."

"I am content to just drink the water."

::::::: CHAPTER 3

Riyadh
Saudi Arabia

The pressure wave hit the Saudi Air Command in Riyadh as a soft thunderclap and a gentle rustle of palm fronds. Commander Haddad watched the expanding black wave approach the command bunker on the green wall map. He knew the wave had lost most of its energy but he still had to force himself not to wince when it hit the bunker.

The 12 men in the control room cheered both in relief and in defiance when the shock wave rolled past them and moved on to further dissipate over the desert on its way to Mecca. Haddad held up his fist in support. Young Omar Salala sat at his control console and nodded to Haddad.

The loss of the satellite had blinded the staff's view of Dhahran and had punched a hole in their early warning system. The dying satellite had sent a death-status message to Riyadh and to the three closest defense satellites in the equatorial orbit. The satellite had taken less than a second to send the death-status message. In seconds the three Saudi defense satellites had retasked themselves and Dhahran was back in their

13

full view. The early warning system returned to full
function in less than a minute.

The satellite strike had no tactical effect on the Saudi defenses. The Saudis lost at least a satellite each
decade when their craft crossed paths with some of
the orbiting fine space debris of past space missions.

Saudi Arabia would have to pay almost a billion
dollars to launch and tune a new satellite to take the
place of the burned one. That would cost but a frac-
tion of the state's yearly oil profits. The Peace Shield
that Hughes Aircraft had helped them build had at
times cost almost 5% of the yearly oil profit. The
Peace Shield had once again helped pay for itself. In
a few more minutes other Saudi TV satellites would
retask themselves and restore the commercial broadcasting to the few homes and offices that had just
lost it.

Haddad knew the loss of the satellite was either a
fluke side effect of the blast or a symbolic act of terrorists. He felt it was the latter. Blinding a satellite
with a blast had played a part in both the popular and
classified works on terrorist techniques since the end
of the 20th century. It was a clear message that few
could send. Terrorists had tried to send it but had
failed during the great economic booms in India and
Siberia. That had been more than a decade before.

Now a blank red screen flashed in front of Haddad.

He palmed the gray command pad to confirm his
ID and to confirm that he had received the NATO
prompt. The gray pseudo-image of a unisex NATO
dispatcher appeared. It confirmed Haddad's ID and
then gave him a brief message that the NATO commander had just approved. NATO AWAC jets and
satellites had confirmed that a small nanonuclear device just blew up in the Dhahran oil fields. The NATO

crisis manager put the odds at over 80% that terrorists had set off the bomb. The message ran in Arabic and then in English. The red screen blinked off.

A new blue screen broke into windows.

On the first window Iranian Air Defense confirmed the explosion in Dhahran and lack of casualties in Iran. The other windows ran the same message from Turkey and the Sudan and from Saudi Arabia's other Arab neighbors. The new radical Islamic state of Egypt sent no message. Omar Salala spoke into his headset to confirm Egypt's null response.

Commander Haddad brought up the royal screen to King Fahd in his Riyadh palace just as the monarch had started to call him. The royal screen set off a noise barrier between Haddad and his staff. The staff could see Haddad only as a blurry mirage. They could not see the monarch or hear either man speak.

Haddad had to choose his words with care. His critics would review this secret session in the days to come. The House of Fahd held over 10,000 kinsmen. All would have something to say about what their air commander did to avenge the Dhahran attack. The king's advisors would also have their say and that was what Haddad feared most.

The king drew most of his advisors from the Sunni *matawwa* religious police. The *matawwa* had sworn to end the regimes of the Shiite radicals in the Sudan and Egypt. They used spies and torture to root out the Sunni radical groups that had formed among the poor and the young in the Saudi empire. The *matawwa* still wanted blood revenge for the Shiite hackers who had once again stolen over a billion dollars from the Bank of Saudi Arabia.

Haddad stood straight with his chest out just as they had taught him to stand at pilot school. He clenched his jaw to keep his face calm and his neck rigid. The smallest mistake now in what he said or did not say could cost him at least his rank. Fahd never let him forget that the king could replace him at will and without cause.

"Haddad!" the monarch said. "Was it a bomb or a missile?"

"Your excellency. It was a bomb. We found no missile track."

"Why not a stealth bomb from Iran?"

"We are at least 95% confident it was not a stealth bomb. We would have seen part of the heat track. NATO is at least 80% confident that terrorists set off a small nanonuclear bomb in our Dhahran oil fields. I agree. The blast blinded one of our TV satellites for a moment. That is a classic terrorist signature that goes back to the 1990s."

"Then what does it mean?"

"It means they can spit in our eye."

"How many killed?"

"We do not yet have hard estimates. But it must be in the many thousands for a city of that size."

"And the royal oil fields?"

"The blast seems to have destroyed the fields and our refinery. We also think it destroyed or at least damaged all the tankers in the harbor."

"Who did this?" Fahd said without moving his head or his watery eyes.

"I believe the Green terrorists did it."

"Why? The Shiites have threatened our oil since I was a boy."

"That is true. But all know this and Iran would face war. This was not an act of infowar. The Greens have sabotaged at least three oil sites in Siberia and

Texas in the last year. We also have the intelligence report I sent you last month.''

"The American CIA report?''

"Yes. The CIA and the National Reconnaissance Office. With help from the Greeks and the Israelis. The report said the Greens in Paris and in Eilat have discussed cutting our optical fiber cables in the Indian Ocean and blinding our communication satellites. The Dhahran blast looks like this kind of information harassment.''

"Commander Haddad. The people demand vengeance!''

"Yes, your excellency.''

"Then tell me. What do you propose?''

"At minimum we can demand that France and Israel make good all damages. They harbor these Green terrorists.''

"As you say that is a minimum. It is not enough. And it is not your place to decide such a political issue.''

"Your excellency. I did not mean to—''

"Do not interrupt. We must respond at once and set a clear example for the world. No one must doubt the resolve of the Saudi people! What contingency plan did you prepare?''

Haddad paused to reflect on just how grave his plight had become.

Weakness now could mean prison or the sword later. The *matawwa* did not like him or trust him because he had studied aerospace engineering in the godless halls of MIT. The West had soiled him with its Coca-Cola and rock music and feminist politics. The older *matawwa* also did not approve of a commander who was only 46 years old. They wore white head wraps and he wore a green cap or no cap at all.

Haddad's judgment told him to err on the side of peace and wait for more data. But his political judgment told him to err on the side of strength. The old Fahd and his rare strain of syphilis could always deny his strike request.

"We can launch a smart strike from El Haql," Haddad said.

"Against Eilat?"

"Yes. We can launch against the desalination plant in Eilat. The Israelis own it but the Greens run it."

"I know that," Fahd said. "I have considered this option. Tell me the numbers. How many will it kill?"

"A spot strike should kill most of those in the main building and kill or wound those within 50 meters of it. There should be about 200 to 300 dead. There may be more than twice that number wounded. We have six cruise missiles programmed for that strike sitting in El Haql right now. At least three should make it through Israeli air defense."

"You are sure?"

"Your excellency, we are dealing in compound probabilities. But yes. It is more likely than not that three of the six missiles will strike the target. There is a better than 90% chance that at least one missile will strike the desalination plant and that is all it takes."

"But the plant is on the Red Sea. What of the tourists there?"

"They will live to tell quite a story."

King Fahd almost smiled but let his face go blank again. He pinched his trimmed black beard and still stared at Haddad with his watery eyes.

"Commander Haddad, give me a good military reason why we should risk killing so many innocent civilians. Even the Israelis may be innocent of this attack.''

Haddad paused once more. The king had with that remark just laid the blame on him for the counterattack. Fahd would claim credit for the strike if it worked and blame Haddad if it failed. The *matawwa* would have the king remove him if he now backed down from the pending violence. That was how power filtered the weak from the strong.

''Deterrence,'' Haddad said. ''A fast counterstrike will deter these types of guerrilla attacks in the future. Killing innocents in such a matter will only show our enemies our resolve.''

''I see,'' Fahd said. ''So why not cut off the hand of the shepherd after the thief has run off with one of his goats? Would that not deter other thieves?''

''It would deter them if they believed the shepherd was a thief.''

''So you think the world will believe that the Israeli Greens are guilty of this?''

''Your excellency, I am a soldier. I do not presume to know the many political facets of such a question. But I believe the military answer to it is yes. The world will see that we swiftly respond to force with force against even a probable aggressor.''

''Very well. Give the launch command. Now.''

The screen and noise wall dissolved as Haddad nodded his assent. Fahd would watch the missile flight paths on his own war room screen with advisors that Haddad would never meet.

Both Fahd and Haddad knew they had answered the most important question without having asked it: *Should they first tell the Americans?* The security bureaucracy of nations was a bureaucracy like any other.

It was larger than most but it still acted like a bureaucracy.

So it would grant forgiveness far more quickly than it would grant permission.

CHAPTER 4

Eilat
Israel

"Jesus. Look at this," Alon said. "It looks nuclear."

Dr. Alon Gorenberg wore a green T-shirt and blue jeans and stood before a small old-style pocket TV that he had brought into the desalination plant and placed on his lab desk. Someone had once told him that there was a plant rule against bringing in TVs and radios and even cellular phones. No one seemed to obey the rule.

Still Alon hid the pocket TV in his desk drawer before he went home at night. He was putting the TV away when he turned it on and saw the Dhahran news flash and then the satellite images of the blast. The lab post-docs had already left for the day. He and the new programmer, Jackie, were the only ones left in the crowded optics lab.

"You can bet they will blame it on the Jews," Jackie Zukor said. "I'm going home. I need some sleep. I don't want to hear the bullshit Zionist spin the Saudis will put on this."

Alon pulled a folded plastic bag of black Moroccan hemp from his back pocket and waved it at Jackie.

She understood and smiled. The plant would not conduct its blood and urine tests for almost a month and her off-and-on romance with Alon was now more on than off. She could wait an extra hour to get home.

"Jackie. A lot of people just died. We should see what happened."

"Well I guess you're right. If it is Dhahran then someone might have bombed the oil fields."

"Who knows? They just might think it was a couple of us Greens."

"I could think of a few of your friends. You think the Saudis have a file on us?"

"Wake up," Alon said. "Everyone has a file on us. I've told you that before. You think our bits are secure? Not in the banana grove on your old kibbutz and not here. Privacy died before you were born."

With that he pointed at the old video camera that hung from the ceiling and that faced the room's largest optics table. Alon had left the wideband plastic lasers turned on. The camera moved back and forth to watch the slowly moving red and blue light beams that shined on a small spiny ball of green glass. The spiny ball itself was mostly hollow inside. It served more as the project's logo than as a reaction housing. It had the same shape as the green rubber ball that John Grant had almost thrown into Lake Mead.

Alon and Jackie stood on the other side of the room and well out of the camera's field of view. They knew the camera's control logic cared less about them than it did about the two platinum cubes that also sat on the optics table.

The heavy cubes housed supercooled atoms of rubidium. The lab team could freeze the atoms at will and lock them into a Bose-Einstein condensate. BEC was a truly uniform state of matter where all the quantum matter waves flattened and merged into one wave. Then a clear atomic laser beam formed between the cubes. The plastic lasers fed fine light pulses to the atomic laser while the computer told the atomic laser how to take apart old atoms and sculpt new ones. The atomic laser was a prototype and the lab team had to share it with the Weizmann Institute. Plant security kept it in view at all times.

"If they know so much then they should be smart enough to know we don't have to blow up what we can replace."

"That's the spirit," Alon said as he packed some of the black hemp into a small smokeless pipe he had made from some plastic hose and a brass gas valve. "Put your faith in technology. First they made soft contact lenses with cross-linked polymers. Now we make smart molecules with lasers and math. We'll remake the world even if we don't make it better."

"Then what are we doing here?"

"Better living through molecular engineering. Look at those satellite images. Who do you think did that? You can bet it was a bunch of engineers. Probably molecular engineers just like us."

Alon held the blue-yellow flame of a Bunsen burner to the pipe's small bowl and sucked at the pipe to light the black hemp. It took him a moment to get a lungful of the thin smoke. Jackie sat on the desk edge next to him.

"Well maybe they are just like you," Jackie said and winked. "But if all this atomic-laser stuff really works, then the next nut will have a lot harder time trying to blow up the world's water supply."

Alon nodded as he exhaled and handed the pipe to Jackie. She closed her eyes as she drew on it and hoped that this time the pot would not lead to an anxiety attack.

"Better than that," Alon said. "If this smart water really scales up, then we won't have to waste time and blood trying to swap our Arab sisters more land for peace. We can swap them the Dead Sea."

An alarm turned on and off in loud shrieking pulses.

"My God!" Jackie said. "Did we set off the smoke alarm?"

"Oh shit. It's an air raid. And we have to run all the way back to the main entrance to get to the staircase. This better not be another drill."

Alarms went off in many places in Eilat. The public alarms cleared the diners and sunset watchers on the Eilat beaches. The dive boats called in their divers and snorkelers and headed back to the hotel docks.

Some of the night divers stayed underwater but turned off their dive lights. Their air could last for most of an hour if they stayed out of the deep water. But they risked facing the shock wave from a stray bomb that might fall in the water. And they risked facing a land blast if they did not make it out of the water in time and back to the hotel bomb shelters.

The strike alarms came at the end of a long chain of sensor processing and number crunching. Israeli Air Defense had seen the six Saudi cruise missiles seconds after the missiles had launched and cleared the hills of El Haql and entered Israeli airspace.

The Israelis' "sight" came from fused sensor suites in low-earth orbit and in the air and on the ground. Each sensor suite computed a threat probability for each object it scanned. Then the Air Defense computers in Tel Aviv computed a final threat probability. They based these odds on their own measurements and on the threat probabilities of each sensor suite.

The early warning system used tens of thousands of equations and nanochips. But its logic still rested on the gambling theorem that the Reverend Thomas Bayes first proved near the time of his death in 1761. Bayes showed the best way to change a gambling belief in the face of new facts about the game. Those facts now changed by the microsecond.

But the Saudis also used the reverend's theorem. And they knew how to confound it. Small turbojets fired in spurts on the sides of their missiles to give them a mildly chaotic path like a gnat jerking in the air up and down and from side to side. The Saudis knew the missiles would seek their targets but even they did not know which jittery path the gnats would take.

Israel first launched 10 surface-to-air missiles from the outskirts of Eilat when the six Saudi cruise missiles crossed the border. Each SAM locked on to its own cruise missile. The 10 SAMs had to split into two groups of five when the Arab cruise missiles began their chaotic jiggle. Before this the 10 SAMs had a fighting chance of hitting most of the six cruise missiles. Now they had to do their best to swat just two of the gnats.

Israeli Air Defense Command launched two more swarms of 10 SAMs each. They were for backup and to hunt down strays and cripples.

The first pack of five SAMs missed the lead Saudi missile. The SAMs had to turn now and regroup. That cost too much time. So now they too would fly on as backup and prepare to attack the next volley that the Saudis would never launch. Soon they would run out of fuel and skid to a shearing stop on the Negev Desert floor.

The second pack of five SAMs converged on the lead Saudi missile as it jittered low over the surface of the Red Sea. The first two Israeli missiles missed the gnat and skidded across the Red Sea before they sank. The third SAM blew up when it neared the gnat. The orange and white blast wiped out some of the gnat's skin sensors but did not stop the missile. Then the Saudi missile itself blew up when the last two SAMs closed in on it.

The blast crippled the closest SAM and it spun and crashed into the Red Sea. Israeli command could not reach the missile underwater before it blew up in a frothing white hill that rose up out of the dark sea. The Israeli command net did reach the second missile. It slid safely underwater and shut down and slammed to a stop in a mound of brain coral and tube sponges. The Israelis would winch it out before sunrise.

The Saudis had just traded one attack missile for five Israeli defense missiles. This type of low-kill ratio was unique to the 21st century and due to its cheap smart cruise missiles. They had overturned one of the oldest principles of war.

It now cost less to attack than it cost to defend.

That did not hold for the Greeks who had had to launch a thousand ships to sack Troy. It did not hold for the 20th-century Afghan mountain rebels who had used handheld Stinger missiles and RPGs to shoot down helicopters. The reason was that the circuit density of chips had doubled every two years or so for decades. More and more machine IQ could fit into the nose cone and even the tail fins and skin of cruise missiles.

The cost of cruise missiles fell as their machine IQs rose.

Cruise missiles had cost over $1 million in the early

1990s. The cost had fallen in two decades to just over $10,000, or less than the cost of a new car. The new cruise missiles stored vast databases of terrain and tactics. They retuned one another's mission goals in flight with math schemes that had once filled book stacks in science libraries. Now all countries could buy large stockpiles of cruise missiles. Even a few large firms kept defense SAMs at some of their branches in Africa and Indonesia and Siberia.

And no one could be sure they could shoot down the smart missiles.

The lead Saudi missile jerked in a last spurt of fuel and acceleration. Then it opened into a cloud of hundreds of small bomblets. The carrier missile had just optimized the trajectories for each cluster of 10 guided bomblets. It had made sure they would hit the long boxlike buildings of the desalination plant and its green lawns and hit them in a uniform pattern of blast ellipses.

Most of the bomblets had sensor fuses to let them first wreak kinetic havoc. They ripped through the plant's walls before they came to a full stop. Then they burst into superhot clouds of chemical energy and metal and plastic shrapnel.

The next three Saudi missiles watched the bomblets explode. The missile eyes watched them explode through almost all frequencies of the electromagnetic spectrum. Their chip minds worked fast at the nanolevel and let them estimate the bomblet damage and discuss it among themselves. Then the missiles jointly picked the optimal point of impact for their own massive payloads of chemical superexplosives.

The joint blasts leveled the main building of the desalination plant and left three smoking blast craters.

The sixth and last Saudi cruise missile watched

these three explosions in its tiny arrays of dead smart eyes. The Saudis had launched this missile for backup but there was no need to waste it. Now the missile flew up and over in a complete eight-g spiral to evade the distant five Israeli SAMs. Then it too jerked and opened into a cloud of smart bomblets and fiery plasma.

The smart attack had pierced the Israeli shield. It had set the entire Israeli defense system on full alert and had cost lives and weapons and honor. The smart attack had not changed the real Israeli defense portfolio. The secret arsenal of 300 Jericho nuclear ballistic missiles stayed hidden and silent in the Judean Hills at Kefra Zekhariya.

And there had been little time to run.

Jackie had run ahead of Alon into the crowd of plant workers who jumped and pushed their way downstairs to the bomb shelters. Alon had stopped at the top of the stairs when he looked down and saw the brass hemp pipe still in his right hand. Jackie had handed it to him when they ran out of the optics lab.

Now Alon walked over to a square green trash can. He stood between the hall video camera and the trash can and then dropped the pipe into the black plastic liner.

That last green act of recycling and a Saudi bomblet cost Alon Gorenberg his life.

Jackie made it down the stairs and lost only her hearing.

CHAPTER 5

Cyberspace

The Saudi bombing and missile attack filled hundreds of channels on the Wireless News Network. The WNN signals were compressed bit streams of 1s and 0s that circled the globe and passed through the labyrinths of cyberspace. The signals moved through both the wired and wireless links of the global internet and of thousands of local and wide area networks. The signals passed through optical cables and between the thin air and bounced off satellites in both high-earth and low-earth orbits.

The WNN signals themselves looked like dim white noise to those who did not pay the WNN code fee and tried to intercept them. They saw only the tangle of randomized signals "spread" out over much of the electromagnetic spectrum. Teams of WNN scientists worked to find the new random codes that made it all possible.

The emblem of WNN was not its bits but some of its atoms. The emblem was the pattern of its thin blue credit cards. Even many children in the Congo and ice climbers in Antarctica had the blue cards. They could slide the cards into a palm panel or desk screen and see who was now killing whom anywhere in the world.

WNN sold new base-level cards each year and sold new deluxe cards each month. Students had to crack old cards to pass some college courses on secure communications and on quantum algorithms that factored whole numbers into primes. Hackers opened encrypted news groups on the internet to debate ways to crack each new WNN card.

WNN's encryption schemes relied on the computer search for new and ever larger prime numbers. This code search drew on the math fact that there are infinitely many prime numbers. Euclid had proved that about 2,300 years before. The trouble was the Prime Number Theorem that humans first proved in 1896 and that machines later reproved many times. This math fact said that the prime numbers thin out and grow rarer as the numbers grow larger. So each day the code search grew a little harder and secure WNN cards grew a little dearer. And quantum computers worked harder to crack them.

❙ ❙ ❚

WNN Channel 5: An Israeli drone patrols the skies near Eilat. The unmanned aerial vehicle looks like a silver kite studded with infrared sensors and other machine eyes. The drone watches the first Saudi cruise missile burst into bomblet clouds. The clouds move forward in a type of slow-motion shotgun blast. The first bomblet clouds pelt the desalination plant and those who run from it. The later bomblet clouds explode just after impact. Three bright flashes of light throw the drone view into snow as it climbs in altitude. The view returns to show three dark smoldering craters. . . .

❙❙■

WNN Channel 12: A panel of eight NATO experts debate whether Israel will launch its own smart tit-for-tat strike against Saudi Arabia. Most of the experts do not believe that Israeli Greens bombed the Dhahran oil fields. They say that Israel will not strike because of new reports of Saudi casualties and Dhahran damage. Israel will not respond for fear that its radical Shiite neighbor Egypt would join the Saudi counterattack and maybe even attack Israel at the first sign of an Israeli launch. . . .

❙❙■

WNN Channel 23: Split screen. The first screen shows a young WNN reporter who stands in front of the Knesset building. She speaks in English and holds her black leather bag to the side to show where she had just held the hidden microcamera. The second screen shows a Knesset debate that turns into a fist-fight and then into a pile of Labor and Likud leaders. . . .

❙❙■

WNN Channel 41: The White House. Green Democrat President Vance Jackson holds a press conference on the conflict between the Saudis and Israelis. He denounces nuclear terrorism and says he has sent Secretary of State Gloria Rosen to Tel Aviv to help mediate the conflict. A young reporter with a shaved head asks the President if he will suspend Intel's contract for smart-weapon support to the Saudis. Jackson says he may. . . .

❙❙■

WNN Channel 64: Dhahran. A large white polymer tent serves as an emergency ward. Soldiers tend to bleeding blast victims who lie facing Mecca on the bumpy floor. The soldiers do not have alcohol or morphine or medical training. A bloodstained and bearded father holds up his armless baby son and screams for the death of all Israelis. . . .

❙❙■

WNN Channel 96: The United Nations. The Israeli ambassador stands as he demands that Saudi Arabia pay Israel for all damage to the Eilat desalination plant and that the UN approve oil sanctions against the Saudis. The Iranian ambassador stands to protest the call for oil sanctions. He threatens Israel with war. . . .

❙❙■

WNN Channel 809: Split screen of the 24-hour London and New York stock exchanges. Both markets have dropped over 4% of their value through e-money transfers as the bond market has fallen. The United States no longer offers a 30-year bond but its 10-year bond has lost 6% of its value. The dollar has jumped from 24 yen to 30 yen in panic buying from central banks in Europe and Asia. The largest gainers are the private currencies Daiwa metal and Zurich fiat. . . .

❙❙■

WNN Channel 810: The Shanghai Stock Exchange. Chinese pit traders stand in crowds and wave their black handheld wireless transactors at a clear crystal spike. The Thailand and Hong Kong exchanges are up over 2%. The Tokyo Stock Exchange has fallen almost 1%. A large red wall display shows that the Shanghai exchange all-stock index has just gone up from 5% to 6%. . . .

CHAPTER 6

Mojave Desert
Nevada

"**G**oddamn Arabs."

John Grant spoke to his windshield.

"I can't believe they bombed my desalination plant. What are the odds of that happening? One in how many billion? Jism. What are the odds?"

The odds are slight.

" 'Slight?' I know they are 'slight.' You can do better than that. You wrote that big thick book on causal inference. You know how many hours it took me to scan in that wordy shit? Too bad you never learned to speak in math like we do now. But go ahead and take a chance. Make a causal guess. Explain."

Eilat was the closest city in Israel at which the Saudis could hope to strike with impunity. They chose a retaliatory path which was both swift and secure.

"Jism. I know that. But why did they choose the water plant? Why *my* plant? Why my atomic laser?"

John. Do not despair. Eytan will call soon and no doubt assure you that you shall still supply their demand. The Saudis saw the desalination plant as both a close government structure of the Israelis and one

34

*which the Greens had put forth to the world as an
emblem of the new postoil era they hope to achieve.*

"So you believe the news?"

So far the news is the only evidence we have and—

"Jesus. I know the line. Always proportion your
belief to the evidence."

John Grant now watched six WNN channels on his
windshield in a holographic heads-up display. The
thin shield of doped diamond housed massive computer and communication networks. The Jism he
spoke to was as much in the windshield or dashboard
as it was in the small brown "raisin" he wore just
inside his left ear.

Jism was the name John used for the nineteenth-
century English philosopher John Stuart Mill.

Sometimes a Jism image would flash on the windshield. John could glimpse the thin Englishman in his
frock coat and see his bald forehead and blue eyes
and thick dark sideburns. The tera-flop image still was
not perfect on the windshield. And John did not like
to think of Jism sitting apart from him or dangling
above the Jeep on the highway.

John liked to think of Jism as in the raisin. Then
Jism lived with John in John's mind. The raisin talked
to John and he could still talk to it when he left his
Jeep or his desert home. The voice of Jism was always
with him. John kept extra raisins in his pocket and
wallet and in his desert trailer. He had buried two sets
of them in the Nevada Mojave Desert that he now
drove through on his way to Los Angeles.

John had trained his intelligent agent on the works
of John Stuart Mill. The training began when John
was a graduate student in molecular engineering at the
University of Nevada in Las Vegas.

John had found John Stuart Mill the smartest man

he had ever read. John had always searched for a personal advisor and knew he had found him when he read Mill's *System of Logic* and his *On Liberty*. John agreed with Mill on science and politics to a very high degree. Then John read Mill's *Biography* and knew that they agreed on religion and life as well.

John viewed himself as something of an elitist among his peers for even reading nonmath books. He took pride in how he had sculpted this English gentleman in his ear. Most people bought packaged versions of Jesus or pop stars or sports figures or motivational speakers and used them to exalt their diaries.

John had scanned in all of JSM's published books and essays and letters he could find. It had taken years and he once went to London to copy 200-year-old issues of *The Westminster Review*. The JSM text streams served as training data for vast networks of neural filters and fuzzy rule banks. These plastic systems learned the patterns of JSM's thought and writing.

John had also fed the intelligent agent each book he could recall reading and had shared with it his secrets and vital statistics. He made sure his Jism had access to the latest science disks and stores of social and legal and medical data.

Correct. Proportion your belief to the evidence.

Jism knew John liked to hear the line. It was a principle that summed up over 2,000 years of Western philosophy. It had special force in the extreme case when there was no evidence. Then it said believe nothing. That extreme case laid waste to many of the belief structures of Western and Eastern man. It abolished gods and souls and public wills and all the other unseen creatures of religion and folk wisdom.

Jism's principle also cast doubt on the claims of many power institutions. It shaved the claims of the church from its bloody track record of group control and bad predictions. It reduced states and governments to mere force monopolies and so reduced them to pools of waste and fraud and group control and warfare. The principle reduced the press to media power. It applied to media-bite reporting and saw only how units of the press compete to share power with states by how the press units shine their spotlights on some agenda items and not on others.

John had lost belief in the lot of them. Now all he had was Jism.

"Try Richard again," John said.

John watched a new blue window form on his windshield. The other windows shrank and shifted from curved 2-D to full 3-D. The windows looked like paintings hanging in a hallway with the new blue window at the end of the hallway. John stretched his legs as best he could in the front seat but still had to bend them down with his bare feet on the floor on the passenger side. He had the car on full autopilot so he could focus on the gallery of screens and windows in the heads-up-display windshield.

John broke off half a gingersnap and sucked at its dry spicy surface. The gingersnap made him think of Ramachandra and all the work he had left to do at home and at the Hoover Dam and how little time he had left to do it. He swished the sparkling river water in its Hoover Dam bottle and gulped down the cool bubbly fluid.

Richard Cheng appeared on what had just been the blue window and it grew in size.

Richard was not 30 yet and sat at his multimedia console in Los Angeles. The smooth chrome device could produce more images than an entire film studio could a century before. Richard spoke so fast that sometimes Jism had to whisper to John and repeat what Richard had just said.

"Have you heard from Eytan?" John said.

"No word. I've almost got the film made for the site visit. It still needs to adapt on a good-looking woman."

"How about your sister?"

"Fuck you. I'm thinking about scanning some old film of gospel singers or cabaret dancers."

"Sounds too cute for the Israelis. And it doesn't sound legal. Richard. Please don't forget that this is a full-blown site visit. It has to impress a lot of people. Let's don't risk anything on dancing girls."

"We'll talk about it when you get here. Adios."

The windshield went back to full view of the purple and gray Mojave Desert.

"Jism. Smart search on the Eilat bombing from the Arab point of view. I don't trust the Israelis. I want to hear what the other side has to say."

Fine idea. Forty programs so far.

"Let's see them."

The windshield display split into two rows of five windows each. All showed video clips and some showed them as holographs.

"Jism! You fuck! Translate!"

English captions appeared at the base of each window image. The system tracked John's eye movements and gave the most sound to the image he looked at. Then the Arabic turned to English and the captions popped off that window.

John could hear the image windows next to the one he had focused on. The display damped and filtered their sounds to keep them within John's preferred signal-to-noise ratio. John squeezed his right hand around the small rubber spikes of his green porky ball as he watched.

Many men owned land in the world. Few owned his own blend of diamond and graphite in a patented carbon molecule.

▎▌ ▌

Window 1: A shirtless scuba diver in the Red Sea points to brown broken stalks of coral. The coral surrounds a twisted chunk of surface-to-air missile. The diver points to the black Hebrew letters on its side. The voice says this smart minicruise missile was the dumbest of the lot and attacked the reef on its own instructions. . . .

▎▌ ▌

Window 4: Orthodox Jews beat an old bearded Palestinian man when he pushes them from his spot near the Al Aqsa Mosque across from the Wailing Wall. A later segment shows the same Jews in a rock fight with Palestinian children. . . .

▎▌ ▌

Window 5: A dark-eyed woman from the Arab Antidefamation League graphs the amount of Israeli versus Saudi damage coverage in the world media. She then graphs the latest numbers of Jews versus Arabs in U.S. and European broadcasting. . . .

▎▌ ▌

Window 7: A Green Senator argues on a U.S. talk show that Congress should ban sales of smart weapons to the Saudis and ban all oil imports from them as well. Her Libertarian colleague in the Senate disagrees. Her colleague claims that both moves would be pointless symbolism and bad economics in the global economy. A weapon ban would just raise the price of weapons and increase the odds that U.S. allies or enemies would supply them. A U.S. oil embargo would make Americans pay more for gas and oil. It would in the end just transfer more wealth from the United States to the Arab states and to Russia and Venezuela. . . .

▌ ▌

Window 9: President Ibn Aminzadeh of Azerbaijan addresses his country through the state-run cable TV network. Aminzadeh demands that Israel pay the Saudi government for the billions of dollars lost in oil reserves in Dhahran. He says the Muslim nations should discuss whether to impose an oil embargo on Israel. . . .

▌ ▌

"Jism. This is just Arab bellyaching. Find something on my desalination plant. Find something on the technology. Associative search on *Black Sun*. Hell. Find something on *me*!"

John. Relax. There is no evidence that anyone wants to harm you.

"Look. These Saudi bastards just harmed me. They blew up my water plant for Christ's sake! That was my laboratory. I knew they would try to get at me through that atomic laser from Weizmann. Big Oil. Big Arab Oil with Allah on top. I never wanted to get mixed up in the old Arab-Jew pissing match. How long will that go on? Another century? I thought science was supposed to kill off religion. What happened? Now look at those Muslims waving guns at that mosque. You have to give them credit for their skill in geometry. But what does waving those guns prove?''

They are the sentimental enemies of political economy.

"Those sentimental enemies blew up the only water plant in the world smart enough to license my patent. So they are my enemies too. Like they say: Even paranoids have enemies.''

Jism laughed at that and so did John.

I can find only one match to your technical work and to Arab extremists. The associative link has a near-random connection strength.

"Fine. What is it?''

It is a recent program on Israeli public television called "The New Varieties of Religious Experience." The program compared Jewish kabbalahism to Islamic Sufism.

"That does sound like noise. I bet the show didn't come up with one claim that you could test. Christ. My faith in cartoons versus yours. They should have called the program 'How to Kill a Man for the Sake of Unobservable Fictions.' No. That's too Western for the Mideastern mind. It lacks a sense of the tribe. Lacks a sense of the all-loving omnipotent *community*. It needs the taste of what they used to call the czar's cake in the first Russian Revolution. Remember that? Yeah. How about 'How We Fool You as We Rule You'?''

The program mentions a Sufi mystic in Iran who once worked on the mathematics of brain function.

"Really? What does he look like?''

The windshield cleared and then one window opened in the center from a small blue dot. The grainy image quickly grew sharp as the car net performed trillions of pixel computations. A pale man with a black beard and white turban walked into a rocky cave. The narrator claimed this was secret footage of a Sufi brotherhood in Turkey on the border with Iran.

"Can you slow down and contrast enhance this guy's voice? I can't make out his name."

The name of the man in the image is Hamid Tabriz.

"Tabriz? H. Tabriz? Jesus! You know who he is? I based my learning scheme on his gradient-projection algorithm. Half the field has stolen from this guy."

I see you referenced him twice in your master's thesis.

"Had to. That guy is pure structure. They say he got out of Tokyo University with just a 20-page dissertation. He published only two letters in the *IEEE Transactions on Neural Networks*. Read them."

I just did.

"See? They're not even full journal articles. And no coauthorship with his Ph.D. advisor. They're beautiful papers. No tech talk or grant talk or any of that bullshit. Just straight theorem and proof. Theorem and proof. Wham bam fuck you ma'am. No one ever met him at a workshop or heard from him on the net. Yeah. I remember now. I did hear that Tabriz was some kind of religious nut like Pascal was. The Muslims get them when they're young. I sure thought he was too smart to believe in cartoons."

A Jism image flashed on the windshield and stayed there. Jism's thin mouth was firm and did not move. His blue eyes looked above John and his forehead wrinkled.

"Hey. Why do we keep watching this pillowhead walk into a cave? I admit I'm a fan but so what? I don't think his ass is cute. What are you doing?

Thinking? You think he had something to do with my water plant?''

He is the only tie I could find between neural engineering and the Saudi bombing.

"I see the neural tie. And I don't need you to make it. How big a machine IQ does that take?''

The same Israeli program says Israeli intelligence has linked Sufism to Islamic militants.

"Sure it does. The Israelis link all Arabs to Islamic militants. They've got whole rooms full of computers that do nothing but test combinations of people for ill intent. You remember. Eytan even bragged about it the first time we met in Vegas. The Israelis run half the planet through their machines. They're more paranoid than I am.''

Jism smiled slightly and his blue eyes sparkled.

Tabriz is a Persian and not an Arab.

"Jism. Don't logic chop. You're the guru on cause and effect. Tell me what you base the link on.''

John. You know that the known laws of pattern recognition are model-free. We can recognize a pattern far more easily than we can explain how we recognize it. We do not even have reliable numerical confidence measures of the patterns we think we recognize.

"I know that but try anyway. A tie to Dr. H.-fucking-Tabriz is too far off even a thick-tailed bell curve to treat it like it's off the curve. Like you said or you should have said: There is no such thing as a statistical outlier. Didn't you say that?''

Words to that effect.

"You said that all right. Listen to the data. Don't tell the data where they belong. Let them tell you. Each datum belongs to at least one pattern. Try to explain the facts and not just explain them away. That's the core of your whole empiricist world view.

So tell me: What makes you think Tabriz and these Sufi men of the woolen cloth somewhere out in a desert cave give a spiritual shit about whether the Saudis blew up my water plant? What do you base that on?''

My neural-network intuition.

"Christ."

CHAPTER 7

Kirovabad
Azerbaijan

The skinny gangster called the Sturgeon sat down at the same table with Joel Davis. The Azer gangster was young enough to still have purple acne splotches on his tanned high cheekbones.

He smiled as he picked up Davis's vodka and sipped it.

"Tell me," the Sturgeon said in perfect English over the loud Turkish rock music. "What is a German doing taking pictures of our esteemed national oil pipeline?"

"Fuck off punk. You need a bath."

Joel Davis watched the man's dark eyes as the man reached in his yellow silk suit and pulled out a flat palm screen. Davis could see himself on the screen. It was footage from this morning. He sat in his brown Honda rental car on a dirt road and held a small clear tube to his eye. Below him lay the sleek olive Tamraz pipeline as it snaked through a red rocky valley. The tube took the light that bounced off the pipeline and valley and burned it into a volume hologram as a sequence of diffraction patterns.

Later tiny chemical robots would convert the doped

lithium jelly of the hologram into a 3-D strike point for an Israeli cruise missile.

"Sightseeing?" the Sturgeon said.

"Who wants to know?"

"The people of the Republic of Azerbaijan want to know."

"Fine. Give me my drink."

Davis reached for the vodka and then slammed the heel of his right hand on the back of the gangster's neck. At the same time Davis grabbed the young man's oiled black rat tail of hair and gently lowered his face to the cedar table. The Sturgeon would have a concussion from the blow but he would live.

Few failed attempts at blackmail ended this well. Davis would have liked to have killed the young man but after all it was his country and his oil.

Joel Davis stood and smiled at one of the nude belly dancers and walked to the door. No one seemed to notice the young gangster passed out in the back of the club. Davis tipped the fat Algerian at the door when the man gave him back his black windbreaker. Davis put it on and felt through the pocket to his cotton pants. The sealed hologram cartridge was still in his pants pocket.

His life would not be safe until he gave the small gray tube to his courier and then left Kirovabad for Baku and on to Cyprus and on back to Tel Aviv. Now the Azer gangster had forced him to abort his rendez-vous. He would have to drive close to the border of Armenia and hide the car and then cross on foot in the night. His monitor at AMAN or what he called *Agaf Modi'in* would have an agent there to pick him up and fly him to Cyprus. Or so he had to bet.

Davis felt them when he hit the cool night air.

He did not see them but his instincts made his

stomach tighten and his nostrils flare. The feeling always made him think of his first mission in Damascus. He and his team had gotten out all right but it had been close. There was the guilt of killing a man he had never met and the fear that at any moment he might have to answer for it.

Joel Davis walked faster to the dirt parking lot and hoped they did not know which small Honda was his. Something moved to his right and his left but moved faster than he could see.

The last thing he saw was a flash of blue lightning from one of the two tasers. Then came the long spasms of pain that shot through all his muscles and much of his central nervous system.

He never knew the darkness when it came.

::::■ CHAPTER 8

Searchlight
Nevada

John Grant's Jeep slowed to 40 miles per hour as he drove through the small Nevada town of Searchlight. He had 10 more miles to go on Highway 95 before he crossed into Southern California.

John always liked this stretch through the gray and purple Castle Mountains and the stark stands of green yucca and Joshua trees and greasewood shrubs. He looked away from the WNN windows on the windshield and out to the Mojave. He often grew tired of the man-made world of bits and longed for the real world of atoms.

The desert was the real world.

The desert was free and open and harsh and full of its own rewards for the taking. Most people could not wait to drive through it or fly over it and get back to a city. John liked the thought of the desert as much as he liked to look at it from his house trailer sunken into the hard red and brown gravel. And there still lay beneath it all that gold and silver slowly working its way up through the crust from the magma. Who would have thought gold and silver would outlast oil?

Searchlight made him think of gold and the hard

men who had long ago tried to bring it out of the ground. John opened his window to let some of the hot dry air shoot in the Jeep. He wanted to feel some of the heat that they had had to live with most of the year. Jism knew not to disturb him at such moments. Jism tried to match John's mood by softly playing a new version of Anton Bruckner's Ninth Symphony. Jism also gave the windshield a soft but dark green tint to match the D-minor texture.

John looked out the other window and saw once again the twisted remains of a gold mine from the early 1900s. The brown rotting timbers and its old pulley system still stood on a desert hill across from the new Exxon station in Searchlight.

Someday he had to go down that mine shaft.

A young man who worked the gas pumps at the station and who spit green mint juice on the pavement had once told him that the old miner who dug the mine shaft went down one day and never came up. John had talked to the young man more than once as he filled up the tank of his Jeep. He used to kid John about buying the mine claim. The young man said no one had ever gone in after the old man. The cops still tried to keep kids from playing near the mine shaft.

The small gold vein had run out but the old man would not quit. John tried to picture the old man at work. The old man had thought he might strike a new vein each time he swung his pick or blasted out a few more cubic feet of granite streaked with white quartz. He had sunk the main shaft and chipped out the side shafts by himself. He had worked for years in the desert just as he pleased. The old man had never paid federal taxes or worn pain patches on his joints or male-hormone patches on his shaved scrotum.

John was not sure if the old man had ever married

and he wanted to know. He faced the prospect of marriage himself. The young man at the Exxon station said no one could ever locate any of the old man's next of kin. So John had to infer the rest.

John did not know what the old man looked like besides being thin and bent and having white hair and white beard stubble. He could never picture the old man's face. But John knew that the old man had never watched the yield on a 10-year bond rise or fall on a car windshield's heads-up display or brushed his teeth with antiplaque enzymes or even felt the cool false breeze of an air conditioner.

John also knew something else about the old man. The old man had been a hundred times tougher on his worst day than John Grant was on his best. And the old man had been a lot freer. He just chose to spend that freedom chipping out a gold mine on a claim he had staked in the Nevada desert. Today the state would likely not even sell him the permit.

John wanted to meet such a man but did not believe they still lived. The best John could do would be to meet a dead one. That was why he wanted to work out a way to climb down the gold mine. Maybe Richard would help him set up the ropes and run a winch that they could rent from the Exxon station. John would climb down the main shaft with a good flashlight and carry a .44 Magnum with bird shot in it to shoot any rattlesnakes or rats.

He would find the old man's bones and try to figure out how the old man had died. What had it been like at the end when the old man knew he had truly dug his own grave? Did a man like that have the courage to take it straight at the end or did he fall back on a cartoon? John would go down and think it through one more time and then give the bones a proper burial.

A man with those balls deserved at least that.

But the young man who chewed crushed spearmint and spit green juice had once said something that seemed to ruin John's plans. He said gangsters and bootleggers used to shoot people in Las Vegas or Los Angeles and then drive out to the desert and throw them down old gold mines and silver mines. He said an old-timer had told him that that was why no one ever went back down the old man's mine. There were too many rotted corpses at the bottom of it.

John still did not know if he believed that. He did not like even the thought of sorting gangster bones from the old man's bones. He wanted to find the old man's white skeleton still holding a pick stuck in the rock wall.

John checked the gas gauge to make sure the tank was three fourths full. He thought about turning back to stop at the Exxon station. His mouth was still dry despite the bottled water. He could stop and buy one of those sour red Tootsie Pops made of fake sugar and fake raspberry flavor. So much of the junk food in the West was fake these days and yet his mouth watered when he thought of it.

John pulled out a gingersnap instead and chewed on it. He knew he did not want to stop for the sour candy. He just wanted to find the young man who spit green mint juice and ask him some more questions about the gold mine. But there was no time for that.

The Jeep picked up speed as it passed the retirement parks of Searchlight.

John thought of the parks as high-tech death camps for seniors. He tried not to think of the old folks and their nearby green desert golf courses that drank their fill from the Colorado River. He never wanted to be old like the boomers. Most were grandparents now but they still played their love songs from the 1960s on their tennis courts and in their nursing homes.

The baby boomers had had it all and then had left their credit-card bills to John's generation. They had grown the largest state in history and got used to its rate of growth. First the boomers had bankrupted the federal government. Then when they retired they drained their mutual funds in a panic and sank the U.S. stock market. John and his friends disagreed on many things but they all despised the old boomers. The trouble was that the old boomers still held most of the power. They had organized well and now they shared the common goal of dying well.

The boomer parks were part of the price of driving on old Highway 95. Interstate 15 would get him to Los Angeles faster than Highway 95 would but he did not like the border crossing on I-15. The Southern California desert patrol there would watch his approach the whole way in. Their laws made it clear that driving there was a "privilege" and not a right. There was no way to escape the wireless eyes of the state. Driving through Southern California just put him in fuller view.

A window panel flashed red with the image of a black old-fashioned phone. The Bruckner symphony died down.

"Jism. Who is it? Eytan?"

No. It is your fiancée.

"Where the hell is Eytan? I sure hope he made it through that bombing. We may be wiped out if he didn't. That's the last thing I need to tell Denise. All right. Put the Dragon Empress through."

Half the windshield turned to high resolution voxels or 3-D picture elements. Denise Cheng appeared in full view. She smiled much the same smile that her twin Richard Cheng had smiled at John a few minutes before. She wore her long black hair straight with long bangs on her forehead. The bangs and microsurgery made her nose look much thinner than Richard's.

The Cheng twins had science in their nature as well as in their nurture. Their parents had met as liberated multimedia engineers at Berkeley. They had kept all but the sex chromosomes the same in the twins. That had put an end to their family dispute over the old Chinese desire for sons.

John liked to look at her face. Its resemblance to Richard's face surprised him when he had not seen her for a few days. Sometimes it disturbed him. Still John loved her smile and had to answer hers with his.

But he hated that he had taken her money.

"Guess what?" Denise said.

"I hope it's good news. The Saudis just bombed us."

"I know. This is much more important."

"Really?"

"Uh-hum. Your son just started kicking again."

"Of course. He's like his father and wants out of his cage. Right now I can't even get out of this moving coffin. Let me see him."

Denise twisted back and around on her yellow-flower divan and looked behind her at the egg shelf on the black wall.

A new window opened on John's windshield. It showed the large clear birthing egg. The egg had a fine clear skin of pseudodiamond. The fluid inside was a mix of dark red blood and yellow nutrient sap. Denise had had the egg custom-made. She and John had both put blood samples into it to seed the fluid. That kept their consciences clear and kept her body in shape.

The pink fetus kicked against the side of the bloody egg and turned itself slightly.

"You're right," John said. "That is more important. Thanks."

John felt the gene thrill of knowing the child was his and that Denise was as good a woman as he would ever find and that he loved her as much as he would ever love any person or thing. But it still scared him now as it scared him at night in his dreams. The child would constrain what freedom he had and freedom was what he fought for so hard. John also feared that money had been part of why he had agreed to have a child.

It was too damn bad that the bond market had wiped him out and his first partner.

Now he had mixed his genes with hers and had taken her money. The two events were less than a year apart. John kept asking himself whether it was chance or design. He was not sure. But he was sure that he who has a partner has a master.

Genes and money.

Jism would see a causal connection between the two events but he never said so and John did not ask him. He had trained Jism not to poke him where it hurt. Now the sharp jolt of gene fear made him want to wipe the screen clean and scramble his comm ports. It made him want to head off the road through the desert to some new place he had never been. There were thousands of canyons out there that he would never explore or camp in.

Then the gene fear made him think of how the old man would just shake his head and go back to chipping away at his gold mine.

"What's wrong?" she said.

"We still don't know if the Arab missiles hit our

lab in the hydroplant. We may be out of business.''

"You care too much about money.''

"It's a great way to keep score.''

"Spoken like a true Rockefeller.''

"Just give me time,'' John said.

He grinned and held up the green porky ball. Denise rolled her eyes.

"When will you get here?'' she said.

"As soon as I go over the damage assessment with Richard. I have to be on-site for most of it.''

"You're not coming by here first?''

"Denise. Did you see what happened in Eilat?''

"Don't you want to come fuck your financier?''

"Jesus. Where do you get that language?''

"How about telling me you love me?''

"You know that. Okay. I should be at Cajon Pass in less than three hours if all goes well.''

"What would you like to eat when you get here?''

"Apple butter smeared over your nipples.''

The windshield blinked red in priority interrupt.

John. It's Eytan.

"Denise. I'm sorry. Have to take this. Jism. Put him through.''

John winked at Denise but she frowned and signed off. He pushed the dashboard to start the transmission but it did not go through.

"What's wrong?'' John said.

We are synching random protocols. It will take a few more seconds.

"Christ. Fiancée and financier. Jism. Never take money from a friend or from his sister. Make a note of it.''

I shall. Synch complete.

The chiseled face of Major Eytan Baum with its old acne pockmarks and endless slight smile looked at John. Baum had captured a tank division in the two-day ground and smart war with Jordan and Iraq. He now ran the group on molecular engineering at two Tel Aviv state labs and ran the smart-water test site at the Eilat desalination plant.

John's contract with the Israelis was part of the licensing agreement. It gave John and Richard a lot of free rein but they had to clear all changes with Eytan. John also had to report to him once a week.

"Did you get hit?" John said.

"*Shalom* to you too. Confirm triple spread-spectrum mode."

"Okay. It's your shekel."

John leaned forward and typed a random code into the dashboard. His contract said that he could not share the code with any person or intelligent agent. But he had told Jism the code for backup and had sworn him to secrecy.

The full windshield screen fluttered in static and white noise. Then the white random dots turned blue and red and dissolved back into Baum's round face. The consulting meter ran in red numerals at the base of the screen. The Israeli government had to pay John for this call even though John had called Eytan first.

"Confirmed," John said. "Do you want Richard to join us?"

"No. He has no need to know."

"Eytan. He's my partner. You license my patent and our netware. I'd say that gives him a need to know."

"Not for this. As you said you hold the patent and he doesn't."

"You were hit that hard?"

"There was damage to the main water line and of

course the mirror banks. Much of our group is still operative. No scuba diving for a while. But that's not the reason.''

''What is?''

''First things first.''

''No,'' John said. ''Back up. What do you mean by 'much of our group'? Is Alon okay?''

''Alon didn't make it.''

''You mean he's dead? Alon?''

''John. This is not the time.''

''Hold on. I don't want to sound cold-blooded. But if the bombs killed Alon, then what happened to the Weizmann laser?''

''Don't worry. We're getting a new one from Ben-Gurion.''

''Jesus. We're wiped out.''

''Nonsense. We'll mourn later. Now let me get to my next point. Ready? The demo next week is canceled.''

''What? I just left the Hoover Dam a half hour ago. Ramachandra said it was all set when I left.''

''It was. I just told him to move it up to Thursday.''

''Thanks. That gives us less than two days. I still have to drive to L.A. to help Richard tune the damn thing. That's not enough time.''

''John. It's too bad you were never in my squad. You might have even made it.''

''Fuck you too.''

''Fact is we have no choice. The good news is our people got your Department of Energy to agree to a five-year contract at Hoover. So congratulations. The trade-off is we have to let three Texas oil partnerships buy in. The demo on Thursday is for the Texas execs. They set the schedule. And frankly after the bombing we need to show your government that we can still deliver. Our people won't sleep until then. Be there.''

"We'll be there.''

"Good. And don't worry about the smart strike. It was political.''

"That's why I worry about it. Eytan. Just what do you do in the government anyway?''

"Wish I knew. Now listen. Here is where you have a need to know. Why don't you put down the cookies for a minute until we're through. Are you ready? Good. We have evidence that your government is watching you.''

"That's what they do. Did you know that Southern California now wants to impose a new communication tax every time you speak in the state if the wireless message you send passes through its airspace? You believe that? Every time you *speak*?''

"John. I am serious. And I mean your federal government. Odds are they are trying to crack this line right now.''

John felt it in his solar plexus. The state was watching him.

He knew they had watched him in college. That much they had not blacked out from the FBI file that he had fought to get under the old Freedom of Information Act. The law said the Federal Bureau of Investigation had to give him his file within two weeks. It had taken them almost three years. They blamed the delay on case backlog. Yet they gave one of John's classmates her file in two months even though she and John had filed in the same week.

The state had files on John all the way back to his birth to an unwed Southern Baptist teenage girl who believed in adoption over abortion and whose name the state would never tell him. John had taken the name Grant from the last of three couples he had lived with by the time he had moved into an apartment in Phoenix with some older friends.

That was when he was 14. The Grants were now an older couple in their early 60s. John had not seen them since they surprised him by coming to his high school graduation. He sent them copies of his bachelor's and master's degrees on the days he got them and thanked the old Grant couple again for their name.

Now the state was watching him again.

"Maybe it's all the time I spend in Boulder City with Ramachandra and those civil servant fucks."

"No. This goes beyond routine security. *Za'hal* confirmed it."

"The IDF confirmed it? So is my government watching Richard too?"

"Not that we know. That's why you have to keep this to yourself. We think it may be industrial espionage."

"On whose behalf? Your Texas oil friends?"

"Who knows? But you have to redouble your security procedures. Don't tell anyone except Richard that we have moved up the demo. No mistakes."

"Not even my fiancée?"

"Not even her."

"Is this why you moved it up? To beat the spooks?"

"John. Try not to be so paranoid."

"Why? The Saudis wiped out your test lab and my government is watching me. Is there anything else I should worry about?"

"No. See you on Thursday."

"Will you be there?"

"By remote. Have to go now. *L'hitra'ot.*"

"Wait," John said.

"What?"

"Did you ever study alpha-stable neural nets?"

"As a kid."

"They didn't have those when you were a kid."

"Is this business-related?"

"Maybe. I'm trying to track down a neural theorist in your neck of the desert. Hamid Tabriz. Remember him? I'm sure you have files on him. Whatever happened to him?"

"You belong to enough cults already. You want to join his?"

"I want to see if he has published any more neural theorems. We might use them for the intermediate reactions."

"John. Never cast a hook at a fisherman. But I will tell you something about Dr. Tabriz that you don't know."

"But not what I want to know."

"If you want to know more, then come join the Israeli Army."

"Then I could really take orders from you."

"Do you want me to tell you or not?"

"Yes."

"Tabriz once killed an old man in a rival Sufi brotherhood."

"No shit," John said.

"No shit. And he was just 13. What were you doing when you were 13? *Shalom.*"

The windshield turned to white snow and popped back to the quilt of windows of WNN channels. A smiling Jism flashed on the windshield and then dissolved.

"Jism. Did you add that to your neural intuition?"

Yes. Dr. Tabriz seems as precocious in his social-

ization as he was in mastering the art of constructing derivations correctly.

"Jesus. I can't believe they killed Alon. And now they're watching us. I told you they were. Can you noise up our comm lines?"

Yes.

"Make sure you don't grow any stochastic resonance. That will just boost our signal strength to them."

Of course. John. I am on your side.

"That's good to know. What about Eytan? Is he on our side? How much did Mr. Potbelly lie this time?"

He spoke the truth only 77% on average in terms of his patterns of vocal stress. The pattern of distruth was almost constant throughout the conversation. In fairness to Eytan I have to point out that we have only a low confidence measure of this estimate. He has exceptional self-control.

"Jism. You are truly a man's best friend. I would sure hate to swim through the multimedia sea without you."

Thank you. Shall I resume the Bruckner?

"Yeah. Thanks."

My pleasure.

"So Eytan and his self-control fed us a stack of 23% lies this time. And he jumps up the demo date on us and I still have to go by and see Denise. Did you hear what he said? 'We'll mourn later.' Alon used to joke that Eytan was his illegitimate uncle. He said Eytan would keep the bad guys off him. Shit. Eytan couldn't care less that Alon is dead. Eytan just wants to do his soldier's duty and turn in a good report at the end of the year. He doesn't even have any equity in the deal. That Eytan is a real son of a bitch."

He has a completely fashioned will.

CHAPTER 9

Boca Raton
Florida

The blue Gulf Stream flows past Miami and then moves closer to shore on its way north. That was why the scuba diving and snorkeling was better at Boca Raton than at Miami. The Gulf Stream kept the water cleaner and bluer and helped feed the coral reefs. Most tourists thought it was because Miami had more trash and nanotreated sewage in its waters.

Now the Cuban oil tanker *El Hombre* sailed up the blue stream on its way from Galveston to an oil refinery in Savannah.

Captain Jorge Alvarez sat in the control room of the *Hombre* and flew over Boca Raton in his virtual-reality headset. Real-time satellite data gave him a true bird's-eye view of the green beach resort city and the old pink Boca Hotel. The view took him back to his youth in Florida with the Cuban exiles.

Alvarez had once worked in Boca Raton as a golf caddie. His baker father had gotten him the summer job from one of his rich Cuban-exile customers. Alvarez loved walking through the soft green golf courses then and he loved flying over them now. The VR system had to interpolate its own fine detail from the satellite data to maintain the privacy of the golfers.

Alvarez swooped down into the soft green fractal grass. He lay in the false grass and touched the ribbed muscles of his false stomach. His real stomach was a poor mix of flab and black hair but it was now hard and hairless to the touch.

A siren pierced his lucid dream.

First mate Ron Garcia ran in the control room and helped Alvarez take off the VR helmet.

"Leaks!" Garcia said. "There are holes in the ship!"

Alvarez followed him to the door and stopped short. Dozens of small gray holes covered the aluminum deck of the green tanker. The holes grew as he watched. The holes dripped gray goo at their edges and left only empty space in their centers. The larger holes grew faster than the smaller ones.

Crewmen shouted and ran around the holes to the two lifeboats that hung on the port side of the ship. Two crewmen held chrome fire extinguishers and sprayed the large gray hole on a steel staircase. The hole ate the white carbon dioxide foam along with the cast steel.

Just then a young black crewman from Guyana screamed when he slipped. His right foot passed through one of the growing rings of gray goo. His boot and foot became part of the goo. The smart superacid ate his leg faster than the gray ring grew. In seconds the goo had eaten through his stomach. Only then did he pass out from the searing burn on his way to full molecular disintegration.

Alvarez knew then that he was up against a superacid and that he would lose.

Superacids had once helped produce high-octane unleaded gas. They froze rapid chemical reactions among charged hydrocarbon molecules and had friendly trade names like Magic Acid. Yet even the early superacids based on fluoride compounds were still trillions of times more acidic than sulfuric acid. The new smart superacids could freeze select reactions and speed up or change others. Computers could program them to destroy target compounds and to ignore or even enhance neighboring compounds.

The smart superacids filtered matter.

Alvarez ran back to the control room and told the chief engineer to send an all-band SOS message and to beam the deck video images of the nanomeltdown to the U.S. Coast Guard Atlantic satellite. He turned and saw a gray hole the size of a nickel in the middle of the floor. He gave the order to abandon the ship and strapped on an orange life preserver.

Captain Alvarez followed the control crew out the door and saw that the *Hombre* had started to sink.

Again he stood at his command post in the doorway and watched the huge holes grow at a geometric rate as the ship jerked now from side to side. He looked down at the deep blue water of the Gulf Stream and saw the black oil pour into it. The oil would paint the rich beaches of Boca Raton black and end his career.

Right now his career did not matter.

Alvarez ran down a staircase to join the men jumping overboard. The boats from Boca would get there in minutes to pick them up. Let the new Cuban government jail him. He just did not want to burn to death as the young black crewman had and who was now part of the dripping gray goo of disassembled molecules.

Twenty crewmen fought to get in the first lifeboat before it had lowered. Captain Alvarez ordered the men to disperse and jump in the sea. They ignored him.

He pushed two of the men overboard. The others still ignored him and the ship made loud wrenching sounds as it rolled and started to come apart. Alvarez wanted to jump but he had always sworn he would be the last to leave the ship.

So he tried to push a third Cuban off the edge.

The Cuban panicked and slammed the metal clasp of a clear plastic clipboard through the bridge of Alvarez's nose. That knocked the captain off his feet. Alvarez stood but just as quickly had a short blackout from the lack of blood to his head. He fell to the deck in his own blood. Alvarez stood and fell three more times and then resigned to crawl to the edge and roll off.

He did not see the blue TV helicopter that hovered above him and filmed his ordeal.

The two women in the helicopter turned to watch two giant holes merge into a large empty figure-8. When they looked back at Alvarez his hands were gone. He found the strength to crouch and jump overboard but that did not stop the superacid. He never surfaced.

The *Hombre* sank in pieces in less than a minute.

The superacid had disassembled each piece long before it would have sunk to the bottom. The word spread quickly among the growing ring of ski and fishing boats that the mysterious acid did not eat oil or water. It did not even eat the crewmen who had made it safely to the salty blue water.

The superacid left only a huge surface puddle of over five million gallons of crude oil.

::::■ CHAPTER 10

Near Homer Mountain
Mojave Desert
California

"Jism! That looks like my molecule!"

I am afraid that I cannot agree. There are no lasers to sustain the intermediate reactions. This molecular agent seems self-sustaining.

"But the shearing force. Look at that tanker!"

John. Stay calm. Mere agreement in effect does not constitute agreement in cause.

"Yeah. You're right. And it leaves the water alone instead of taking it apart."

John Grant watched the gray goo eat and sink the *Hombre*. The image took up half his windshield. Most of the windows on the other half showed the meltdown from other points of view. One small window still showed the WNN report on overpopulation in Africa and South America that John had been watching before Jism brought him the news flash on the *Hombre*.

John looked up as the Jeep slowly braked for the border crossing.

The Jeep worked its way even more slowly to the

system of small brown air-conditioned guard booths. Two electric cars shot past from the other side of the highway as they crossed into Nevada without stopping. John's Jeep was the only car to enter the state of Southern California from the Nevada side.

The Caltrans Authority computer took control of the Jeep's road sensors and navigation units and guided the Jeep to the one manned guard booth.

"I still don't like the timing," John said. "Why this kind of environmental nanoterrorism just after a nanonuclear blast at the Dhahran oil fields? It looks like a pattern with the same cause."

I share your suspicion. The use of a new nanodisintegrator is disturbing in the extreme.

"That smiling crook," John said as he looked through the border crossing to the welcoming sign on the other side.

Governor Juan Torres smiled at the left side of the large clear plastic sign that read

---

WELCOME TO THE 51ST STATE IN THE UNION!
SOUTHERN CALIFORNIA
THE COMPASSION STATE
PLEASE FOLLOW ALL RULES

John could just glimpse the four signs behind it that listed the rules for driving through the East Mojave Desert Park. The glimpse made him shake his head.

He would never make it at this rate.

John needed a full million dollars to buy his freedom from the United States federal government. That would more than pay for his share of the national debt. And it would pay for the stiff exit penalty that a Green Democrat senator from Montana had charged for his swing vote on the bill.

A million dollars would free him of federal sales and income taxes. It would also free him of almost a third of the laws in the hundreds of thousands of pages in the Federal Register. The FBI could still arrest John if he robbed a bank or kidnapped someone or broke some other federal law against fraud or violent crime. But they could not put him in their active files until then. The buyout came with one free use of the FBI and a discount rate for services after that. He would still have to obey all the laws of his state of residence. That was least hardest to do in Nevada.

Now the Saudis had bombed his Eilat test site. John suspected something else was wrong but he was not sure what.

There was always the problem of money. John had no more savings left than when he had gotten his master's degree. The patent had gone through after three years but John had had to borrow from Denise to pay for it and to build and market the prototype software system.

Denise sat with Richard and John on the three-person board of their three-person company. She held only stock options now and no stock yet. John never knew if she would side with him or against him on the board. She and Richard had already made him change the firm's name from Black Sun to *Water Dragon*. Soon the child would come and Denise would goad John to marry her and live with her full-time in Southern California. He feared she would do many things to his fleeting liberty and do them in the name of the child.

"Jism."

Yes?

"Did you ever think I would get married? Or have a kid?"

Jism's blue-eyed image flashed on a small windshield window. Jism smiled.

Of course I did. A family will help you grow.

"The old ball and chain. I'm too young to get married. Jism. You got married. I've asked you this before but I keep coming back to it in my head. How did you estimate the costs and benefits of that loss of liberty?"

John. Those brief years made up the happiest moments of my life.

"You don't hear that said much these days. Hardly anyone gets married except Mormons and Catholics and movie stars. But people sure don't let that get in their way of putting new branches on their gene trees. Just keep adding a couple hundred million more babies a year to the world. Jism."

Yes?

"There still is something you have never told me. How old were you when you lost your cherry?"

Jism only grinned.

"You don't know how many goddamn biographies on you I read looking for the answer to that. Not one mentioned it. And you know damn well that when and how you lose your virginity is one of the bricks in a man's character. I think you married as a virgin but I can't prove it. But let me ask you a serious question. Why didn't you and Harriet Taylor ever have children?"

There was not enough time.

Jism faded and John felt like a fool for talking to his intelligent agent. He knew he should not pry into the private life of another man. And he felt sorry for the great mind that had never passed on its genes.

John wanted to turn back and just let Richard send him the movie and the dam demo programs. There was still time to go back to Searchlight and hike up the hill to the old man's gold mine. But that would risk the whole deal with the Israelis.

It would also defy Eytan Baum's new orders about the demo and their contract also forbade such public transmissions. Israeli intelligence would find out. Then Baum would find out and that would be the end of Water Dragon. Baum joked a lot but he would not stand for someone ignoring his orders. John knew he had to go Los Angeles and prepare the demo for Baum and sleep with Denise and get back to the dam. He had less than two days to do it and do it all right.

The Jeep stopped next to the manned brown guard booth.

"Window," John said.

The window went down and John swung his feet around and sat up.

A thin old man in a green uniform leaned out of the booth. He pointed a black MRI gun at the left side of John's head and kept his eyes on his console screens. The gun pulsed radio and magnetic waves that realigned the hydrogen atoms in John's head. The raisin in John's ear could detect some of the electric field that the atoms sent back to the gun.

"Don't be nervous," the guard said. "Nervousness shows up in purple. Okay. Any fruits or vegetables?"

"No."

"Just a moment please."

The guard turned back to his control booth but left the glass door open. John felt the cool air tumble out the booth and into hot desert air just as it flowed out of his Jeep. He had to strain to see the floating brown image of his brain on the guard's monitor.

Signal processors had taken his brain's field measurements and mapped them into an electroencephalogram. The EEG was the first step in the system's parallel match of stored EEG brainprints. The EEG waves rolled across his brain in shades of blue and green and red. A massive neural network matched the 3-D brain pattern to millions of like patterns stored in the tangled webs of its trillions of software synapses.

The guard looked puzzled.

"You're not Maria Ramirez are you?" he said.

"No. John Grant."

"Hmm. John Grant. You know it's been a while since we got any new netware out here. Budget cuts. That don't stop them from packing this thing with new scans. Been misclassifying for nearly two months now."

The old man stroked his whiskers with his left hand while his right hand typed in John's name on an old-style keyboard.

John had a bad thought and he wished he could see how it looked on the brain scan. He thought that this old guard might be what would have come of his old miner if the miner had been born 100 years later.

The console screen showed a new brown brain image that turned slowly in orange three-space. The guard spoke the words "John Grant" twice to the screen to confirm the brain image. The teacher signals also helped tune the neural net.

A neural net forgot things much as real brains did. The neural net would learn the new pattern of John's brain but would forget small parts of the other brain patterns spread over its tangled virtual synapses. There was no way to tell what it would forget.

A neural net could match patterns well if it did not store too many patterns. But it could not explain where it stored the patterns or how it matched the new pattern to the stored patterns. The neural circuits left no audit trail. They spun around in massive feedback cycles and then converged on a fixed pattern or nearest match. The full neural system answered questions just as humans did. And like humans it could not explain how it answered them.

John watched the guard's console screen scroll through his tax returns and his medical and banking data.

The state had kept this data on him since his college days when he had used the school's medical plan and then had taken out a small loan. He regretted that now and had since paid off the loan. He could not wipe the ongoing files unless he bought out with the million dollars that so few could afford. Even then he could not be sure SoCal would wipe its files.

The lower third of the guard's monitor flashed in red. John knew it was a warning. It told the guard that John Grant had a high-risk profile in the eyes of Southern California. John tried to read the message. He turned his eyes so hard to the left that they hurt and his contact lenses bunched up. He could read only something about how state employees should remain courteous but cautious when they dealt with him.

"Hey," the guard said. "I see that you patented your own molecule."

"Jesus. How did you know that?"

"Son. You don't want to know. Sure would like to know how you patent a molecule. Never heard of that before. Figured the Orientals had all the patents now."

"You have to work out a novel molecular structure. It can't occur on its own in nature or the state won't even look at the patent."

"Amazing. Mr. Grant is it? I'm sorry. Looks like you have some unpaid speeding fines and some consumption taxes from your last visit here. No sir. You can't beat those new asphalt sensors. Please drive right over there to secondary inspection. Just step on the gas a little bit."

Jism flashed on the windshield and nodded to John to calm him. Jism blinked off the windshield before the guard saw him.

John tapped the accelerator.

Caltrans took over and drove the car to a metal hut behind the welcome sign. Two border patrolmen in green and brown came out with .357 Magnums strapped to their sides. They held wire wands in their hands. They were younger than John and that just added to the humiliation. It also made him feel a little old and far away from the buyout. And it made him feel both lonely and sad at the loss of Alon Gorenberg.

"Sir," the shorter patrolman said. "Please step outside the vehicle."

John stood in his shorts and T-shirt as the man moved the wand over his bare knees and back and chest. The other patrolman passed a longer wand over the roof of the Jeep. The longer wand made a loud bell sound. He passed it over the Jeep twice more to locate the target.

"Go ahead," John said. "It's in the glove box."

"We'll need your driver's license."

John gave the license hologram to the shorter patrolman. He ran it through a small wireless monitor and gave it back to John.

The taller one came out of the car with a pack of *Zensin* marijuana cigarettes.

"What's this?" he said.

"You know damn well what it is. And look at the seal. It's not broken. That means it's legal even here in Southern California. So put it back."

The patrolman gave the pot back to John instead.

"Mr. Grant. You got quite a few speeding violations from I-15 last month. What was the hurry?"

He held the display pad so John could see the green dots on the desert highway and the date and time and the amount of the fines.

"You know these fines compound at 10% per month. That puts your fine total at $856 and your consumption tax total at $203. So as of today you owe $1,059. State law says you have to pay any fine over $500 on the spot. If you can't do that then we have to impound your vehicle for future auction."

"I have a credit card," John said.

John pulled the Visa card from his wallet and handed it over. The short patrolman ran it through the wireless monitor.

"Sorry. You're overdrawn. You know the state has the right to fine you for that?"

"I know."

"So we impound the car?"

"No. Let's get my girlfriend on-line. She has the American Express card. It has no balance limit."

"Let's hope she is home."

::::■ CHAPTER II

North of Tabriz
Iran

The young guard Jahangir sat with his wood flute and Japanese submachine gun. He sat outside a cave high in the brown rocky Qareh Dahg Mountains of northern Iran.

Jahangir was 19 and had tended sheep and had cut pine trees as a boy in the valleys far below. He and his older brother had fled Azerbaijan as children when an Armenian shell fell on their house while he was at school. The explosion killed his parents and his baby brother. He had joined the Sufis a few weeks after the Armenians captured and shot his brother in the war in the Nagorno-Karabakh enclave that lay to the north across the border in Azerbaijan.

The young *shayk* Hamid Tabriz had pitied the boy and let him live with the brotherhood. Tabriz had taught Jahangir many things. Tabriz taught him to pray and fast and meditate. This helped Jahangir ease his grief and then leave it in his past. Most of all Tabriz had taught the young man to love life and to love Allah.

Now Jahangir sat close enough to the cave entrance so that he could hear the singing and the synthesized music within. The music made him feel warm and excited. Many times he flipped the machine gun's safety off and on and then off again. Tabriz had promised him that someday soon he could join the brotherhood. He thought about that now as he listened to the music and watched the rocks and the dark sky.

Someday Jahangir could even become a dervish like the young initiate Barat Berdiev from Baku. The initiation would come at the supreme cost. But it would secure him a life in heaven. It would be his wedding with eternity.

Heaven was worth any cost.

Tabriz sat at the back of the ancient cave. He kept his back to the granite and kept the cave entrance in clear view. Twenty Sufis in old white wool sat on the dirt floor in a large circle with Tabriz at one end. All had fought for the Muslims in Nagorno-Karabakh or Kazakhstan or Turkmenistan.

The tanned boy Barat spun and shouted at the center of the circle.

Barat had found the rapture early in life at puberty. Tabriz loved the boy but would not have sex with him because he had not yet become a man. Some of the Sufis swayed with him and shouted to the many rhythms of the wild music. The shouts came in Farsi and Turkish and Azeri. A few came in garbled Russian. Four Sufis sucked on red cords from a large brass water pipe filled with a brown brick of smoldering hashish.

Tabriz did not shout or move or smoke. He sat still and watched both the boy Barat and the rock mural across from him. He had made the mural when he was 15 and had founded this brotherhood. The other Sufis had carved the rocks and woven the red and black rugs with polygon designs and sketched in charcoal the portrait of the ancient Sufi master and poet Jalāl-ad-Dīn ar-Rūmī. The Sufis had also placed computer consoles beneath the mural and stacked superconducting battery packs between the consoles.

Two older Sufis laughed and blew hashish smoke at the Israeli AMAN agent Joel Davis. The Sufis had beaten him below the neck and tied his hands to his boots.

Davis had lost the Game. He puckered his cracked and dry lips and sucked in as much hashish smoke as he could. That helped ease the pain and helped him to rest amid the Sufi frenzy.

The whirling dervish Barat spun to a stop.

The Sufis went silent. The mood music softened and reduced to just three lines of fast counterpoint. The young guard Jahangir looked in the cave to watch the final celebration. Barat looked at the ceiling and sang the lines of ar-Rūmī in Farsi:

> *It is the day of great great joy.*
> *Let us all now become friends.*
> *To mystery's side. To the side of mystery!*
> *We go dancing as God's guests.*
> *My death is my wedding with eternity!*

Hamid Tabriz stood as the dervish sang the last line.

Tabriz had the tall thin body of an ascetic. He held an ancient scimitar across his white robe.

"Let us become friends," Tabriz said in Farsi.

Barat looked at Tabriz and then looked back up at the cave roof. He screamed in ecstasy for over a minute. The other Sufi members in the brotherhood shouted and screamed in support. The music grew louder and added more lines of counterpoint.

Tabriz spun with the curved sword and cut off the boy's head as it still screamed.

Two Sufis rose and caught the wild-eyed head as it fell. The other Sufis jumped to their feet and rushed in and danced with the jumping headless body. They smeared their white wool robes and faces with its pulsing blood. The music screamed with a distinct line of counterpoint for each Sufi.

Joel Davis watched the blood dance and fought to keep his head clear and to keep his courage from turning to panic. He knew that Israeli intelligence would conclude that he had died. They would only worry whether he had talked first and whether they could still use his latest reports. Davis had resolved to tell the Sufis only lies and then only when he could no longer stand the pain.

At least he had had the hashish.

Joel Davis had always known that someday his death would come. He would never again sleep well or make love or read the London *Times* on the porch of his flat in Tel Aviv. The Sufis would not even let him drink water. Now his life would end like this and no one would care.

Tabriz lowered the bloody scimitar and turned to look at the beaten but stoic Israeli.

Davis just hoped it all had some purpose.

:::::▪ CHAPTER 12

San Gabriel Mountains
California

John Grant cleared the Cajon summit on I-15 at sunset and began the long descent down the mountains to the L.A. basin.

John had taken the wheel at Barstow when I-40 fed into I-15. He could brake and steer and control the throttle. He could not replace the collision avoidance system. The road sensors now measured his speed and how much his Jeep veered from the midpoint of his lane. The state would fine him for a high speed or a wide dispersion from the lane midpoint.

The heavy traffic on the freeway was a mix of old gas cars and new electric cars and buses. They all drove on smart lanes that billed and fined the driver by the second. Satellites and road sensors helped each car navigate to within a millimeter of its goal path. The system worked much as the air traffic control system worked for airplanes and helicopters and unmanned aerial vehicles.

John watched the road and only glanced at the new tract homes. The homes covered much of what had been the Angeles National Forest before the Great Quake. Southern California and the federal government had both sold much of the forests and foothills to land developers. Now only the steepest peaks remained wild.

John tried not to think about how the land had changed or how the people had changed. He could not blame them for wanting more. They made do as best they could in the face of the huge state and federal debts from the past that still grew each year.

The world had long since learned not to index its debt in dollars.

First Japan and Germany had called in their U.S. debt and dumped their U.S. treasury and municipal bonds. Then the Chinese and Mexicans and Brazilians had switched to Swiss francs and to the new private commodity currencies. The United States had had to sell land and highways and offer ever higher bond yield rates to attract buyers. That pushed up the cost of capital and increased the kill rate of start-ups like Water Dragon. There were now more people than ever and they had to pay more taxes for fewer state services than ever.

John relaxed and tried to let his mind float and yet not fall asleep. He thought of Denise and the child and the old gold miner and of the slight thrill he felt as he watched the river of gas cars and smart cars.

The black phone symbol appeared in red on the windshield. Jism appeared and reached over and answered it.

John? It's Richard.

"Put him through," John said.

Richard's face broke through the green heads-up display of the freeway traffic. John tried to watch Richard and the real traffic at the same time.

"Good news," Richard said. "I just finished the first draft of the movie. You'll love it."

"Good. Don't forget I have to present it."

"I didn't forget. I packed it with 36 ports for you to blend in. Of course you do have to practice your lines."

"Sounds like more work," John said. "But I'd rather do that than just sit in this damn car. I have to stop in a few minutes and see Denise. Can you last awhile?"

"Sure. When you get here I'll show you something else you'll like. We just got the new bill for this month's CPU tax."

"How much?"

"Almost a grand."

"Jesus. There's nothing like paying a tax for a loss of liberty. Do you have the money for it?"

"No."

"I don't either. They just hit me for over a grand at the border. My card bounced and I had to call Denise. Sure hate to ask your sister for more credit. It would be a lot simpler if you just changed your Y chromosome to X!"

"Fuck you."

"Not till you change. Oh shit!"

The word VIOLATION flashed in red on the windshield.

John's Jeep had just passed the state speed limit of 70 miles per hour for the second time in five minutes. The new $400 fine would add to the 37 small fines he had accrued since Barstow when his Jeep's lane variance passed the state's lane dispersion limit in fixed five-minute intervals.

The state could suspend his license with the next ticket. It could impound his car with the next ticket after that.

"Jism?"

Yes?

"Move us into the smart-car lane. I quit. You're back in control."

Thank you.

:::::■ CHAPTER 13

Wrightwood
California

The sun had set when John's Jeep pulled up to Denise's cabin in the pine suburbs of Wrightwood. The cabin was over 7,000 feet up in the San Gabriel Mountains and looked out over part of the L.A. basin far below. The L.A. lights now glowed orange and yellow through the basin smog and the local pine trees. Most of the glow came from millions of barrels of oil a year. Only part of it came from the lone nuclear power plant down the Pacific coast at San Onofre.

John jumped out to stretch and felt the good crisp chill from the cool thin air. He always liked the tall western yellow pines and ponderosa pines. Only mesquite and paloverde shrubs grew near his desert trailer. John did not look forward to driving to Richard's lab down in the heart of that orange and yellow glow.

"Jism. How much time can I spend here?"

Enjoy yourself. Take at least two hours.

"Don't try to act like my father. I never had one and never will."

Please forgive the suggestion.

Denise stood at the cabin door and held her new green silk robe closed with both hands. Her long black hair swirled around her neck to the left side. She was barefoot and John could see she wore nothing under the silk robe.

He ran up and kissed her.

"Good trip?" she said.

"Are you kidding? The whole world is coming apart and I've been stuck in that goddamn car. Defenseless. Nothing to do but watch it happen."

"Mr. Rockefeller wants action? Maybe I can give him some."

She wrapped her legs around his and made him carry her into the brown pinewood cabin. John waddled with her past the open door and into the cabin where he smelled the Vietnamese fish oil of her cooking. He carried her past the blue fake Ming vases in the hall and into the pine-log living room.

Large red and purple flowers slowly blossomed on the smart walls. Denise had picked them to celebrate his coming. Their son had his pink left foot at the edge of the egg of red and yellow sap on the new egg shelf. Denise had just bought the shelf for the final gestation.

John carried her next to the egg.

He wanted to see the red status numbers at the base of the egg stand. He could not make sense of the DNA codes and nutrient ratios but he mumbled them softly to himself for Jism to hear. He did see that the fetus was now 14 weeks old and had a fuzzy degree of life of 41% alive.

"Look at him," John said. "He looks a third like you."

"And a third just like you."

"Yeah. But a third like whom? Sure hope you

know what you're doing with this gene search.''

"You're just like all men," Denise said as she kissed his neck and rubbed her firm breasts on his shoulder. "All you want with a girl is to propagate your genes. Your big white ego can't give up that sixth of the genome for the child's own sake."

This was true and it cut John in some new place inside himself that he could not name. It was that place where Jism knew to stay out of. John still could not fit a wife and child into his view of his future or his view of himself and he did not want to part with that extra portion of his genes. Yet he longed for both Denise and the child. He felt the warmth grow in his loins and felt the first tingle on his back.

"But momma can," John said. "She can give up anything for her little Barbie doll in a fish tank."

Denise did not answer. Instead she drooped her head in a half pout. John leaned in and kissed her on the cheek.

"Sweet Denise. What's the gene search done for our little precious today?"

Denise pulled away to boot the egg computer with her right palm print. The black console beneath the egg displayed ADAPTIVE GENOME in gold.

"50-50 gene mix," Denise said softly to the voice sensors in the egg stand.

A blue sheet appeared in 3-D perspective.

John knew that the blue sheet stood for genome space compressed down from its billions of dimensions to just the two of length and width. He had given the device his blood and spit and urine and had told it his medical history.

Each point on the blue sheet defined one genome or unique set of human genes. It stood for a list of over four billion base pairs of nucleic acid. These base

pairs defined the person's DNA blueprint. A bright
red dot named Denise appeared close to a bright blue
dot named John. A black line formed from the red dot
to the blue dot. A bright purple dot formed at the
midpoint of the line. That meant the system had finished its many teraflops of computations.

"Face at age 30," Denise said. "50-50 gene mix."

The smiling face of a young man appeared on the
console. He had dark hair and John's hawk nose and
her soft Asian eyes and cheekbones and lips. The
computer had run millions of Monte Carlo simulations
to compute this statistical average of the parents' genomes.

"Hi folks," the face said.

John felt again the strange mix of joy and fear.

"He sounds just like you," Denise said.

She hugged John. Then she again palmed the console. The face popped off and the console screen went
black.

"We can still stay with the 50-50 mix if you
want."

"No. We agreed to this. Let's see what science has
done for us."

"Gene search to date," Denise said to the console.
"Mix in thirds."

The blue plane popped back on with the red and
blue dots and the purple dot between them. This time
a line did not connect the red and blue dots. The purple dot moved slowly at random out from the midpoint of the red and blue dots. Then a new green dot
appeared in the center of the other three dots.

The green dot stood for the child's new gene mix.
The gene search had perturbed the parent midpoint in
its search for a DNA blueprint with higher IQ and a
better and more fluid mix of nerves and muscles.

The green dot slowly moved outward as the purple dot moved outward and came to a stop. The search system had optimized some measure of the purple genome's health and IQ. The system had constrained the result to stay near the parent dots in genome space. So each parent still had a third of his or her genes in common with the new gene set. Denise and John had also given the system a set of 25 body features that picked out preferred directions in the genome space.

"Face at age 30," Denise said.

A new face popped on the screen. It looked much like the first face but had larger eyes and forehead and thinner lips.

"Dad," the face said. "What is my name?"

"Jesus," John said.

"Oh. I like that name."

John. Relax. This means a great deal to Denise.

Denise palmed the console once more and the console screen returned to black.

"What do you think?" she said. "I know it shook you a little. Shall we keep him?"

John looked her in the eyes and held her shoulders but did not answer. He did not want Jism to feed him the answer either. He knew Jism sensed that.

He did his best to think of her now as his fiancée and not as his financier.

"You know," she said. "It's still legal to abort him. He's only 41% alive."

Answer with care. Pause and think.

"Get rid of the flowers," he said and kissed her.

"Wall: Paint. New van Gogh and Picasso."

The red and purple flowers popped off the three walls of the room. Classic van Gogh paintings popped on and off in large squares on two walls. Classic Pi-

casso paintings did the same on the third wall behind
John.

Then the paintings changed.

Van Gogh's *Starry Night* swirled into a cosmic
spacescape of galaxies that spiraled out while massive
black holes at their centers ate them from within. Picasso's flat horse and dog shapes turned to alien faces
and starships and cubic planets. Soon all three walls
crawled with hybrids of the two masters and with new
paintings in their styles. John wondered if the old gold
miner would see it all as magic.

"Wall," John said. "Add some Dali and Escher.
And some music."

"That won't work. I trained the walls to my voice.
You know that."

"Last time you were still watching the manual
disks."

"I've come a long way since then. Watch. Wall:
Paint. Add Dali and Escher. Wall: Compose. Varia-
tions on your Beethoven's 51st Symphony."

The walls changed to the seething surreal land-
scapes of Dali and the fractal symmetries of Escher.
Loud orchestral chords in G Major came from the
walls. The complete works of Beethoven had trained
and seeded the system's neural autocomposer. The G
Major chords sounded like the E-flat Major chords
from the start of the *Eroica* Symphony. Yet they had
their own feel to them that John recognized but did
not like.

Denise pulled back from John to open a chrome
drawer. She pulled out a thin tube of pink sponge and
held it under John's nose as he helped her green silk
robe fall to the floor. The stick gave off the sweet
smell of bubble gum.

Denise held an outlawed pea stick.

John's eyes watered as he sniffed the sweet out-lawed pheromone compound based on phenylethy-lamine or PEA. He felt the "pea brain" further charge his sex and adrenal hormones and further fire the erotic visions in his mind's eye. He and Denise did not need the sex booster but it would sharpen their feelings and lessen the time between bouts. Liberals and Greens had outlawed the pea compound as a cause of date rape.

"No no no," John said. "Not Beethoven. Give me something with balls in it. Something like Wagner. And not that damned 'Ride of the Valkyries.' "

"Okay. Wall: Compose. Wagner but no preludes or overtures."

Denise turned back from the wall. She stood naked as she faced him.

"John?" she said as she sniffed the pea stick. "Sure you don't want to talk about that new United Nations tax on my futures trades? You love to talk about taxes."

John pulled off his sweat-stained black T-shirt and felt the full rush of the pea brain. The wall music began as "Entrance of the Gods into Valhalla" and grew on its own from there to something grand and orchestral with string tremolos and harp glissandos.

"Fuck the UN and fuck me," he said.

The two fell to the sleek black floor in an animal frenzy of sex.

The wall art changed faster now. The wall figures grew and shrank and merged and split. The music grew louder and faster and more contrapuntal. It drifted further from its Wagner seed music into com-plex patterns of orchestration that would have taken a human days to write out on 40-line score sheets.

John had not slept with Denise for over two weeks.

So he found his frenzy coming to a quick end. He clutched her in Darwin's rhythm and soon saw the white flash of orgasm in his mind's eye and felt the hot contractions of his nerves and muscles.

John's frenzy ended with him behind Denise and his right hand pulling her twisted long black hair. But John and his pea brain were not yet spent. His climax had been too hot and too strong to fade so fast and Denise had still not reached her climax.

John looked down at the smooth arc and ribs of her back. The music grew with her mounting frenzy. He saw out of the corners of his eyes the more complex patterns of colors on the walls while he watched her supple spine writhe up and down. She flexed her vaginal muscles and her small fine white ass cheeks faster and faster and kept him hard despite himself. She moaned more and shook her head so fast from side to side that it seemed to vibrate on her neck.

Her orgasm came in a taut shimmering spasm.

Denise clenched her cheeks and all her muscles one last time and held it like the last breath of someone drowning. Her moan passed into a soft scream and then died off in a broken laugh.

The music and walls still tracked Denise's mood but they did not slow after her climax. Her clenched cheeks and vaginal muscles still held his hardness and now it almost hurt. Still John felt the calm roll over him and felt the clearness of mind that always came after sex.

He thought of Jism watching him. Or at least listening to him.

John looked past Denise's fine ribbed back to his raisin lying on the floor. He felt truly naked without Jism in his ear. It had fallen out in the frenzy. The wild music and swirling colors irritated him and he wished it would soften or stop. His hardness withered.

Denise did not see John grab the small brown device. She also did not see him pause when he pushed the raisin into his left ear and then stared in shock at her scalp.

John thought he saw pink worms on her scalp.

"Jism."

Yes?

"What about jism?" Denise said with a laugh.

John pulled the twist of her coarse black hair to the side. Denise moaned and he got a good look at the thin pink scars and tiny stitches that ran across the back of her head. The raisin could sense John's adrenal flash.

"Jism! Christ! Look at these fucking brain scars!"

"What do you think of them?" a voice said that began as Denise's and ended as a man's.

John jumped up and grabbed for his pants.

"Wall: *Allahu Akhbar!*"

A placid face appeared on large squares of all three walls. John recalled the face from the cave video that Jism had played for him a few hours before. The face was that of his neural math idol.

It was Hamid Tabriz.

The music turned into the wild Arabic music from Tabriz's cave in the Qareh Dahg Mountains. The driving music further confused him.

Denise's naked body jumped to its feet.

"Let us be friends," Denise/Tabriz said in unison with the wall images of Tabriz.

John. The Jeep. Run to the Jeep.

Then the small lithe body of Denise leaped across the room. It spun and backfisted John in the mouth. The blow split the side of his lower lip and loosened a tooth. It almost knocked him over backward. Denise grabbed John by the neck and the two fell back against the black console and egg shelf.

Denise yanked the egg free of its mount and raised it above her head to throw. Blood nutrient sap poured from a trailing hose.

Blind her if you can.

John dove at her instead. He drove his head into her stomach as she tried to crush his skull with the egg. She missed and fell over backward.

The egg bounced once on the floor and dribbled more blood and sap from the ripped clear plastic cord. The wide end of the eggshell cracked on the second bounce. Then it broke on the hard pine floor and spilled its bloody contents. The pseudodiamond casing itself did not break.

John's tiny son thrashed his small wet hands and feet for only a moment and then he lay still.

John's lunge had made Denise fall backward against the edge of the egg shelf. The back of her head cracked in pieces along the pink scar lines. Chunks of black sponge spilled out and bounced twice on the floor. Denise's eyes crossed and rolled like a lizard's in separate directions.

The wall images of Tabriz spun off into wild fractal curves of all colors. Millions of colored dots blinked on and off in waves of color. The music screeched into fast parallel lines of atonal dissonance.

"There's no blood!" John said to Jism.

Reach in and shut her down. Quickly.

John tried to reach and grab the split head but he froze.

He saw Denise lying wounded. He looked away and saw his son nearby in a puddle of red and yellow sap. John turned back and knew this was no longer Denise but still he could not bring himself to defile her ruptured skull. She was not his enemy and she needed help.

Denise/Tabriz did not agree.

The young girl snapped forward and backfisted him twice more in the face and chest.

The wall art slowed and mixed with flashes of Tabriz's calm white face. The music calmed somewhat too and returned more and more to the pulsing Arab cave music. Denise's eyes fell into synch and turned hard to look at John as she kicked him in the stomach.

John. Shut her down. Now!

He knew Jism was right and must have patched into Denise's computer system and watched the struggle from the room sensors. Jism might even have made contact with the Tabriz system.

John saw in a flash that in the next instant Tabriz would fully self-organize and take control and kill him. The head blow had only stunned the Tabriz system.

There was a price for living and he would now have to pay it.

Denise tried to bite his hand as he punched her in the left temple. The blow knocked out more of the black foam. Then John reached around into her cracked head and tore through the foam and heard the music scream in a whistling roar.

Then his fingers found it and he yanked out the small golden nanochip.

In that instant Denise froze and the walls went black and silent.

CHAPTER 14

Highway I-10
Southern California

"Jism. He's going to pull me over for murder."

Please relax. The officer sensed us with only standard police radar as he did all the other cars in a 40-yard radius. We can infer at most that the central police computer in Los Angeles has now run our data and recent travel history and has found no reason for the officer to stop us.

John let Jism drive the Jeep through the stop-and-go traffic on the new 10 freeway that still ran from Florida to Santa Monica. The Jeep would take half an hour to reach Richard Cheng in the inner city.

"Jism. I'm worried about leaving the fetus. Little Stuart. I loved my son. You know that. I didn't want to leave him there."

John. There was nothing you could do. He died before the fight ended. Just try to relax.

"I am trying. Did you ever kill anyone? You'd be paranoid too."

No doubt I would be. Yet the evidence suggests that Dr. Tabriz or his followers killed Denise well before we arrived at her cabin in Wrightwood.

John tried not to think about how she died but he could not push the thoughts from his mind. He still saw Denise with her skull cracked open. He saw her naked body thrashing in the chaos of random neuro-muscular contractions.

Did Tabriz kill her quickly? That would have risked some injury to her body or scalp. Did he cut out her brain in one stroke? Or did he cut it out slowly with some sick new technique he had devised? There was no way to tell from that last image of her on the floor. It all left open the real question: What did she feel at the end? How horrible was it to lose your brain and see at least some of it happen?

The Jism image appeared on the windshield but did not smile.

"But *why*?" John said. "Why?"

Of course he must view you as a threat. He went to such great lengths to deceive you.

"You mean he went to such great lengths to *kill* me."

We don't know that Dr. Tabriz wished to kill you. He could have killed you when you entered the cabin. He certainly could have killed you before you two engaged in sex on the floor.

"Hey. I had sex with her. Not him."

I should think we can safely say you had sex with both persons if the term person *has any meaning beyond the flesh. The point is that the Denise automaton—*

"Jism. Don't call her an automaton. We're all one of those if you look at it in terms of differential equations. We're all made of meat and we do just what the equations of physics say we will do and no more. Christ. You know that. What the hell are you? There is no Markov process in nature. No future is free of the past. Look. I'm guilty of a lot of things but I have never violated the law of conservation of energy! I should take some kind of pill to calm down. No. Denise was a chiphead. She literally had a chip for a brain! How can they do that?''

Very well. Denise was a chiphead. The point is that the Denise chiphead displayed no aggression toward you. Indeed it behaved in such a way as to suggest that it would never have harmed you if you had not found the scars on the back of its head.

"Are you saying I caused this? Tabriz attacked *me*! Look at this lip. It burns every time I talk. Why would he want to deceive me?''

Surely it relates to your Black Sun patent or your contract with the Israeli government or perhaps both.

"So you think it's about hydrogen?''

In any case it seems to relate to oil. The terrorists attacked the Dhahran oil fields. That led to the expected outcome of a Saudi tit-for-tat strike against Israel. Then terrorists dissolved the oil tanker Hombre.

"No tie to Israel there,'' John said.

None that we can see. Then terrorists murdered the financier of Water Dragon.

"Jesus. Have the respect to call the company Black Sun in my presence.''

Please pardon the synonym. Your words are yours to use as you see fit. I just wish to present the recent events and advance a conjecture. For I believe you are now in the greatest of danger.

"No shit. The cops will think I murdered Denise. My prints and semen are all over her. I'm sure I left some blood on the floor.''

You did.

"So they'll have my DNA match in minutes. I should call Eytan and tell him."

I advise that you wait to call Eytan at least until you arrive at Richard's warehouse.

"You don't trust the Israelis?"

Richard has more secure communications. The police will wonder why you called the Israeli government before you called them.

"You're right. I'm too nervous to think straight. I'd also like to get out of this Jeep and into a bed sometime before the state grabs me and puts me in line for lethal injection."

John. Try to relax. You might eat some more of those bagels to keep up your energy.

"Your personal intelligent agent. Man's best friend. The bagels are a week old and hard as rocks."

I want only to help you maximize your utility.

"I know that and I love you for it. You'd know that if only somehow I could get you laid."

I return to my conjecture. You may have been in little danger if you had not found the scars on the chiphead's scalp. Tabriz may have wanted only to infiltrate the operations of Black Sun. We may never know. But we can be sure that those who killed Denise and installed the chip will know that you have discovered them. The odds are good they know already. You thwarted their plan.

"So this time they will try to kill me?"

Yes.

"Can't the police protect me?"

John. I am surprised that you of all people would expect refuge from the state bureaucracy. The guilty parties here are both highly intelligent and vigilant in their cause.

"What about Richard? Do you think I should trust him?"

Only if you cannot find like scars on his scalp. You should not tell him about his sister unless you are sure of his identity.

"I hate to play games like that. But you're right again. If he is a chiphead then he'll be waiting to kill me. Hell. They are twins or were twins. Richard a chiphead. That would be just like his high-tech fanatical ass to end up like that. He'd likely love it."

You must prepare yourself for that outcome. And you must proportion your belief to the evidence no matter how strange the evidence appears.

"You still think we should go to Richard's?"

Yes. The other alternative is to return to Nevada. But you need rest and there is little safety in this vehicle. Most of all you need to explore the nanochip you hold in your hand.

"Bet they would like to kill me to get this back."

No doubt.

"Think about that. I hold in my hand the mind of the great Hamid Tabriz. At least I hold some of his mind. You can bet that murderous fuck backed this up."

You may also hold in your hand the soul of your fiancée.

::::: CHAPTER 15

Downtown Los Angeles
Southern California

John let Jism park the Jeep in a deep underground lot in downtown L.A. Jism had found no news
of Denise's death in the media but John still thought
the police had followed them. So John risked the
longer walk at night through the old cracked streets
where the homeless lived after almost a decade of
large earthquakes. The Big One never came and released the pent-up stress energy but a series of lesser
quakes did.

Some of the homeless sat or slept on the ground.
Others watched old TVs that they had mounted with
small satellite dishes. Many of the homeless stood in
long lines outside the green city outhouses or in front
of the new welfare vending machines. Only one griz-
zled old man asked John for cash as John walked by.
John shook his head and walked on to the old subway
in the Rebuild L.A. Science Park.

Richard Cheng rented part of a warehouse in the
park behind Figeuroa. There Richard had set up the
L.A. branch of Water Dragon. In minutes John stood
outside the old gray warehouse made of cracked concrete and particle board.

John now felt sure that no one had followed him.

"Jism?" he whispered.

Yes?

"Can you port to Richard's computer net as soon as we walk in?"

I always have in the past.

"I just want to be sure that you can see as well as hear. I'm going straight for that Glock."

Please be careful. The gun control laws are severe in Los Angeles and quite so for an unlicensed nine-millimeter semiautomatic sidearm. Have you had fire-arm instructions?

"Cork it."

Imagine what would have happened if you had had the Glock in the Jeep when the border patrolmen searched it.

John found the plastic key in his pocket and slid it through the door slot. The door opened to darkness and John could hear Richard talking to someone. John walked in on the balls of his feet. He saw Richard taping himself in front of a blue screen for the Hoover demo.

A second screen showed the Black Sun process as a glossy cartoon. Lasers pulsed to time and to energize and even to program the porky ball carbon molecules. The porky balls split the precious hydrogen from the oxygen molecules in water. H_2O poured in one tube. Hydrogen and oxygen poured out their own tubes at the end of the process. Waste hydroxy radicals poured out a third tube that fed back to the splitting system.

On a third screen a porcupine wore sunglasses and had chrome quills that stood on end. The creature moved its lips to track Richard's lips as he synched the voice-over. The system used the latest netware for motion estimation but it still had to train on Richard's patterns of speech and body language.

John wanted to shout that there was no way he would get in front of the Boulder bureaucrats and the Texans and the Israelis with that talking porcupine. But he knew that in the end it was his fault for coining the term *porky ball*.

John had nicknamed his carbon molecule that because of the hundreds of electrons in its outer shells. He thought of the fleeting molecule in the math sense as a hypercube with trillions of corners or quills. The name had stuck and even the Israelis used it in state documents. The Israelis were also the first to create a porky ball long enough to split water before the outer electrons peeled off and the molecule cooled to a new energy minimum.

John thought of this and saw once more how much he missed Alon Gorenberg and his research team in Eilat.

Richard seems to have prepared a multimedia surprise for you.

"This is what happens when a kid watches too many cartoons," John whispered. "Is the Glock still in the safe?"

It should be. No one has opened the safe in four days.

"I just hope I remember the combination."

I remember it.

Richard saw John as he crept to the safe and kneeled and opened it.

Richard stopped the taping and the lights came on in the warehouse. His own raisin had spoken to him.

"What do you think?" Richard said. "This could launch porky as a lunchbox franchise!"

"It's all right."

"So you like it? Wait till you see the whole animation. I've got the hydrogen molecules lining up and spinning just like the light fairies in *Fantasia*!"

"Jesus fucking Christ. How old are you?"

"John boy. My raisin tells me there's a problem."

"What did Sun Tzu say?" John said.

John walked up to Richard along the far wall of the warehouse and kept the Glock low at his right side.

"He says you just picked up the pistol. What happened to your face?"

"You tell me."

"Hey. You're serious. What's wrong? Is Denise all right?"

"She's just fine."

Then John tackled Richard and pinned him to the floor with one of the first grappling holds he had learned in wrestling. John had over 30 pounds on Richard and most of it was muscle. He took a muscle enzyme tablet once a week to slow the breakdown of the muscle mass he built in a gym every third week.

"What the hell?" Richard said.

"I just want to see if you still have dandruff."

John moved the Glock's barrel through Richard's thick black hair. There were no scars on his scalp.

Jism learned from the tackle. Jism had watched John for more than two years and knew most of his likes and dislikes. The likes and dislikes formed a bumpy choice surface or preference map in his software. Hills stood for likes. Valleys stood for dislikes. Jism had never seen John assault someone. Now the agent had to learn and reshape part of the choice surface to account for the evidence.

Richard is not a chiphead. Please do the right thing and let him up.

John jumped back from Richard and stood up.

"Sorry. I thought you might have a chip in your brain."

"What!"

"Jism. Tell Sun Tzu the story."

Richard looked worried now as well as ruffled in his khaki outfit. Sun Tzu had already told Richard that Denise was dead. The background on Hamid Tabriz and recent world events would take longer.

"I will tell you. But you'll trust Jism more than me and this is life and death."

Richard's eyes watered and he lowered his head for a tearless cry.

John suspected that death hurt more the closer two people were in gene space. Nearly identical twins were as close as two distinct genomes got.

"Why the hell did I get involved with you?" Richard said and he broke down and cried outright.

"Knock it off. I did not kill Denise. The great fucking Hamid Tabriz did."

"You just left her body on the floor?"

"Richard. We are in danger. They killed Denise and they tried to kill me. And they sure as hell will try to kill you."

You don't know that.

"Sure I do. Richard. Save the grief for later. I loved Denise too."

"Bullshit."

Richard lunged at John and punched John in the solar plexus.

John crumpled in a pain spasm and saw the flashing blue lights that he sometimes saw on hot desert days when he stood up too fast. John tried to speak but the blow had knocked the air out of him. Richard had studied kempo karate for years and knew how to throw a front punch. John dropped to his knees and tried to breathe. He still held the Glock to his side and rubbed it against the nanochip in his pants pocket.

Richard moved his fingers through John's short brown hair.

"My turn," Richard said with most of his old self back. "I have to make sure you don't have a chip in your brain."

:::::■ CHAPTER 16

Outside of Kirovabad
Azerbaijan

"Show me where," Captain Bavarian said.

Both men sweated in their shirts in the midday heat. The Sturgeon tried not to look the dark young captain in the eyes. The Sturgeon's ribs hurt from the captain's beating. He did not want the captain to see how much he wanted to kill him. The Sturgeon just wanted to get free of the man and leave Azerbaijan for good.

Captain Bavarian tapped the Sturgeon's chest with his balled right fist. A herd of tan goats stopped chewing the thin grass to watch them.

"I told you," the Sturgeon said. "He sat in his car right here where I stand."

"Little fish. Listen to me. I think you have so many purple spots on your face because that bull goat kicks you when you suck him. Maybe we should see. Look at me when I talk to you! Coward! You know what else I think? I think you made a deal with the Israeli and then you killed him. Maybe you used your friends and maybe not. We'll find out. Either way you have betrayed Azerbaijan!"

"Look what he did to me! My head!"

"Your friends could have hit you on the forehead.

Maybe you tried to double-cross them too. I think I will have you shot. I will have you interviewed first but then I will have you shot."

"I am telling you all I know! Please!"

"Why did he leave the lithium tube in the club's parking lot? Where did he go? We have no intelligence that he tried to cross the border. You took our money and then you took his. You are a whore as well as a traitor!"

Bavarian slapped the Sturgeon so hard that the young gangster began to cry.

"Little fish! Look at me! I am not even convinced he was an Israeli spy. Why would he care about this pipeline? Israel buys its oil from the Sibers and the Americans. Liar! I should shoot you right here."

The Sturgeon saw the pipe rupture before Bavarian finished his threat.

Sweat poured down his neck and back. The sweat stained the yellow silk suit that he had bought with the proceeds of his first Turkish opium deal. He wanted to speak but did not want the captain to slap him again.

Bavarian pulled his Beretta M-92 from his black leather hip holster.

"Yes," Bavarian said. "I think I will shoot you. I think I will shoot you now."

"No! No! Look! Look at the pipe. It's melting!"

Captain Bavarian turned to look at the olive Tamraz pipeline.

The gray goo had eaten through two sections of the pipe and left a lake of brown-black oil in the reddish dirt. The pipe had shutoff valves every 50 meters. Terrorists had bombed it for years. Bavarian had twice seen bombed sections of the pipeline but they did not look like this.

The gray goo moved toward Bavarian and the Sturgeon and the rest moved away from them. New oil jets shot out as the nanoacid ate through the shutoff valves on a new stretch of pipe. Two families of shepherds ran their sheep and goats off at right angles from the melting pipe.

"My God," Bavarian said. "They're attacking us! It's some kind of sabotage! Like that oil boat!"

"I told you," the Sturgeon said. "The Israeli came here and set it up. I told you he was a spy!"

Bavarian shot the Sturgeon point-blank in the breastbone.

The impact slammed the skinny young man on his back next to the captain's green Jeep. The Sturgeon's eyes bulged in shock and looked down at the black rent in his suit. He could not breathe but he still tried to speak.

"Why?" he said.

"Why do you think? Because you let this happen!"

"I helped you," the Sturgeon tried to say.

"Not enough. Traitor!"

Captain Bavarian had already worked out the day's report in his head. He still had many seconds before he had to go to the Jeep and call in the meltdown. The pipeline sensors would already have sent their report to the National Oil Company of Azerbaijan and to the army's headquarters in Baku. Soon the NOCA computers would pay one of the Chinese or Japanese satellites to retask and watch the meltdown. The state troops and NOCA repair squads would arrive a few minutes later.

Bavarian squeezed the trigger on the big nine-millimeter. He marveled at how fast he got off the next four rounds.

:::■■ CHAPTER 17

Downtown Los Angeles
Southern California

"Richard," Eytan said on the secure screen. "Your sister was a fine woman. You have all our condolences."

Richard nodded at the screen and returned to the golden chip on the console.

The chip had the standard design of one main input port and one main output port. Richard used light to act as the input and output fiber bundles. Each color or wavelength defined a data path the chip could use. The computer searched through trillions of such schemes for wavelength multiplexing. A few would unlock part of the chip while too many wrong guesses played out in light might break a code and scramble the chip.

"John," Eytan said. "Have you finished the water demo?"

"That's the least of our problems," John said.

"I appreciate your loss. We have suffered many losses here as well. Meanwhile the demo is a little more than a day away."

"Don't you ever sleep?"

"Plenty of time for that in the grave," Eytan said.

"We'll have the demo done in time," Richard said without looking up.

John. It may not be safe for you and Richard to attend the demo. Remember the 77% truth rate from Eytan's last transmission.

"I don't know if it is safe," John said. "Why didn't you warn us about Tabriz?"

"I told you he killed a man when he was 13. What else can I tell you? They also say he had committed the entire Koran to memory by age five. But they say that about many mystics."

"The trouble is my vocal-stress analyzer said you lied 23% of the time in that same message. Reply."

Eytan laughed and held the slight grin.

"All I can say to that is get a new stress analyzer. Or go back and read the manual on the one you have. I thought a word to the wise was sufficient."

"You know what I mean. This chiphead business. Israeli intelligence had to have had something on it. It's too radical a biotechnology for you not to hear of it. And it's too much of a potential threat to your side of the world. You knew a hell of a lot more than you were telling. I'm sure you still do."

John. Relax. Anger hands the advantage to the calmest contestant.

"It's a matter of security classifications and need to know. You would understand if you were in the army. How could we foresee that Tabriz would target your fiancée?"

"I had a need to know yesterday when I asked you about him. I bet you guys have connected all the Tabriz dots by now. And your goddamned security classifications almost derailed the project."

You don't know that. Indeed Eytan may have

wanted to watch how you and Richard dealt with the chiphead.

"John. I appreciate your anger but this won't bring back Denise. And come to think of it. Tabriz may have saved Denise's brain on some other chip or file cube."

"We already thought of that," Richard said.

Snow speckled the screen with Eytan. The lights in the room went dim and then returned to normal.

"What was that?" Eytan said.

"Power brownout," Richard said. "Don't worry. We've been getting them in L.A. almost every day now for a week. We have backup battery packs for the computers."

"Eytan," John said. "You're still not coming clean with us. I read about the tests on rat brains. We all did. All the tests destroyed the brain tissue when they tried to decode it. What technique did Tabriz use?"

"Who knows? The most I can tell you is that Tabriz seems to have had a lot of practice. And that's just rumor."

"This is bullshit," Richard said. "We have to call the police right now."

"Once again," Eytan said. "You don't want to go to jail for murder. Call now and they will book both of you for murder. They will confiscate all your files and all of hers. You might get off in time but it would not be for a long time. Meanwhile all you have worked for will be gone."

His veracity factor climbed to 96% on this last statement.

"I bet your people have already cleaned up her cabin," John said.

Richard looked up from the chip to watch Eytan's expression.

"That's a bet I won't take," Eytan said with the same thin smile.

"We won't be safe if we drive back to Nevada," John said. "The cops or anyone else could stop us."

"You're not safe where you are."

"I know that. Why don't you send some of your people to get us out of here?"

"I've been working on that. Have to go now. Sit tight and don't lose that chip."

Eytan cut the transmission on the Cauchy beamformer.

The image of Eytan had not been as clear and vivid as it had been the day before on the road from Hoover Dam. The Cauchy beamformer made up for that in security. An eavesdropper had no more chance of catching part of the signal than an airplane pilot had of knowing where lightning would flash next in a storm.

"Good," Richard said when the screen turned to snow. "Now let's see what the chip wants to show us."

The screen scrolled through thousands of learning modules.

Richard stepped through some of the movement and speech modules. Some modules learned with adaptive filters and others used straight neural networks. Some used neural nets to learn and tune fuzzy rules and to grow complex logic trees of binary rules.

Richard and John could not grasp the coding schemes that someone had used to map body movements and speech to strings of numbers. The modules all seemed to interlock and feed back onto one another. A few command modules used logic trees to control the learning modules and to assign the right mix of spectral algorithms. They seemed to be the roots of the command tree but Richard and John could not be sure. The wiring diagrams of the modules looked as tangled and confusing as did a brain's wet tangles of neural circuits.

Richard copied the chip output to his console. He also made a backup chip as he scrolled through the modules and the Arabic command text.

The lights dimmed again in a brownout and stayed dim.

"Shit," Richard said. "We'll lose some data in the transfer."

The lights came back to full power and then flickered twice more.

"Got it," Richard said. "Watch this. Right from the top of the buffer. A Tabriz-eye view of the world. But no sound."

The screen turned red and then stabilized on the red and yellow sap inside the baby egg. New images tumbled across the screen with greater speed as Richard's system locked onto the chip's coding schemes and hyptertext transfer protocols.

John's Jeep pulled into the driveway at sunset. John's lips moved in speech and puckered for a kiss. Red and purple peonies flowered on the wall. The image blurred and then focused on Denise's naked white breasts pressed against the black floor and her chest rising and falling with John's thrusts.

"You son of a bitch," Richard said.

"We need to show this to the police," John said and touched his swollen lip.

"What? You fucking my sister?"

"No. This fight scene. It proves self-defense."

Richard shook his head and watched the room spin as Denise back-fisted John in the mouth.

Richard does not believe that the police will find

him in any way responsible for his sister's death. He is still in shock.

"I know that."

"What?"

John shook his head.

The image sequence slowed as Denise fell to the floor.

"Oh no," Richard said. "We tripped something. It must have sent a self-destruct message. Look! The cells are dissolving!"

The image turned to black and Richard ejected the chip from the console.

It was too late. Even the chip's outer skin had changed from gold to brown as many of the chip's 3-D stacks of cells had dissolved. Richard handed the chip to John so he could see the damage for himself.

"We need Eytan's nanoscopes," John said. "What we really need is for Alon to take this apart."

"Can we get it to him?"

"No chance. The Saudis killed him when they bombed the Eilat plant."

Richard looked down again and paused.

"You think we should give it to Eytan?" he said.

"Not right away. And we sure as hell will keep the backup."

"If Eytan wants the chip he will get it. He'll send some kind of Israeli secret agent to get it. We can't stop that."

"You're still in shock," John said.

"Don't dismiss what I say. We can't stop the Israelis."

John put the chip in his T-shirt pocket and pulled the Glock nine-millimeter from his waistband. John could see from Richard's blank face that his Sun Tzu raisin was saying something important to him.

"Dr. Glock can stop them," John said.

"You desert sociopath. Don't even think about pulling that gun on them."

"I'm not going to pull it. I'll keep it in my hand the whole time when they get here. That's why they used to call these things peacemakers."

"Why did I ever get tied up with you?"

"The expected payoff."

::::: **CHAPTER 18**

Baku
Azerbaijan

"**N**o," Aminzadeh said to Mosarian. "I won't bomb Israel as the Saudis did."

Ibn Aminzadeh was president of Azerbaijan and a Muslim who did not believe in Allah. His father had taught him to honor Mecca and its culture but not the god many believed had dwelled there.

Young Ibn had read the Islamic relativist Abdol Karim Soroush. He had proudly told his classmates in petroleum engineering at Tehran University that he was a Muslim but not a fundamentalist. His Shiite enemies had then started a file on him. They shared the data with the Islamic Revolution in Iran and the Islamic Jihad in Egypt and Lebanon and the National Islamic Front in the Sudan.

Shiite radicals now ran these countries and ran Algeria.

The Shiite radicals made up a growing portion of the world's three billion Muslims. Azerbaijan was the only Shiite state that still held true multiparty elections. Aminzadeh led the Islamic Democratic Party in a coalition government of theists and socialists.

115

General Atef Mosarian was both a believer and a socialist.

Mosarian had made it clear to his Azer troops that Aminzadeh had given too much license to the American and Russian oil firms and thus had weakened Azerbaijan. He favored closer ties with the Chinese and Japanese. He now had something he could throw at the Israelis if not at the Americans. He held in his hand Joel Davis's hologram tube.

He laid it on the dark oak desk in Aminzadeh's office.

"Mr. President. This spying device is standard Israeli issue. We took it from a known Israeli agent."

"From whom? Show him to me."

"I cannot do that. The Israelis snatched him from us in Kirovabad. We do have a room full of witnesses and the taped report of one of our agents."

"The gangster they call the Sturgeon?"

"Yes."

"Your room full of witnesses is a barroom in a whorehouse," Aminzadeh said. "Where is this gangster agent called the Sturgeon?"

"He proved a security risk. He was after all a known thief and extortionist."

"I see. So you taped him and then shot him? The world would laugh at him as a witness."

"I don't care what the world would laugh at. The Israelis have destroyed the Tamraz pipeline."

"You have not proved that."

"I know they did it. Look at this tube! We processed some of the 3-D images. They are all of the Tamraz pipeline. We lost over two hundred thousand barrels of oil!"

"I know what we lost and what it will take to clean the spill. But you do not know that the Israelis sab-

otaged the pipe. You only believe it. I will not say
that you want to believe it because I cannot prove that.
I also cannot take your belief to Parliament or turn
your belief into a strike command."

"We know the Greens did this," Mosarian said.
"It was the same superacid that destroyed the Cuban
oil tanker! That cannot be a coincidence."

"I agree. It is not a coincidence. Environmental
terrorists commited both acts and there is a good
chance that the same terrorists did it. I too have read
the intelligence reports. I too saw the WNN report. I
understand that over 10 Green groups have claimed
responsibility. I also understand that Israel supports
the Greens. But the chemist report I read said the two
superacids differed."

"Whoever made one could make the other."

"I agree with that too. But we need proof. Right
now there is no proof that links the Tamraz pipeline
to the bombing of the Dhahran oil fields. Greens have
bombed our pipelines since I was a boy."

"So you will do nothing?"

"General Mosarian. I will not launch a missile attack that could ignite a Mediterranean war just to
please you. You will recall that I was the first Muslim
leader to denounce Israel's support of the Greens after
the Dhahran bombing. I was the first to demand that
Israel pay damages to the Saudis. You will also recall
that I called for the Muslim nations to discuss whether
to impose an oil embargo on Israel."

"But Israel buys most of its oil from the Americans
and the Russians and the Canadians."

"I know that. They also buy several hundred
thousands of barrels from us directly and from us
through Cyprus. So I still call for a Muslim embargo.
Meanwhile I have decided that we should move ahead

on our own and ban all Azer oil exports to Israel and
Cyprus. There will be no military reprisals because
there is no proof of direct Israeli involvement. No
proof and so no reprisals. That is my decision."

"You already decided this before I came in?" Mosarian said with a forced smile.

"Yes. I signed the executive order over an hour
ago."

"Then why did you call this meeting? You did not
want a military opinion?"

"Of course I value your military opinion. But this
was not a military decision. I felt you should be the
first to know."

::::: CHAPTER 19

Tel Aviv
Israel

Colonel Avi Hurwicz sat before a wall map of the Mediterranean and listened to the briefing.

Hurwicz had already scrambled the first wave of Israeli fixed-wing aircraft. He also sent a dozen new Lockheed-Martin ECs over the Mediterranean to gather electronic intelligence from the air and from low-earth orbit satellites. Israel's 200,000 active soldiers had stayed on alert since the Eilat bombing. About 80% of these troops still served as conscript labor. That worried Avi Hurwicz more than he would ever admit.

Avi Hurwicz and many other Israeli officers opposed the growing demands for a volunteer military. The demands came from a new mix of ultra-Orthodox Jews and pacifists and Palestinians and conservative free-market radicals. One claim was that the draft was slavery. The state should not suspend someone's freedom to protect someone else's freedom. The more popular claim was that even a state gets no more than it pays for. If mortal enemies surrounded Israel and if a strong national defense was so dear to the people of Israel, then the people should pay dearly for it. If that

119

meant still higher taxes then so be it. Talk of patriotism was mere propaganda and only hid the real social costs.

Avi and the officers did not agree.

They believed that the force of the state and the patriotic spirit produced better fighting men and women than would simply raising their pay to the market wage rate. They also believed that a draft was cheaper even if the wage gap imposed a net social loss on Israeli society. So what if most of the drafted young men and women could or did earn more than the state paid them for their forced labor? The state paid out less cash and used less tax money. They believed in any case that a draft was fairer because it shared the pain among rich and poor and among smart and dumb. And misery loved company. They had sacrificed some of their freedoms for the state. So could the next generation.

But Avi still had doubts about being a colonel over a largely conscript army. He was not sure that the draft still produced the same will to fight that he had seen in the older officers or that he had heard of from the early days and battles of Israel almost a century ago.

Avi gave little weight to the draft debates on the internet and on the TV talk shows. He did not care that more American Jews than ever married outside their faith and so fewer foreign Jews came back to serve a term in the Israeli Army. Few came anyway. What worried him was that too many young men openly opposed the draft and still managed to get good jobs and get girls. That would never have happened in his youth.

Now Avi Hurwicz had to digest the intelligence report and then brief the Prime Minister in less than five minutes. This was not the time to doubt the chain of command that reached down to the pool of conscripts. The conscripts would die for Israel if the command chain said they would.

"The odds," Hurwicz said to the young intelligence officer. "I need the odds."

"We put the probability at 76% that the same people who bombed Dhahran also sabotaged the *Hombre* and the Azerbaijani pipeline."

"What is your confidence in that estimate?"

"Somewhere between 80% and 90% depending on the prior probabilities."

"You mean depending on how you guess?"

"Yes. In the end."

"So 'in the end' the odds are better than 50-50?"

"Yes."

"One more thing," Hurwicz said. "Major Baum's chip theory about Davis. Has he found any hard proof yet to support it?"

"He claims he has."

"But no one has seen it?"

"No. But Major Baum claims he will show us soon."

"What does 'soon' mean? I can't go with that."

"That is all we know."

"Thank you," Hurwicz said and rose.

He walked next door to a secure booth and sat before the blue screen.

Avi Hurwicz had called the Saudi response wrong because there had been too little time to make the call. He could not afford to miscall this one. He rubbed his eyes and felt the nerves in his right foot twitch from the six cups of coffee he had drunk in the last two hours. The old cooling system did not cool the air in the booth enough to keep his white shirt from sticking to his back and chest.

Then the rough old face of Prime Minister Ezekiel Sharon appeared on the screen.

"Well?" Sharon said.

"It's the same group. We can't be sure *which* group. We can be reasonably sure the same group destroyed the Tamraz pipeline. The odds are better than 50-50."

"The CIA report says that the Azers believe your man Davis did this."

"I have seen the report. It's true that Joel Davis was there. We believe he had imaged the pipe for routine strike planning."

"Why was he there at just this time? That looks suspicious."

"Joel Davis was under deep cover there for over a month. He was pursuing many contacts he made through the Azer criminal underground. We keep many such ears in the mud. Of course we did task Davis with watching the pipeline. That was routine. We don't know the details of all his pursuits. We know only that he failed to report to his contacts in Baku and in Turkey."

"So the Azers may be holding him right now?"

"It's possible. We can't be sure he ever got out of Kirovabad. The odds are that he is dead."

"Colonel Hurwicz," Sharon said. "Will they strike?"

Hurwicz knew he could not hedge the answer with a probability. He had to call it all or none and stand by it.

He could always get back part of his job as a consultant.

"No," he said. "The Azers won't strike."

"Why?"

"The Azer damage is less than the Dhahran damage. And the Azers have far less strike capability than the Saudis have. Their missiles would have to fly across the airspace of Iran and Iraq or Turkey and then across the airspace of Syria or Jordan. That is too far to fly. It would take too many permissions. We would also have more than enough time to lock onto the missile trajectories. The odds are very good that we could repel such a missile strike. We could at least undermine their control and navigation logic."

"I need more than your good odds. You think that if the Azers strike they will not use long-range cruise missiles?"

"That is correct," Hurwicz said. "I would expect a terrorist bombing if they strike at all. I don't think Aminzadeh will approve that."

"Can you read his mind?"

"I can read our intelligence reports. So far Aminzadeh has kept the military under control. I would expect a strike only if there is a coup."

"Avi. A coup is just what we might have here if you are wrong. The young people hate both of us."

::::■■ CHAPTER 20

Diamond Bar
Southern California

Richard had been right.

Eytan had sent an Israeli agent to pick up the Tabriz chip. The agent's name was Daniel. He had come with a second agent named Raquel who posed as his wife. Now the two agents sat in the front seat of John's Jeep and John and Richard sat in the back. They drove east on the 10 freeway toward the pink and orange sky of the desert predawn.

Richard had the Tabriz backup chip in his pocket.

He held in his lap the master optical tape of the Black Sun demo. Raquel kept a backup copy of the optical tape in her black fake crocodile jacket. John held the melted Tabriz chip in his left hand and held the Glock nine-millimeter in his lap with his right hand. Jism worked to get Eytan back on-line in the heads-up display on the windshield. Daniel refused to yield his manual control of the Jeep.

Daniel and Raquel had come to the warehouse and slid their ID cards through the door slot. John had brought Eytan Baum on-line to confirm their IDs and to watch as John drew the Glock and let the two agents in. Baum had ignored the pistol with a slight grin and had gone over a checklist of items for John and Richard to bring for the demo. The agent couple also had ignored the gun and helped Richard pack the demo supplies. John had refused to ride in their old green Bronco and they just nodded. John still had not heard either one speak a complete sentence.

The windshield fluttered in snow.

John tried to guess what Raquel looked like without her black jacket and with her brown hair down from its tight bun.

John. Eytan is coming on-line. He has twice ignored our request for comm synch.

Eytan appeared on the main window. The bags under his eyes had turned black from lack of sleep.

"*Shalom* all," Eytan said. "John. I hope you have calmed down."

"I'm calm. What about Denise's cabin? Have your people been there?"

"We took care of it. The town of Wrightwood is still sleeping."

"What did you do with Denise?" Richard said.

"We took her to a private mortuary. You can see her body when they finish."

"Thanks."

"And my son?" John said.

"We took him to the same mortuary."

Eytan's veracity has fallen below 40%. Do not believe him.

"Make sure he arrives in Nevada before the demo."

"I don't know if we can do that."

"Then forget the demo."

"Calm down. We'll see what we can do. And Daniel. Don't drive so fast. Stay out of the platoon lanes."

Daniel nodded and slowed the Jeep to 60 miles per hour.

"Good. I'll check back with you when you are in the desert."

"Wait a minute," John said. "Are the police looking for us?"

"You should always assume that someone is looking for you."

The screen turned back to snow and then gave way to the clear windshield and the growing orange dawn.

Daniel moved away from the two far-left platoon lanes. Each car could join a single-lane platoon of less than 10 cars. It could become a platoon leader if it drove over 80 miles per hour and if at least two cars chose to follow it rather than pass it. John liked the high speed of the platoon lanes but did not like the extra protocols and the legal liability. Drivers in a platoon wreck tended to sue one another.

John watched the extra fees grow in red at the bottom of the windshield.

The state already counted this time as near-peak transit time even though the dense traffic came from the other direction. The westbound traffic had already slowed to a near stop. Most of the cars still had their headlights on. Much of rebuilt L.A. lay to the east of old L.A. Its people jammed its freeways from morning till night.

John felt the need to sleep and knew his eyes were as black as Eytan's. The car passed through Far East L.A. now. He would wait to sleep until they passed Palm Springs and its suburbs and studios that housed the new film industry. Richard had already closed his eyes.

"Pull over! Now!"

It was a loud voice that came from the dashboard.

"What the hell is that?" John said.

"LAPD," Daniel said.

A small blue ultralight aircraft flew above the Jeep.

"Pull over! Your freeway space ends in exactly 10 seconds!"

Daniel wove between cars and pulled over to the far-right shoulder just as the wheels began to lock on the smart asphalt. Momentum carried the Jeep onto the green ivy and on up the embankment. The wheels unlocked and Daniel flipped the four-wheel-drive switch to climb the rest of the steep hillside. The jerk and bumps had twice slammed John forward to the full extent of his lap and shoulder belts.

The ultralight followed the Jeep over the embankment and onto the grid of streets.

"Goddamn it!" John said. "Where are you going?"

Daniel did not answer him. He spoke in Hebrew to Raquel and into a small black personal digital assistant he pulled from his gray fake deerskin jacket. John kept the Glock in his lap but pointed it at Daniel through the seat. Richard looked at the pistol and shook his head.

The Jeep drove and turned through the mostly empty suburban streets of Diamond Bar. The blue ultralight stayed above them and still sent threats to the sensors in the plastic skin of the Jeep.

The police gained voice control for a few moments as the Jeep crossed some of the main streets. Daniel still spoke to his PDA and received messages from it that played out through the raisin in his ear. Soon two LAPD cars chased the Jeep through the streets. John could see their flashing red and blue lights. The Jeep canceled all sounds from their sirens and loudspeakers.

*The police say we are under arrest and have com-
pounded our crime by fleeing. I see no way that we
can outrun or outmaneuver them. We should surrender before they open fire on us. The transit authorities
have also suspended your license.*

"Daniel," John said. "Where are we going?"

"Police have roadblock ahead," Daniel said with
a strong Israeli accent.

"So where the hell are we going?"

"Roadblock."

John soon saw the roadblock. Six LAPD cars
blocked the street. The cops stood behind their cars
and had their .357 Magnums drawn. One aimed a 12-
gauge shotgun at the Jeep.

John turned to watch the two LAPD cars behind
them when he felt the violent turn and saw the two
LAPD cars off to his right side. Daniel turned sharp
again and then slammed the brakes to stop. Richard's
side slammed against a parked red pickup truck.

The Jeep stopped in a soft but abrupt crunch.

Daniel turned and grabbed the Glock from John just
as John recoiled from the whiplash. Daniel whipped
the short barrel across John's left temple and eye.
Then Daniel grabbed the Tabriz chip from John's left
hand and tossed the Glock to Raquel. She aimed the
pistol at Richard. She took his laser tape and fished
through his pocket until she found the backup chip.

Then the Israelis ran from the Jeep.

John watched them through his right eye. He saw
them run to a small black car and jump in and speed
off.

A can of tear gas broke the window on the driver's
side.

A black cop in riot gear pulled John out to the hard
cool pavement. John's eyes watered when he opened

them and looked for Jism. The raisin had once more fallen out of his ear. He brushed his hands across the sandy pavement but found nothing.

John turned his head to see Richard's face hit the hood of the Jeep.

Then he felt the stinging heat of the baton across his back and felt the first convulsing flash from the taser stick.

:::∎ CHAPTER 21

Baku
Azerbaijan

Ibn Aminzadeh drove with his four bodyguards to a new nightclub called the Gusher. It was
far north of Baku on the Caspian Sea. That night the
53-year-old president of Azerbaijan had left the palace
through the back entrance.

He now walked into the Gusher through the front
door.

Nude belly dancers writhed on the main stage and
watched him as he walked next to the bar and through
the crowd to his own room in the storage area. Two
of the nude dancers wore wigs of wriggling green
snakes with four heads each. Nanochips studded the
plastic snakes and let them writhe in unison and in
novel patterns. The girls had learned which patterns
most pleased the crowd of Russian gangsters and oil-
rich Shiites and Japanese businessmen.

Joel Davis sat at the old-fashioned zinc bar and kept
his face close to his glass of vodka. Davis did not
look up when Aminzadeh walked past with his four
bodyguards.

One of the guards had a thick black beard and massive chest and stayed at the zinc bar. He ordered

champagne and vodka and the rare and expensive yellow caviar. Davis did not look up at him either.

The bearded guard paid for his order with four Singapore dragons from the year 2016. The one-troyounce coins were pure gold. The bartender felt their weight in his hand for a moment before he put three of them in the bar safe. He kept the other dragon as a tip. Then the bearded guard tipped all the girls who came by and kissed him on the cheek. He tipped them in Azeri cash.

A second guard with broken front teeth came out and paid the floor manager for two of the girls. One girl was a fake blonde from Cyprus and the other was a thin dark teenager from Baku. The Iranian owner of the Gusher had paid for both girls to have homeobox gene implants. The new genes let the girls slowly grow much fuller breasts than they had been born with. The new breasts had no scars and no Cooper's droop.

The girls followed the second guard back to Aminzadeh's private room. The bearded guard returned to the bar to drink a dry martini.

Joel Davis finished his vodka and ordered a mug of Ukrainian honey ale and a plate of fresh green mussels. He also paid with precious metal but in the small heavy platinum coins from Yakutsk that the gangsters preferred to use. He had drunk eight vodkas so far tonight and the bartender thought he would pass out soon. Davis used to get sick after drinking only five vodkas.

Now it did not matter.

His flesh and DNA mattered no more to him than did the gray pinstripe suit he wore to look like a Russian tough. The chic silver baseball hat he wore covered the fresh plastic scars and nanostitches in his scalp. A thick egg of lead enclosed his chip brain to protect it from bursts of high energy.

The Joel Davis who had once played in the salty waters of the Dead Sea and had scored the winning goal of his high school soccer team had lived in a three-pound brain. That great knot of neural networks now lay far to the south in thin slices on a rock in the Qareh Dahg Mountains. The young shepherd boy Jahangir now played his flute and sat next to the rock and the dried brain slices that the hawks and ants had not yet eaten.

The Davis chiphead waited five minutes from the time the second guard had paid for the two dancers. The guard had walked back to the private room with one girl on each arm. Davis finished the plate of mussels and then pulled a black ball the size of a golf ball from his coat pocket.

He left the bar for the men's room. He went into one of the new chrome stalls and threw up the mussels and ale and vodka that churned in his stomach. That cleared the room of the lone man at the urinal. Then he touched the leads of a small million-volt taser to the black ball. The taser charged its small core of iridium and charged the plasma trapped in the magnetic plastic sphere.

Davis left the men's room and walked back toward the storage area. The three guards stood outside Aminzadeh's door and took turns kissing one of the older dancers with wiry red hair. They stopped when they saw Davis.

"Wrong way," the guard with broken teeth said.

Davis did not answer. He threw the ball with great strength at a clear section of the plastic floor in front of them.

The magnetic sphere broke on impact and let loose

a growing cloud of blue-green plasma. The plasma
cloud was largely stable but had an unstable corona-
like surface where the ionic gas met the air in the
room. The cloud's core was a fleeting superhot fireball. The extreme temperature produced a large pressure wave in the air much as lightning produced
thunder in the sky.

The tiny shock wave destroyed the eardrums of the
three guards and the redheaded dancer. The Davis
chiphead could see the electrical explosion as if in
slow motion. He blocked its auditory nerve paths as
the pressure wave burst his own eardrums.

The blue-green plasma ball gave off a sharp electromagnetic pulse as it expanded outward and de-
cayed. The three guards and the dancer were close
enough that the intense EMP energy burned out their
retinas and scrambled the neural circuits in their
brains. The EMP bounced off the lead casing of the
Davis chiphead and burned out only a few of the rods
and cones in his eyes.

The EMP knocked out the power and lights in the
Gusher. It killed the fake green snakes on the heads
of the two belly dancers onstage.

Joel Davis ran past the thrashing guards and dancer
and kicked opened the door to Aminzadeh's room.
Two long white candles gave off the only light in the
room. A stunned and naked Aminzadeh tried to dis-
mount from the teenage dancer but was too close to
orgasm to withdraw. The blond dancer jumped from
the couple on the bed and tried to pull the dark bed
sheet up to cover her breasts.

Davis drew a pellet pistol and loaded it with an ice
heart dart from a small Dewar flask. Davis shot Aminzadeh in the right buttock with the dart. The blond

dancer dropped the bed sheet and screamed at Davis. He stood still to watch.

The thin ice dart melted in the warm muscle tissue of Aminzadeh's buttock. There it released a mix of brucine and potassium into the married man's bloodstream. Aminzadeh fell from the screaming Baku teenager and convulsed on the bed in a massive heart attack. His face quickly turned white from lack of blood. Then he lost consciousness.

The blond dancer knocked over the white candles as she and the Baku teenager ran naked and screaming past Davis.

The bearded agent from the bar ran to the room with his Redhawk .44 Magnum drawn. He found only his president lying still. The guard lost all light when he stomped out the carpet fire that the candles had started.

::::■■ CHAPTER 22

Walnut
Southern California

Major Eytan Baum paced the length of a large white freezer truck parked behind the Hong Kong Market in Walnut. Baum paced to help him think and to reduce the paunch he had grown in the last decade.

An elderly Jewish couple in Walnut held the California license on the freezer truck. Baum had used it twice before for U.S. operations and both times felt his mild claustrophobia grow to a slight panic.

This time it was worse.

He had been in the gadget-packed truck when the Saudis bombed his desalination plant in Eilat and when AMAN had lost Joel Davis and when the Azers had lost their pipeline. He did not trust Avi Hurwicz in Tel Aviv to keep him fully informed. So he and his U.S. crew might be at greater risk than the risk they already took as spies on U.S. soil.

A small black Mustang parked in front of the Chinese market to let out Daniel and Raquel. The couple had shed their fake leather jackets and now wore blue and green T-shirts and blue jeans that matched the warm sunny morning in June. They had coffee and sweet buns before they walked around back to Baum's unmarked freezer truck.

They found the back gate unlocked and quickly let themselves in.

"The chips," Baum said.

Daniel gave him the burnt Tabriz chip and Raquel gave him the backup chip. She also pulled the two small optical tapes from her shopping bag and gave them to one of Baum's three crew members.

Eytan held the Tabriz chip to the panel lights on the green wall. He shook his head and handed the chip to his lead technician Schlomo Ravin. The young Israeli smiled. He took the small square of burnt silicon and melted gold to the optical display at the front corner of the truck.

"Good," Baum said in Hebrew. "Now you two go back to Catton and help him put Cheng on ice. We'll cover all expenses for the transport. It's the least we can do."

Daniel nodded.

Raquel was not so sure.

"Will the CIA ice Grant too?" she said.

"Not if you can help it. And they know better than to do that to an Israeli. They think Grant works for us."

::::■ CHAPTER 23

Baku
Azerbaijan

Azerbaijan had the biggest airport on the Caspian Sea. The terminals were spacious and clean. Their motif of silver and black gave no hint of the squalor found in much of Baku. New robotic conveyor belts brought luggage to passengers after they landed. Many of the walls seemed to swirl with 3-D art. Some of the holographic images showed the oil history of Azerbaijan and the Great Game many countries had once played there. Other wall images showed the nation's grand vision of a future based not on oil but on science and worker cooperation.

The airport also had the best security on the Caspian.

When each person arrived they gave a palm print to a flat black sensor board on a customs desk as they passed into the customs area. Gabor wavelets first compressed the palm pattern. The wavelets picked only the brightest leaves on the palm print's abstract transform tree. The wavelets ignored the duller leaves that described less of the pattern. Then neural nets stored the compressed palm pattern in the Azer police database. There the state computers matched it against the hundreds of millions of other compressed palm prints in the shared databases of over 100 countries.

The visitor saw only a green light or a red light after he gave the palm print.

The green light meant that he could pass freely through customs and that the computer search had found no active police warrants for him or warnings about him. The red light meant that the so-called "probability mechanism" had randomly picked him for a complete search of his person and his luggage. Then he would walk to the search area and hope that the armed Azer guards found him too rich to harass or too poor to extort. The random system chose on average fewer than 1 in 20 persons to search.

Ticket holders went through much of this process in reverse when they left the airport. They passed their carry-on luggage through clear rectangles of neural shape detectors. Then they gave their palm prints and walked through a metal detector. The palm print again flashed a random green light or red light that told the guards whether to ignore the person or to search him and his carry-on luggage.

Then the palm pattern soon circled the world and told member governments where the person was at that moment.

The Joel Davis chiphead had no chance of passing safely through the metal detector. The device would detect its chip encased in the egg of lead.

The eyes of the airport watched for Joel Davis. Makeup and a white Shiite headwrap had so far deceived the security cameras and guards who scanned the airport crowds for the assassin. Half the staff and customers of the Gusher had given their images of Davis to the handheld artist of the Azer police. Soon Iranian intelligence had matched the final image to the images they had on file. They learned at once that the image was that of Israeli AMAN agent Joel Davis.

Now the Davis chiphead waited in line and gave its palm print. Alarms did not sound and no one seemed to notice him.

The light came up green.

Joel Davis did not walk through the clear frame of the metal detector. He instead walked over to one of the two young Azer guards who had thin black mustaches. He opened and held out his brown fake leather satchel. The guard nodded and put both hands in the satchel.

The young guard stopped when he came to a thick stack of Azeri bills wrapped in a paper tissue. Davis nodded. The young guard searched with his left hand while his right hand rolled up the bills and cupped them in a fist. Then he waved Davis on to rejoin the ticketed passengers.

The bribe did not work.

Azer police and airport guards rushed Davis from the front and back. Two Sufis joined them in the disguise of green-clad airport guards. Davis saw the bearded bodyguard of Aminzadeh who had the massive chest and the pocket full of gold Singapore dragons. The bearded guard pointed at Davis and screamed at him in Farsi. The guard ran at Davis and called him an Israeli dog in a great shrieking bellow.

One of the policemen shot Davis in the back of the right knee.

The soft copper bullet passed through and destroyed most of his kneecap. The chiphead fell to his left knee. He looked up at one of the video cameras that had tracked him.

Davis ripped open his white cotton shirt. He dug his thumbnail deep into his belly fat. He screamed as he tore out the red arsenic capsule that an AMAN physician had long since implanted.

Davis bit it just as the first batons fell on him.

The chip melted and the flesh died long before they stopped beating him.

CHAPTER 24

It took the meltdown of the *Hombre* to push aside the bombings of Dhahran and Eilat on the Wireless News Network.

The *Hombre* had even beaten out the meltdown of miles of the Tamraz pipeline. Azerbaijan was just too far from Florida to matter much to a media culture still centered in Los Angeles and Washington.

That changed with the deaths of Ibn Aminzadeh and Joel Davis. Images of the two corpses filled the wireless skies of the world and the wired hubs of the internet.

| ■ ■

WNN Channel 2: The New York announcer warns that the next images are graphic. Children should not view them. A coroner shows the buttock wound on Aminzadeh and then blood assays that list the levels of brucine and potassium. Joel Davis looks straight ahead and tears open his shirt and digs out the arsenic pill and bites down on it. Azer police beat him with clubs. The next scenes come from Azerbaijan state TV. Joel Davis hangs upside down outside the Azerbaijan palace. Young men and old women push and

141

shove to get close enough to spit on the corpse. The
Azer parliament meets to choose a new leader and to
decide how to respond to the Tamraz pipeline disaster
and the assassination. The Parliament at once declares
martial law in Baku to stem protests and looting. The
announcer returns and reports that the Azer government seems to have lost the corpse of Joel Davis. . . .

▌▐ ▌

WNN Channel 5: Saudi ambassador to the United
States Mohammed Akhdar explains the new OPEC
position to a WNN journalist in Washington. "The
facts are clear. Israel opposed President Aminzadeh's
call for an oil embargo. Then the Greens destroyed
the Tamraz pipeline. Israel is responsible for the
Greens it supports. Israel knew it risked an embargo.
So it sent an agent to kill Aminzadeh. We have em-
bargoed all oil to Israel and to its main suppliers. Let
the spot price of oil rise to $600 a barrel. We do not
care. We will decide soon whether to embargo oil to
the United States as well. . . ."

▌▐ ▌

WNN Channel 12: Six NATO experts debate
whether Russia will invade Azerbaijan. The panel has
split on the issue. Half the experts think Russia will
invade to secure its own pipeline and to lay hold of
the rich oil fields in Azerbaijan and offshore in the
Caspian Sea. The other half does not think Russia will
invade under the pretext of stabilizing the country or
under any other pretext. That would risk revolt along
the long southern frontier of Russia. It would risk reprisals from Turkmenistan and Kazakhstan and perhaps from Uzbekistan or Afghanistan. One expert
suggests that it is more likely that Iran will invade its

rich Shiite neighbor or launch a small tit-for-tat strike against Israel itself. . . .

■ ■ ■

WNN Channel 18: A French news crew interviews the owner and bartender of the Gusher. The two men match their smart-art image of Joel Davis to the passport photo the French have retrieved from Air France. The program shows older video clips of the dance stage in full swing. It shows the wigs of burned-out green snakes and the melt hole in the black plastic floor where the EMP thunder ball went off. Only two white candles burn in the guest room where Aminzadeh died among the pillows. . . .

■ ■ ■

WNN Channel 23: Israeli prime minister Ezekiel Sharon holds a press conference in Tel Aviv. He denies that Israel sent an agent to assassinate the president of Azerbaijan. He dismisses the video footage of Joel Davis as doctored and challenges the Azerbaijan police to prove their claims and surrender the corpse of the alleged assassin. He further denies any link between Israel and the bombing of the Dhahran oil fields or between Israel and the nanomeltdown of the Tamraz pipeline. Israel will not fund their repair. Sharon accepts the OPEC oil ban but demands an apology from Azerbaijan. . . .

■ ■ ■

WNN Channel 37: The teenage belly dancer Astrad from Baku sits on a Moscow tabloid show and tells of having forced sex with the president of Azerbaijan. She shows the gold ankle band Aminzadeh gave her and the nude photos his men took of her and him and other dancers. She says she forgives Aminzadeh. Astrad of Baku holds up a smart-art image of the assassin whom she saw shoot Aminzadeh with the heart dart. She cries and then begs the Russian people to help her troubled country to the south. . . .

▌ ▌ ▌

WNN Channel 40: Green Democrat President Vance Jackson announces that he has signed a presidential order that bans Intel from selling military software or hardware to Saudi Arabia or Yemen. He says the United States will ignore embargoes against it and will ignore calls for it to join in an oil embargo against Israel. Jackson sees the recent near doubling of the spot price of oil as all the more reason to proceed with plans to fully wean the United States from oil. He says he is still reviewing the report of a special energy panel that has called for a ban on gasoline in the United States. . . .

▌ ▌ ▌

WNN Channel 45: Azeris riot in the Tabriz region of northwestern Iran. The crowd burns an effigy of Ezekiel Sharon. Crowd leaders call for the bombing of Tel Aviv and the death of Sharon. Teenagers set fire to a row of Iranian shops. Other protesters call for Tabriz to secede from Iran. Support riots erupt in the Kazakhstan oil fields of Tenghiz. There protesters burn the main office of Chevron. Other support riots break out in the lesser oil fields of Chelecen on the coast of the Caspian Sea in Turkmenistan. Azer tanks shell the region of Nagorno-Karabakh as the Armenians make a new armed bid for independence from Azerbaijan. . . .

❘ ❙ ■

WNN Channel 76: The Shiite ambassadors from Azerbaijan and Egypt and Iran hold a press conference at the United Nations in New York City. They announce an oil and gas embargo on Israel and all countries that sell oil or gas to Israel. The Azer ambassador says this includes the United States and Great Britain. The Egyptian ambassador says that the Israel Defense Forces killed Aminzadeh to end Saudi pressure on Israel to pay for the bombing damage at Dhahran. He says that Egypt and Iran may take further action against Israel for the murder. The Iranian ambassador agrees. A reporter asks him what Iran will do if OPEC members do not support the oil embargo against the United States and Japan. He says Iran will "deal" with them. . . .

❘ ❙ ■

WNN Channel 91: A panel of graduate students and post-docs at MIT's Artificial Intelligence Lab discuss the nanoscience of the *Hombre* and Tamraz meltdowns. A teenager with long blond hair shows his equation of the *Hombre* decay rate and argues that standard nanoengineering could have produced the superacid. Other students feel the terrorists botched the meltdown since only Azer sections of it melted. They all feel the two meltdowns mark the start of nanoterrorism in the age of postinformation warfare. . . .

❘ ❙ ■

WNN Channel 165: Indians from the southern Mexican state of Chiapas hold Pemex staff hostage at an oil field in the coastal city of Paraiso. The Indians wear red and blue bandannas over their faces. They demand that Mexico share its oil wealth with its southernmost state. The rebel leader swings his machete and cuts off the head of the Pemex manager in plain view of the news cameras. He threatens to cut off one head per hour until Mexico meets his demands. A reporter from TV España claims that the Chiapas Indians have taken over much of the prostitution and slave trade in Central America. He also claims that they plan to take over oil rigs in Guatemala and Venezuela. . . .

▌▐ █

WNN Channel 189: Istanbul state news runs a profile on the clean-shaven General Atef Mosarian of Azerbaijan. Old news clips show Mosarian in talks with President Aminzadeh at the Baku palace. Mosarian watches a parade of army troops and long-range cruise missiles in front of the palace. Then he meets with the commander of Sudan's army. Recent news clips show Mosarian walking through the oil spill of the Tamraz pipeline. He addresses his honor guard in a speech and calls for retribution against Israel and its sympathizers. The program suggests that Mosarian arranged the assassination of Ibn Aminzadeh. . . .

▌▐ █

WNN Channel 307: A BBC reporter stands outside the night lights of the Kremlin. The reporter claims the Kremlin is in special session to deal with demands from the restless Siber province in the east. The Sibers want to force an oil embargo against Israel and want the United States to back it or face the partial nationalization of the 23 U.S. oil firms in Siberia. Yakutsk may make like demands. The reporter claims the Sibers have not threatened to harm the Japanese and Chinese oil firms in Siberia. . . .

■ ■ ■

WNN Channel 472: U.S. Secretary of State Gloria Rosen sits in a Tel Aviv studio and takes call-in questions on a Washington-based talk show. A caller from Tangiers asks when the United States will end or at least reduce its foreign aid to Israel. Rosen defends the $9 billion it gives each year to Israel and the $2 billion it gives to Lebanon as an investment in Middle East peace. She says it is a cheap way to further peace talks among Jews and Palestinians and thus to further American interests in the region. A caller from Calcutta asks if the *Hombre* oil spill will help make the United States join India and the Netherlands and outlaw the gasoline engine. Rosen says the U.S. economy is not ready for such a radical step. . . .

■ ■ ■

WNN Channel 668: Graphs show how the internet betting markets view recent events in the Middle East and the United States. 93% of the world's net gamblers believe Israel played a key part in the death of Ibn Aminzadeh. 76% believe there is a link among the Dhahran bombing and the *Hombre* sinking and the Tamraz meltdown and Aminzadeh's death. 43% believe that Russia will invade Azerbaijan. Only 23% believe Iran will invade Azerbaijan and only 6% believe Turkey will. . . .

■ ■ ■

WNN Channel 803: Precious metal prices continue to climb. Gold has just reached $1,400 per troy ounce and platinum has crossed the $2,000 mark. Palladium hovers around $800 per troy ounce. Private currencies based on gas and oil continue to fall. The Ukrainian eagle and Thomson petrol have both lost over 8% of their value as the spot price of oil has reached $460 per barrel. The dollar has risen from 31 yen to 34 yen based on heavy buying from African and South American central banks. Daiwa metal and Zurich fiat still lead the private currencies. . . .

▌▐ ▐

WNN Channel 809: The Shanghai Stock Exchange. Tired Chinese pit traders wave their wireless dealmakers at the crystal spikes in the rows of trading pits. Trading volume has more than doubled in the past 24 hours. Chinese investors have raised the value of the Tokyo Stock Exchange by 2%. Japanese and Korean investors have in turn poured much of their new capital into the stock exchanges in Shanghai and Taipei and Hong Kong and even Sydney. The volatile Shanghai Stock Exchange has increased a record 19% in value since the Dhahran bombing. . . .

CHAPTER 25

Southern California

"Tell us about the Israelis."

"Fuck you," John Grant said. "Give me back my raisin."

"Not yet."

"I know my rights. Give me my goddamn raisin!"

"We matched the blood on your hands to the blood of Denise Cheng in her house at Wrightwood. The DNA match was better than 99%. They used to gas people in this state on less evidence than that. It sure as hell will keep you in Chino until you're old and gray and have grown bitch tits from the steroids."

"Who are you guys?"

John was tired and sore. The two men had not fed him or let him sleep or drink coffee. The baton welts on his ribs hurt each time he took a breath.

John still did not know where he was. He had been in this small bare room when he came to after the beating and the taser jolts. The two men sat at the cheap white table across from him. They wore trim black suits and white shirts and dark blue and black striped ties. The quiet one on the far end sat with a small black taser in his right hand and John's raisin in front of him.

149

John did not know if they had tried to decrypt his raisin. He could only hope that if they did then they would trip the raisin's self-destruct routines. Both men watched John and did not smile or try to make small talk.

"I told you. I am Carsten Catton and this is Mr. Pierre Rittenhouse."

"You guys are with the CIA?"

"We support many of the intelligence agencies. The Central Intelligence Agency is one of them. Tell us about the Israelis."

"I'm sure you know more about the deal than I do. The Israeli government licenses my patent on a light-laser method to extract hydrogen from water. The learning scheme might also work for an atomic laser."

"You mean the Israeli government used to license your patent."

"You think you scared them off?"

"The United States government has suspended your patent pending your arrest for murder."

"That's bullshit. I filed and paid for that patent fair and square. And I am not under arrest for murder."

"Let me explain a bit of patent law. The government has the right to use the technology you patented. It has to pay you only a fair fee for that right and it gets to decide what fee is fair. Your criminal behavior complicates the issue. That behavior began when you and your vehicle fled from the highway patrolmen this morning."

"You know this is make-believe. I wasn't even driving."

"It was your car. The state will argue that you drove it or that you gave instructions to your PDA here to drive it for you. Then you resisted arrest at the blockade in Diamond Bar.''

''I didn't resist. The bastards shot tear gas through my window.''

''The state will argue that you fled the murder scene after you killed Denise Cheng in an equity dispute.''

''You lying fuck.''

''I am only telling you what the state will argue. Look at the screen. We have the source and some of the contents of your wireless transmissions for the last two days. That's right. We've been watching you and we have every legal right to do so. You are a threat to the nation's security.''

John looked up at the white board on the wall as it came alive with the date and time of his calls in the Jeep and in Richard's warehouse.

The screen fluttered and showed a noisy image of Eytan Baum as he spoke to John in Nevada the day before. John had never heard of signal processors that could eavesdrop even partially on a signal sent with triple spread spectrum. The white board did not play the sound of Eytan's voice but it did not take much science to read his lips.

''You guys bugged me?'' John said.

''That's classified.''

''I want my lawyer.''

''Not until we're through.''

''You can't do that.''

''I continue,'' Catton said. ''We know you work with Israeli intelligence.''

''I work with the Israeli *government*. Are you guys really with the CIA? Show me your badges.''

''We know the Israelis approached you about working with some businessmen from the Texas oil firms of Green O and Energon. We have transcripts of their conversations as well."

"Whose? The Israelis or the Texans?"

"The state will argue that you acted on the news of the deal. You at last saw profit coming from the Texans and you wanted to beat your partners out of it. The state will argue that you tried to buy or perhaps even extort shares in Water Dragon from Ms. Cheng. You did this after you already swindled her out of over $400,000 of her proceeds from trading financial futures."

"Swindled?"

"Yes. You took her money and promised to marry her. You even got her pregnant to secure the deal."

Now there was no reason not to do it.

They had him and had thrown at him all they needed to throw so that they could keep him as long as they wanted. So what the hell. He might as well throttle this neat middle-aged man in a suit and take as much pleasure from it as he could.

John jumped over the table and jabbed at Catton's upper lip with his right fist.

The fist only grazed Catton's mouth. By then Mr. Rittenhouse had slammed his left palm down on the small of John's back and juiced him behind the ear with the taser.

John shook in an all-body spasm and did not pass out this time. He had already started to forget the searing pain of the first taser stun in Diamond Bar. Now the pain suspended him somewhere over a fire in empty space. John seemed to have come back to where he would always be.

There were no neural nets like pain nets and the signals would never end.

Catton did not even wipe his puffed-up lip. He just

stood up and pushed John back to the other side of the table. Then he sat down.

"John? Don't go to sleep yet. Are you still with us? No?"

Catton nodded.

Mr. Pierre Rittenhouse reached across the table and stung John with the taser in a short tap on John's forearm. John jumped and sat upright in his wooden chair. He hated to obey them. He hated the taser pain even more.

"Are you still with us?" Catton said.

"Cocksucker. Put away that taser and I'll kill you right here."

"That is in character with what the state will argue."

"Fuck that. I will kill you."

"Mr. Grant. Understand that we are taping this interview. And the tape is fully admissible in a court of law."

"Court? Shit. This is a kangaroo court or at least the start of one."

"The state will argue that you murdered Ms. Cheng when she refused to go along with your stock scheme. Your greed made you premeditate the killing. So it was first-degree murder."

"It was self-defense."

"So you admit killing Ms. Cheng?"

"I'd sure like to stick that taser up your urethra."

"Answer the question. Did you kill Ms. Cheng?"

"I killed the thing that was in her body. She had a chip for a brain."

"You are a hard one to the end," Catton said.

"I told you. It was self-defense."

"You have almost 80 pounds on her."

"I want to talk to counsel."

"The state will argue that you panicked. You killed her and lost control. Or you lost control and then killed her. Either way you became unnerved. You acted in a hasty mix of cunning and cowardice. Then you went to see Denise's brother to try to build an alibi. Or you tried to involve Mr. Cheng in the scheme. I suspect you did both."

"For the last time. Charge me with murder or let me go. And for the record no one read me my Miranda rights. Give me back my goddamn raisin!"

"Right now murder is not the primary issue. National security demands that we prosecute each action according to priority. I assure you that we are following legal procedure in this case."

"Sure you are. What is your top priority? What are you charging me with? Driving across the fucking grass?"

"No. Treason."

::::■■ CHAPTER 26

General Feng Pei rode a large red Mongol pony across the packed orange-red dirt of the Gobi Desert.

His staff could not believe that the old man wanted to be alone now with his horse. Too much was happening. The politicians in Beijing and Shanghai were meeting to decide if they would punish Israel. His young aide watched the old former Communist on the many surveillance cameras that studded the remote army supply center near Abaq in Inner Mongolia.

General Feng had no need for his staff or their ceaseless concern for what the politicians thought. The old man had seen China go from Mao to freedom and back to something in between.

Now Feng was just over 100 miles from the small Mongol village of Erenhot where he was born and where his name was Ulan. There he had scored so well on an IQ test as a child that the Chinese state moved him to Xian. The Chinese bureaucrats gave him his Chinese name Feng Pei. The state examiner had simply made up the name one day.

The Chinese also made the stoic boy a Red Guard.

He was taller and darker than most of the boys in Xian. And he had the wide flat face of his Mongol ancestors. That face had earned him a childhood of Chinese nicknames but they ended in *Hong Bao*. The Red Bun. The Red Guard boys used to beat him when he ignored that name.

But he had always been smarter than the many schemers around him.

It began with horses. The young Feng was too smart to give up his love of horses. Horses were living grace and speed and wealth. And he never gave up the horsemen's lama gods for their god of Mao. Mao was a god of ants. He was the god of scheming and devious ants.

But the Red Guards had taught him something. The schemers had taught him that he could kill Chinese with impunity if he knew which rule to cite. Their "radical" politics came to no more than that. It was just the latest power game of the Chinese bureaucrats. The right words and actions let him kill some of the ants.

That was a small price to pay for such a privilege.

Young Feng had dreamed of killing Chinese since the day they took him from Erenhot and put him on the old train to Xian. His Chinese teachers were so devious they had never known that he would kill them as gladly as he helped them kill others. He was just their Mongol pawn with the wide flat face.

Feng and his people had always hated the Chinese to the south. His whole village had hated the Chinese overlords even more than they loved horses.

He still hated them at Beijing Normal University where the horsemen had learned the way of math and the sciences. It had taken him until his senior year there before he found a Chinese girl who would have him. Her parents had approved the marriage only when they learned she was pregnant. She and the child died in childbirth the next year and he had never remarried. He still believed her parents had forced her to have a country abortion. They had twice mentioned his Mongol face at the one dinner they had invited him to in their small high-rise apartment in the old Maoist ghetto in Beijing.

It did not matter. Feng had no desire for a new Chinese marriage. The brief marriage had brought him little joy beyond the first pleasures of the flesh. His only joy came from his work and that he turned to with full force.

He joined the Red Army.

Feng let the party and then the people send him where they needed him to kill their enemies. He helped them crush the Tibetans. He could still taste the Tibetans' foul yak milk and rotten cheese. Feng had drunk yak milk and eaten yak cheese in his own village but never so putrid. He suspected that the bad food helped drive the Tibetans to their extremes of religious nonsense. He had no patience or mercy for a grown man who still spun a prayer wheel.

Later Feng had helped the Chinese conquer northern Vietnam down to Vinh. That secured the Tonkin oil for China. It did so in a way the Americans could have never allowed. Feng had had even fewer qualms about killing the small Viets than he had had about torturing and shooting the old counterrevolutionaries in Xian and Kumming. He thought the Viet language sounded like birds fighting over a nest site. Still the Chinese made him learn to speak and write the Viet language.

Feng never felt he understood the Vietnamese as he did the Chinese. He had once watched Viet villagers roast large green grasshoppers on a rice-stalk bonfire and then pray to their gods before they ate the burnt insects. Feng did not like their hot sticky air or their primitive food or their lack of horses. But the Viets had fought well with the few weapons they had. A jungle sniper had even blown out three of his left ribs with an old deer rifle. He and his troops had in the end killed thousands of Viets for each of those ribs.

Feng had spent his life helping the Chinese empire grow and the Chinese had rewarded him. They had made him a general in their army. Now they had shipped him back to where he had come from. The old schemers must have laughed at that. Maybe they would try to kill him here. Feng could accept that if it came to it. His had been a full life even if it had in some small way helped them build their empire.

And the bureaucrats had conquered and patched together quite an empire. This Feng had to admit. But he believed that no one knew what to do with the empire but make it grow. That was the final logic of all their devious power games. Grow it bigger.

Feng knew what he would do with the empire if he ever had the chance.

Now the old man stopped and let the red pony pull at some thin green plantain leaves. The cold north wind blew light dust in his face but did not chill him.

The old man would have loved to have ridden hard to the hills to the north and see his old village of Erenhot the way it had looked when he was a boy. He still had not been back there. He did not want to see what the Communists and the capitalists had done to it. He had not heard from his parents or anyone in the village since the Chinese had taken him away to Xian.

Feng often thought of his uncle Rago. He wondered

if Rago was still famous in the village for his horsemanship. His uncle had taught him to ride and play goat-head polo with the older boys. But now the question still hung in his mind and would not go away. Had the younger generals in Beijing sent him here to his old land as a favor or as a way to get rid of him? That too did not matter.

Young Ulan was back now and he had never forgotten.

The schemers had told him he was to protect China from the Russians and Japanese and Koreans to the north. The Chinese always looked to the north now. Feng had watched as millions of Chinese workers went north in the last two decades in the greatest land rush and oil and gold rushes in history.

Millions moved past his old lands and on up to the vast lands of Siberia. The great northern territory still held the world's largest reserves of most natural resources despite its massive strip mining and diverted rivers and its forests of oil derricks and pipelines.

It was the Wild East.

Cheap Chinese labor poured in from the south. Investment capital poured in from Japan and later from Korea and Taiwan. This time the Americans and British had come too late. Even the Germans and the Russians fell behind the Japanese and their hordes of Chinese laborers.

The Russians and Sibers controlled the vast Siber province in name only. The Russians had lost real control of the province to the Japanese. Now many in Moscow regretted that they had not sold Siberia to the United States when the Americans had offered them dollars and citizenship for the land. The Russian nationalists had killed any chance of such a land swap.

Now the Russian nationalists wanted to send in the

Russian army to rout the Japanese and Chinese from their new towns and factories. The Russians also wanted to drive them from the aquafarms and fisheries along the coast and far into the Pacific. But Moscow received over half its hard currency from the Japanese and Chinese. The two countries held almost half of Russia's debt as bonds. The Japanese and Chinese also traded over half the shares on the Moscow Stock Exchange.

There were a billion and a half Chinese in China and almost 100 million in the Siber regions. There were less than 5 million Japanese in Siberia. But the Japanese still ran it. Chinese workers worked for both Chinese and Japanese firms. Japanese workers worked only for the Japanese.

And the Chinese still hated the Japanese more than they hated anyone else.

General Feng almost smiled at that. But the smile died before it tightened his face muscles. His uncle and the Red Guard had taught him to never say or show what he thought. Never show them.

It was a simple lesson and most people never learned it. They might practice it for a minute or for an hour. They did not have the strength to practice it for a lifetime. And it was so simple. Never show them no matter what they said or did or threatened to do.

Only fools let others read them. That let others predict them and thus control them. Feng could not decide whether the fools were so weak because of their genes or their training or their will. The cause did not matter. Their actions did.

Never show them.

Feng had no special hatred for the Japanese. He had always admired them. They were the one group in his world that his Mongol ancestors had failed to conquer.

His uncle Rago had told him the stories of how the Japanese had once conquered the devious Chinese. He had wished he could have seen that.

And General Feng did not hate the Russians or the Siber tribesmen who had grown rich in the oil and gold and platinum fields. He did not care that they stripped the forests and dredged the rivers and wiped out whole fisheries in the sea. Let them make their money. Let them buy their BMW Jeeps and import wives from Indonesia and dress like Americans.

In the end he felt about them as he felt about the Chinese.

They all needed killing.

::::■ **CHAPTER 27**

Sa'ad
Israel

Michael Riesman had flown the old B-2 stealth bombers against Jordan and Iraq. He had made the rank of major and lost all the red hair on his head by age 40 when he had left the Israeli Air Force for the Mossad. Now he had a paunch and a red mustache to balance his shining round head.

He thought of the many screens and windows before him as an old man's version of the inside of a stealth bomber. He did not have the clearance or desire to keep up with the new stealth cockpits. This panel of screens was the best he would ever do and it was all he wanted to do. And right now he had stumbled on the intelligence find of his career.

He had Hamid Tabriz on his main screen.

The Sufi radical had come to pray at a new mosque in Gaza.

A field agent had told one of Riesman's agents that a major figure in the Hamas underground would come to the small mosque. The figure would meet a teenage recruit and maybe give him a weapon and a mission. The Israelis did not have clear intelligence on this point. Riesman had the mosque bugged and taped earlier that evening.

Now he saw an older Palestinian man praying with a dark-skinned teenage boy. He had the complete Gaza file on the boy but no match on the older man. Tabriz had walked into their prayer session and sat next to the older man. So far they had not spoken.

Riesman did not notify his cell chief. That could only lengthen the chain of permissions and increase the chance of a leak. This takedown was too important to cross lines of authority.

He would call Avi Hurwicz himself when they had Tabriz in hand and had made a positive ID. Riesman knew the capture would stun his old friend Eytan Baum. It would put to rest the dozens of questions the Mossad and AMAN had about the elusive Sufi leader.

He gave the verbal order to proceed.

An old man with a long gray beard and white head wrap and white robe stood outside the mosque. He watched his two colleagues in gas masks as they kicked open the door and ran inside.

The Palestinian boy jumped to his feet and drew the stiletto his father had bought for him in Cyprus. One commando fired an automatic tear gas gun. A can of the white gas hit the boy in the chest. It knocked him backward over a brown wooden stool as he struggled to hold on to the stiletto.

The other commando shot taser darts at the older man and Tabriz.

Both commandos ignored the small old bearded cleric who ran the mosque. The cleric shouted at them to leave as he rubbed his eyes and coughed.

The commandos subdued Tabriz and the older man in seconds. They kicked the two men in the solar plexus to knock the air out of them. Then they tied their hands and feet with blue bungee cord and taped their mouths and eyes with gray duct tape. The teenage boy ran outside past the old man in the white head wrap and away into the night. The Israelis knew where to find him if they needed him.

Riesman lit a cigarette and rubbed the sweat on his bald head. He watched each commando run from the mosque with a bound and gagged man over his shoulder.

The commandos dropped the men into the trunk of an old black oil-burning Mercedes they had just stolen from a Palestinian taxi firm. Riesman lost sight of them as the car drove off to his command station.

Riesman used emergency access to get through to Colonel Hurwicz. He had never done that before. He lit a new cigarette as he waited for the comm link to open.

:::::▪ CHAPTER 28

Southern California

"You have quite a file," Catton said. "Do you recall this image?"

The white board showed a news tape from 10 years ago at the University of California at Berkeley where John and Richard had met as undergraduates.

Hundreds of young men and women shouted at and gave the finger to the Republican presidential candidate who had come to the school to campaign. The candidate had short-cropped black hair and claimed to have been a Navy SEAL. The crowd of extreme free-market anarchists had crashed the rally of the Berkeley Republicans to protest the baby-boomer buyout of Social Security. A few students threw eggs and water balloons made from red and white and blue rubbers.

"So what?" John Grant said. "Somebody had to kick the fucking Republicans back to third-party status. My generation did it."

The Republican Party had splintered after Social Security collapsed and a rare coalition of Democrats and Libertarians legalized many drugs. Most older ex-Republicans joined the Green-leaning Democrats to secure the vast state subsidies that still went to those over 50. Most younger ex-Republicans joined the Libertarians to fight those subsidies and to fight the massive centralized bureaucracy that gave them out and taxed and borrowed to fund them.

The religious right made up both the core and fringe of the Republicans.

"That's you right up front with the blue water balloon. Here is where you lob it. You know what? That lob got you an agent assigned to you."

"You?"

"No."

John's ribs still hurt but he did not feel the twitching pain that had followed the taser stuns.

John thought he had gone through the worst of it and now even smiled at Catton and Rittenhouse. He just hoped they had not taken the extra raisin from his wallet. He might get to his other backups but that one had stayed in wireless contact with the raisin on the tabletop.

The next image showed John at the front of a crowd outside an Oakland post office.

He screamed back and forth with a fat middle-aged man who still wore his red Generation-X ball cap backward. Then the screen showed dozens of John's e-mail posts that attacked the latest stop-gap taxes to bail out Social Security and Medicare. Other e-mail posts called for private health and retirement accounts and for an end to the legal and medical monopolies.

"Big deal. That stuff bounced all over the net along with hundreds of thousands of flames just like it. What matters is that we finally privatized Social Security. You two civil servants should thank me."

"The state will argue that there is a pattern here that goes beyond politics and a student's thirst for reform."

The screen showed a more recent image of John at

the University of Nevada at Las Vegas. He stood at a podium and denounced the Libertarians first for not cutting defense and energy subsidies and then for not abolishing the FBI and CIA. Crackling sound came with the image as John said "The CIA must die!"

The screen froze on the image.

"I bet you spooks liked that one."

"The pattern is that of a sociopath," Catton said. "You were an antigovernment zealot at school. Then you went to work for a foreign intelligence agency on crucial energy technologies."

"You guys could too if you had real college degrees."

"You have even inquired about how to surrender your citizenship."

"That's legal."

"It's legal but extreme. It also fits your profile of a traitor-for-pay."

"Is that what this is about? A goddamn profile?"

"No. You made a mistake. You murdered someone. Now the house caves in and we sort through the rubble."

"This is no murder investigation."

"This is evidence. And we agree with your friend's epistemology. We too proportion our beliefs to the evidence."

"You guys are civil service at its best. Give me my raisin and let's cut to the deal."

"Deal?" Catton said.

Catton nodded to Rittenhouse.

Agent Rittenhouse set down his taser and picked up the brown raisin in front of him and dropped it on the white tile floor. Then he ground it under the heel of his black shoe. John could see the raisin in the agent's own ear when he turned his head.

"That's your deal," Catton said.

John felt a wave of relief. There was a good chance that they had not even tried to decrypt the raisin even if they had intercepted some of its transmissions. He had other Jism raisins but they did not.

"That will look just as cute in court," John said. "Tell me what you want."

"I already told you. We want to know about the Israelis. We want to know about the Texas firms Green O and Energon. We want to know what you have passed to the Israelis from the staff and computers of the Hoover Dam. What were you and Dr. Ramachandra discussing on the Hoover Dam yesterday? You promised him a position in your company. We want to know about that. Most of all we want to know why your partner says you are a spy."

"Richard said that? Bullshit."

"He said it under oath and has just signed the transcript."

"Show me the transcript. Not that I would believe it was authentic. Look. Enough. I have allowed you pricks to question me without a lawyer. No longer. Go ahead and taser me some more if you want. Nothing happens from here on unless I see a lawyer."

"We have something else to show you first."

::::■■ CHAPTER 29

Keiko Yamaguchi kneeled next to the dark red teakwood table. She poured Turkish coffee into the two small white porcelain cups. Keiko was 23 years old and wore a red silk kimono and long brown wooden pins through her knotted hair.

General Atef Mosarian sat cross-legged on the floor across from Iranian ambassador Mossan Esfahani. The president of Kodo Electronics had given Mosarian the teakwood table and Keiko when Azerbaijan had bought 25 mobile missile-defense platforms.

Mosarian watched the man's eyes as Keiko left the room. He would let the Iranian in the tall white turban have her for the night if he wanted her.

The Iranian showed no interest.

"I admire your office," Esfahani said.

"Thank you. I fell in love with Japan when I first went to Kyoto University to visit my oldest son. Very peaceful."

"Yes. General. Let us be frank. Tell me how can I help you."

"My country is in chaos. Thieves walk down the streets of Baku with shopping carts. The oil spill

169

grows worse and the Armenians steal more of our land each day. Parliament has lost control. The people demand order and justice. Parliament just bickers like a washroom full of wives. It worries only about the media. Half the members still worry about what the Americans think. The other half worry about the Russians. I confess I too worry about the Russians. I fear the Russians will take advantage of our troubles. I grew up under their boot and do not want to die under their boot."

"And if Iran can protect your people from the Russian boot?"

"Then Azerbaijan can punish those who need punishment."

"How can you be sure what your Parliament will do?"

"All disbanded parliaments act the same."

Mosarian heard himself say it and knew he had crossed the line.

He did not trust the Iranians and now they had him. Somehow the wily ambassador would record or transmit this meeting. The Iranians could expose him or lead him into a trap. They could even replace him with one of his own Shiite commanders.

"That is true," Mossan Esfahani said. "Coalitions are fragile. But what of the oil that lies on the ground? Who will put it back in the barrel?"

"I hope Iran can help us repair the damage and build a new pipeline. Of course Iran would have a right to some of the oil."

"Of course. Or Iran could simply invade and have it all."

Mosarian laughed with the ambassador and both men drank the bitter Turkish coffee.

CHAPTER 30

Riyadh
Saudi Arabia

"Commander Haddad," King Fahd said. "The Jews killed over 3,000 of our people in Dhahran. They left an entire oil field radioactive! Now the Jews refuse to pay us for the damage. The Iranians and Egyptians laugh at us and so does much of the world. Your missile retaliation was not enough."

"Your excellency," Commander Haddad said. "We took a reasonable risk with the attack on Eilat. A larger attack might risk war. It would surely draw the censure of the United Nations and the Americans."

"Haddad. We risk war if we look weak to the Egyptians and the Iraqis. The Iranians are spreading lies to the people of Dhahran so that they will challenge the monarchy. Our kingdom could fall because of this internet creature of the Americans!"

The king paused but did not blink his watery eyes.

Haddad wondered if the old man had his arm-IV needle in him now. He also wondered what the king put in his IV.

"Your excellency. I recommend that we wait at

least 24 hours to see if either Iran or Azerbaijan takes action against Israel.''

''Wait? This is the strength of your counsel? The kingdom is at risk! You said you would cut off the hand of a shepherd if the thieves believed the shepherd was a thief. You called that deterrence.''

''Yes. I did.''

''Then plan to cut off the hand! I have discussed this with my cabinet. Do you understand?''

''I do.''

''Good. We would indeed risk war if we struck *after* the Shiites did. The United Nations will tolerate only one strike. I want you to plan it. Now.''

''As you command.''

CHAPTER 31

Sa'ad
Israel

Michael Riesman lit a fresh cigarette as the old black Mercedes cab parked in the garage of the small Mossad building in Sa'ad.

Colonel Hurwicz watched the cab on a screen in his war room. He did not have the time for this but catching Tabriz was something he had to see for himself. Then he would report it to the Prime Minister.

Riesman knew the value of his find. Tabriz could help them prune some of the scenario branches on their decision tree. Tabriz might even be the mastermind behind the Dhahran bombing as Eytan Baum and his team believed. Riesman had also caught an unknown man he claimed was a senior Hamas terrorist. The man might help them prune even more branches and maybe grow a few new ones.

The two commandos opened the trunk and pulled out the bound men.

The trunk had banged them as the old car drove through fields and a fence and over poorly paved roads. The Hamas man had fierce brown eyes and gray streaks in his short wiry black hair. Tabriz had red welts on his pale face but no expression in his eyes.

Riesman thought Tabriz was shorter and thinner than he would be. He searched both men himself. They had no weapons or ID. Each man had a blue WNN credit card and the Hamas man had a thick wad of Swiss francs in his pants pocket.

The commandos untied their feet and held small black short-stock Galil III submachine guns to the backs of their heads to prod them to walk. More Mossad and IDF agents joined the men as they walked upstairs.

Riesman led them to the chairs in the white make-shift interrogation room. His bald head had started to sweat from the stare of the cameras and the heat that the crowd of men and women gave off.

Riesman pointed to the young analyst Ariella who stood behind the Hamas man and Tabriz. She had trained in mechanical engineering at Ben-Gurion University of the Negev when she left the Israeli Army and now spent most of her time reading stolen e-mail messages that other analysts had judged suspicious. She ran the messages through text processors and pattern matchers and wrote reports on which messages other analysts should try to answer or steal.

This was a new experience. Ariella had never seen her work produce a concrete act of intelligence. She sometimes felt guilty about how much the state paid her for her work but still laughed about it with her girlfriends and her programmer husband. Riesman's pointing finger was the first field assignment of her career.

She reached around Tabriz and ripped the duct tape off his mouth.

The tape came off with small pink strips of the dry

lip skin. Tabriz did not flinch or change his forward gaze. Then Ariella reached around the Hamas man and did the same thing.

It was her second concrete act of intelligence.

"Little bitch!" the Hamas man said in the Queen's English.

One of the commandos slapped the back of the Hamas man's neck with his Galil barrel.

Ariella felt guilty about that and stepped back to stand along the wall with the rest of the staff. She had heard that Colonel Hurwicz was watching them from one of the security cameras. She did not know how best to reply to the man's insult and the gun slapping in front of someone of Hurwicz's stature. So she just stood at attention as she had in the army and hoped they had caught the right men.

"Palm prints," Riesman said. "Quick!"

Ariella helped them force the Hamas man's right hand down onto the glowing red pad. The man still fought them and tried to shake his hand slightly to confuse the laser-based matching software. The commando slapped him again in the back of the neck. This time the man kept his hand still.

"No match," Riesman said to one of the cameras.

They could all read the same thing from the wall monitor and Hurwicz could see it as well. Riesman did not care. He had stumbled on this intelligence find and he would stay in charge of it. He thought that by now even the Prime Minister might be watching him.

"You have no match and I have committed no crime," the Hamas man said. "I demand that you let me go."

Riesman ignored him and looked at Tabriz.

It took only one staffer to move Tabriz's limp hand to the red pad. Riesman thought Tabriz was trying to show them some sort of false Sufi calm. Riesman was not even sure he knew what Sufism was in practice. He had once studied kabbalah with his old uncle but viewed it now as no more than numerology and spiritual double-talk.

Riesman looked hard at Tabriz's dead eyes and tried to break his Sufi mask. Tabriz had to know that his mask could not last. The stakes were too high. They would make him talk.

"Match," Riesman said. "Hamid Saleh Tabriz. Age 38. Confirm with retina scan."

Two staffers wheeled the large white machine before Tabriz's chair. It was an old device and they had to adjust its height to Tabriz's eye level.

Ariella watched them fiddle with the height knob and felt the alarm grow in her. She had heard many stories of the Sufi cleric and had never been so close to such a potential enemy. Riesman had just told them that the thin man was a fiery Islamic radical. He said Tabriz had killed Arabs and Persians since he was a teenager.

Riesman had also said that Tabriz might have helped kill Joel Davis. Riesman had not said why he thought that. He had just volunteered it when they watched the WNN broadcasts of Davis's death. The whole office had watched the footage in silent horror. They were part of an international event.

Ariella had met Joel Davis once in this same room when he briefed them on the location of Turkish missile sites. She had drunk coffee with him and laughed at his coarse jokes about the intelligence bureaucracy. Davis was muscular and confident and acted the way she thought a real spy and killer should act. Ariella could not see how the pale quiet man before her could have beat him.

Then she turned to look at the back of the man's head and saw it in the light. It took all her strength to stand still.

"Sir," she said.

"What?" Riesman said in his command voice.

"I suggest we do an MRI scan at once."

"One step at a time. First we get the retina ID."

"Sir. He has scars on his scalp."

The staff and commandos leaned over to see. Even the Hamas man squinted and turned to stare at Tabriz's thick short black hair.

Colonel Hurwicz walked closer to his screen and so did the staff in the war room.

Riesman pushed the retina scanner aside and moved next to Tabriz to see his forehead and white scalp under the black hair. He wished Eytan Baum could be here to watch. Maybe Tabriz was not faking a Sufi trance. Maybe he did have a chip in his brain and not just a mood implant.

This was truly the find of his career.

"Bring an MRI scanner," he said. "Quick!"

One of the staff had already gone to get the oblong black gun. He turned it on and pointed it at the wireless port on the main wall monitor and then handed it to Riesman. Riesman held the MRI gun with both hands and pushed it to Tabriz's forehead.

The monitor showed a normal skull case and brain.

Riesman waved the MRI gun back and forth in front of Tabriz's forehead and turned to watch the wall monitor. Red and green lines of energy streamed from inside the brain and swirled into the butterflies of chaotic attractors.

"What the hell is that?" Riesman said. "Ariella. Check his scalp."

It was the last thing she wanted to do but she did it.

She moved her fingers through the man's coarse hair. She felt the plastic scab lines and saw the pink scars like thin worms on his scalp.

Tabriz still did not move or change his gaze.

"They look like scars," Ariella said.

"Stand back."

Riesman moved closer and held the MRI gun straight down at Tabriz's crown. The monitor showed a solid sphere the size of an orange at the center of the brain. It was the source of the swirling red and green lines.

"Someone get me a pattern match on this!" Riesman said.

"I can tell you what it is," Tabriz said in a soft voice.

Riesman jumped back and so did the staff. Ariella felt her heart race.

"What?"

"It is a superdense variant of what you call C-4 explosive."

Riesman looked at the security camera in panic but could not move his feet.

Tabriz smiled and looked up at the ceiling camera.

"*Allahu Akhbar,*" he said slowly and calmly.

The explosion leveled the small Mossad compound and the office suites on each side of it.

::::■■ CHAPTER 32

Southern California

John Grant thought of cool green honeydew melons.

He had not slept in a day or eaten in half a day. The stress had at first kept him alert and taken the place of food. Now he was stiff and sore and tired and felt the first dizziness of fever. John closed his eyes to take fast microsleeps even as agent Carsten Catton spoke to him. He tried not to think of his son or Denise or their last moments.

Mr. Pierre Rittenhouse typed something on his palmtop. The sounds of the key strokes soothed him. John loved the fresh melons of SoCal and tried to think only of their sweet green flesh.

"Let me show you an advance copy of the *L.A. Times*," Catton said.

The white wall screen showed John on page three of the electronic version of the newspaper. He wore an orange jumpsuit and handcuffs and walked next to a sheriff's deputy with a thick brown mustache.

The headline read "Boyfriend Arrested in Brutal Slaying."

The orange jumpsuit kept him from having more microsleeps.

They had him at last. There would be no million-dollar buyout from the bastards. There would be no Water Dragon or Black Sun companies and no royalty stream from the Israelis and no more green melons in his desert home near the cool blue Colorado River. They would put him in prison for murder and maybe for this trumped-up treason charge. They would strip him of what little freedom he had and feed him to the race gangs in the cage. He tried not to think of that or whether they would give him the death penalty. The fever was working on him and he needed to hear the sound advice of the English gentleman in his ear.

"What do you think?" Catton said.

"I told you what I think. I will kill you someday. The same goes for your fat-assed friend there with the taser."

"Tough talk for a man who will surely face lethal injection. This is interracial murder. Let me show you a different version of the same issue of the *L.A. Times*."

The screen split.

The left window showed the image of John in the orange jumpsuit. The right window showed an excerpt from page 55 of the *Times*. It was one of the obituary pages. There was text but no images. A short paragraph said that Denise Ann Cheng had died at home of a brain aneurysm and gave details of the cremation.

John looked at Catton's confident face. There was a deal after all and so there was hope.

He wished he could hear what their raisins told them.

"Which will it be?" Catton said.

"How about the truth?" John said.

"How about you going to Leavenworth for treason

and murder? They have a program there for sex-crime rehabilitation.''

''You are with the CIA. Someday we'll abolish you cocksuckers and then start the new Nuremberg trials.''

''Let's review your options. You can go to Leavenworth and get fucked up the ass and fucked in your skull for the rest of your natural life. Or you can cooperate with us and walk out of here. You might even walk out of here a rich man.''

''Something has happened. What? You have the Tabriz chip.''

''I can tell you something about Dr. Hamid Tabriz. He is an expert in neural engineering as well as a Sufi holy man in parts of Iran and Turkey.''

''We all know that. They're feeding you old data.''

''What you don't know is that he is dead.''

''I don't believe it.''

''He is dead.''

''That means at most that someone found his body.''

''That usually is enough. And that body just carried a suicide bomb into a government office in Israel and detonated it.''

''The body but not the brain,'' John said. ''He lives in chips. Okay. I see what's happened. The Israelis have panicked and they want revenge. They have put a lot of pressure on you crooks to let me go. Right?''

''We did not murder your fiancée. You did.''

''The Israelis have corroborated my story. Haven't they?''

''Look at the two articles. Which one do you want to run?''

''You know which one. What do you want?''

''Mr. Rittenhouse has prepared a bill of conveyance for you to sign.''

"Fuck you. What happened to talking about the Israelis?"

"I can tell you something about the agencies we represent. They care a lot more about business than they do about intrigue."

John had seen the claims on the net that the CIA had tracked down and shot the leaders of the Chiapas rebels in Mexico. The Indians posed little threat to the Mexican government but they had disrupted oil drilling and metals mining in southern Mexico and Guatemala.

The Indian rebels and bandits had grown rich in the drug trade. Drug legalization ended their wealth but not their demands for change and their networks of crime and terror. The CIA focused on trade and foreign investment to justify its yearly budget of $80 billion. New rebels took the place of the Chiapas rebels the CIA had killed and gave the CIA further cause for its mission.

So it did not surprise John that they wanted to buy him out. He just wished Jism could tell him if it was a trick.

"What do you want me to convey? My shares in Water Dragon?"

"That firm ended with the death of its financier. Probate law bogs down in the case of murder. We want you to convey the molecule patent to Horizons Technology."

"Is that a CIA franchise?"

"Horizons Technology is a limited liability company in Southern California. It pursues start-up ventures in alternative sources of energy."

"What do I get?"

"Your freedom and a fair-use settlement. You trade your patent rights for a trust fund worth 5 to 10 million dollars over the next five years depending on investor interest.''

''And a lot of fine print,'' John said.

''All you have to do is consult for Horizons as needed.''

''The Israelis have a legal right to their patent license,'' John said.

''Yes. But the licensee has a sequence of milestones that the licensee must pass to the satisfaction of the licensor. Horizons may not prove as lenient as your firm was.''

''I see,'' John said. ''I sign and then you shoot me?''

:::■■ CHAPTER 33

The White House
District of Columbia
United States

President Vance Jackson sat at his oak desk in the Oval Office.

His staff had advised against his holding a live press conference or even a remote one. Jackson had already acted. Now he would present that action to the world before the press and the Congress and the world financial markets could challenge him.

Jackson had waited all his career to play the card he had just played. He had joked about it in college with his dorm pals as they smoked pot and hashish and watched reruns of *Beavis and Butthead*. He had researched it in law school when he had first met the woman he would later marry. And he had refused to discuss it during his campaign.

Now Vance Jackson held the power to make a Green dream a moment of history. He did not need notes or a TelePrompTer.

"Good evening. I want to speak to you about a problem we all face and have faced all our lives. That problem is fossil fuels. The world is simply running out of oil and coal and even natural gas. We all know this and deplore it. Yet there has been very little we could do about it.

"The number of cars and trucks on our roads has grown steadily since the 1970s. More wealth in more hands has meant more cars on the road and more fossil fuels converted to the electricity that runs our homes and offices and computer networks. Yes. We have made cars more fuel efficient. We have reduced their drag or wind resistance to almost the lowest limits of what the laws of science allow. And we have seen the welcome growth of electric and solar and even hydrogen automobiles.

"But more than half the cars on American roads still burn gasoline. Each gallon of gasoline we burn gives off a full 20 pounds of carbon dioxide as well as a wide range of dangerous hydrocarbons. It is no surprise that the world's carbon dioxide levels have also grown steadily since the 1970s as has the very real warming of the earth's atmosphere.

"Our nation still burns millions of gallons of gasoline each day. And we have paid dearly for that limited fossil fuel in terms of the environment.

"The people of Florida know just how dear a price we have paid. The world watched as a Cuban oil tanker melted before our very eyes. The Federal Bureau of Investigation has already made a preliminary determination that terrorists destroyed the oil tanker. The Florida coastline will suffer an incalculable environmental loss even though we are using the very best chemical techniques to clean the oil spill. The world has also just watched oil disasters unfold in Saudi Arabia and Azerbaijan.

"And generations to come will still have to contend with the dangerous loss of ozone in the stratosphere from a foolish and elitist fleet of supersonic aircraft.

Ozone depletion remains a leading partial cause of both global temperature warming and the global rise in the incidence of skin cancers.

"Let us remember that the people of the United States make up a little over 3% of the world's population. Yet we consume over 15% of the world's oil and we consume nearly that much of the world's coal and natural gas.

"This cannot continue.

"Americans have led the world into the oil age. We drilled the first modern oil well in Pennsylvania in 1859 in a small town called Titusville. We set up the first oil refinery in 1861 as our nation entered its bloody and only civil war. American inventors and merchants developed the automobile and the airplane and the refrigerator. These and many other American products changed the world. They also made the world depend more on oil and its by-products.

"That oil shaped much of America's legal and political and military history. We outlawed the great oil monopolies in 1911. Decades later we led the world when we repelled Iraq's 1990 invasion of the Kuwaiti oil fields. We did so again in 2015 when Iraq invaded the Saudi oil fields. And America has supported our oil-laden neighbors from the Middle East to Mexico.

"Now the time has come for America to lead the world *out* of the oil age and into a safer and cleaner future. We cannot pass this burden on to our children and our grandchildren. We cannot ask the other nations of the world to reduce their use of petroleum and hydrocarbon products if we do not do so ourselves. And we cannot risk the security of our great country or the security of our allies each time a conflict breaks out in the Middle East or in Siberia or anywhere else on this small planet.

"We must break with the habits and the complacency of the past.

"So tonight I am announcing a new policy and I am asking our colleagues in NATO and Central and South America to join us in this effort. I have signed this Executive Order Number 184,326. That executive order bans all use and sale of gasoline in the United States and in its territories. I will ask both houses of Congress to help implement this ban by passing a host of support measures.

"But make no mistake. I have signed this executive order. The ban is now law.

"The ban will take effect in three phases. Phase one bans the use or sale of gasoline and heating oil in automobiles. That ban takes effect exactly two weeks from today. Phase two bans the use of crude oil derivatives for the heating and cooling of homes and buildings. That ban takes effect six months from today. Phase three bans the use of crude oil derivatives in the generation of electrical power. It takes effect one year from today.

"I realize some of you will have to make rapid and painful adjustments. So I have approved $10 billion in relief funds for public transportation and home heating. I will also ask Congress to speed up passage of its package of tax breaks and research supports for those companies that invest in alternate energy.

"We stand at the threshold of a new and better future. Today we have taken the first step toward that future. Together we can show the world how to make that future the reality of tomorrow.

"Good night and God bless you and God bless America."

CHAPTER 34

Cyberspace

President Jackson had shocked the world.

Each person on the planet had an opinion about the gas ban. They formed their opinion from the hundreds of TV channels they or their agents scanned and the hundreds of on-line net groups they surfed.

A few even acted on their opinions.

| | |

WNN Channel 4: A reporter stands in front of the well-lit White House and interviews the Democratic Senate majority leader and the Libertarian Senate minority leader. The Democrat applauds the President's leadership and vows to support some version of the gas ban and pass the tax breaks for alternate energy. The Libertarian denounces the ban as unconstitutional. She promises to help the oil firms appeal it to the Supreme Court. She also calls for the end of punitive taxes on gas and heating oil. . . .

| | |

WNN Channel 9: Late afternoon traffic slows and jams in Los Angeles as cars form long snaking lines at filling stations. The lines block streets and spill out to freeway exits and onto some freeways. A helicopter news team lands at a Shell Oil station and talks to those stuck in the long lines. The drivers curse President Jackson and the Green Democrats. One driver accepts the gas ban as in her long-term best interests but admits she would not vote for Jackson again. Many drivers call for civil disobedience and the impeachment of Jackson. . . .

▌▐ ▌

WNN Channel 17: German youths march through the streets of Bonn and Berlin and Frankfurt. They carry signs that demand the German government ban gasoline and coal even though most German cars use batteries or hydrogen fuel. Crowds of Green youths sit to form a human roadblock on the autobahn. Many of the youths throw rocks at the German police in riot gear who try to move them. Students overrun a small gas station in Munich. They set it afire for the cameras but not all survive the fireball. . . .

▌▐ ▌

WNN Channel 38: National Guardsmen pitch tents outside of highway patrol offices around the country as they prepare to help the mobile policemen enforce the gas ban. Members of private militias drive their trucks in circles around the tents and shout taunts and threats at the guardsmen. A reporter says most federal buildings in the country have received bomb threats. Texas vandals have firebombed department of motor vehicle buildings in Austin and College Station. The reporter shows excerpts of conservative militia e-mail messages that debate a nationwide attack on DMV buildings. . . .

███

WNN Channel 62: A Moscow special report shows a burning oil well in the Republic of Yakutia in central Siberia. It claims Yakut mining extremists have bombed the oil well and threaten to bomb other Russian-backed wells. The Kremlin now meets to decide how to protect Russian investments in the oil-rich republic that has twice the land of Alaska and much of the world's diamonds and gold and platinum. Yakutsk Mayor Vasily Bychkov says he thinks Russians or even the Chinese might invade soon to grab the Yakut gold and diamond fields as the U.S. demand for Siberian oil falls. The Moscow station cites its own poll that 81% of Muscovites think Yakutia still belongs to Russia and 54% would not oppose the use of Russian force to secure the republic. . . .

███

WNN Channel 93: Students burn Uncle Sam dolls at the University of Tehran and call for a new *jihad* against the Great Satan and its Zionist stooges. The same Uncle Sam dolls burn outside the U.S. embassies in Algiers and Cairo and Khartoum. Firebombs and plastic explosives have destroyed the U.S. embassy in the Pakistani city of Islamabad and the Venezuelan capital of Caracas. Canadian Green radicals from the University of Saskatoon march on the oil fields south of Regina and try to block oil trucks by sitting in the roads. The students yank a driver out of one truck and beat him to death when he drives over four students. . . .

███

WNN Channel 165: A Chiapas Indian in Paraiso cuts off a young Mexican woman's head with a machete. He picks up the head and stacks it on the Pemex chief's desk with four other heads. The leader repeats his demands for social justice in the southern Mexican state. He tells a remote reporter from TV España that the Chiapas guerrillas survived when the United States legalized drugs and now they will survive the U.S. ban on gasoline. The image flickers for a moment as Mexican commandos set off a case of C-4 and level the small Pemex office building. . . .

❚❚❚

WNN Channel 664: Graphs show how the internet betting markets view the U.S. gas ban. News that 62% of Americans oppose the ban while only 21% of non-Americans oppose it has switched much of the betting from invasion to U.S. elections. The bettors think President Vance Jackson has only a 23% chance of re-election. They think the Democrats have only a 32% chance of keeping their majorities in the House and Senate at the midterm election. Now only 36% believe Russia will invade Azerbaijan. Only 4% believe Iran will. . . .

❚❚❚

WNN Channel 803: Metals prices have jumped up on news of the gas ban. Gold has reached $1,630 per troy ounce and platinum has hit $2,230. Private currencies based on gas and oil still fall as the spot price of oil has dropped to $390 a barrel. The Ukrainian eagle and Thomson petrol have now both lost over 14% of their value. The yield on the U.S. 10-year bond has risen above 10% and depressed all major U.S. stock exchanges. The dollar has collapsed from 34 yen to 28 yen based on heavy selling from European and Mideastern central banks. The basket of pre-

cious metals that backs Daiwa metal has pushed the
private currency far ahead of all others. Analysts
claim that Chinese and Japanese oil traders buy the
private paper bills to hedge against the risk that the
Russians might invade the Yakut or other Siberian oil
fields. . . .

▌▊

WNN Channel 809: The Chinese government has
threatened to close the Shanghai Stock Exchange to
stem investor panic and the drop in share prices. Trading volume has grown as traders sell energy stocks
and buy metals stocks and technology mutual funds.
The Tokyo Stock Exchange has held steady and lost
only half of its 2% gain. The increased value of the
Shanghai Stock Exchange has fallen to a gain of 14%
from its peak gain of 20% since the Dhahran bombing. . . .

▗▄▄▖ CHAPTER 35

John had refused to sign until they brought him a honeydew melon.

Catton would not let him use a carving knife to cut the green melon. John had to use a dull steel butter knife and yank the knife up and down to split the white rind. Then he scooped the wet pale-yellow seeds onto the table and sawed the halves into slices. Rittenhouse brought him a brown bio-sack to put the seeds and chewed rinds in.

John ate the whole melon and washed his hands and face on a wet towel. He felt the warm start of the blood-sugar rush as his body absorbed the fructose.

Then he signed the two copies of the bill of conveyance.

Catton brought him a shoe box that contained his wallet and Swiss army knife. John felt the raisin through the doeskin of the wallet but did not pull it out. He put the wallet and knife back in his pants pockets. He still did not know if anyone watched him through the whiteboard.

"Where's my copy?" he said.

"Of what?" Catton said.

"What I just signed."

"Don't worry. The documents are valid. The patent office will send you a processed copy within three weeks."

"The hell with that. I need something to take to my lawyer right now."

"Mr. Rittenhouse will have to make a copy for you on your way out."

"You're not coming?"

"I'm done here. I have to catch a red-eye back to DC tonight."

John did not want to hear about Catton's red-eye flight to Washington. He wanted to get free of these men and call Eytan and then get some sleep. The melon still raised his blood sugar but that was not enough to fight the soreness and the deep fatigue. He knew he had forgotten something and now it hit him.

"Shit. Where's my Jeep?"

"Mr. Rittenhouse will drive you to a hotel or to Richard Cheng's warehouse if you want. Your Jeep is not functional."

"You mean you tore it up to search it."

"That's a small price to pay for your liberty and a trust fund."

"What about the speeding tickets I had on it?"

"I don't know about them. You'll have to contact the Department of Motor Vehicles."

"You son of a bitch."

Catton ignored him and left the room.

Pierre Rittenhouse stood up and held a black briefcase he had brought in the room with the melon. The stout man in the dark suit fiddled with his blue and black striped tie. That made John think of the taser stuns and the baton welts that hurt deep into his back and ribs. It also made John think of the Swiss army knife in his pants and how much he would like to use it to carve up Rittenhouse's full stomach.

"Let's go," Rittenhouse said. "You can give me directions in the car."

"Where are we?"

"Gilman Springs."

"That's where we are? It's an hour outside of L.A."

Rittenhouse shrugged and left the room. John followed him out. They had been in a new office suite the whole time.

They walked to the elevator at the end of the beige hall and passed the offices of a tax lawyer and a pediatrician. John thought they had been in a warehouse or the holding room of a police precinct. They rode the elevator down to the parking level and John thought of the Swiss knife again. Catton had said that Rittenhouse would make him a copy before they left. Now was the time to test whether he had lied.

"Wait a minute," John said. "You're supposed to make me a copy of the conveyance."

"We'll stop at the hotel and use their machine."

"You have the original with you?"

The man nodded and tapped his briefcase.

John wanted to dig out the raisin and put it in his ear before he made a move. He could do that as they walked to the car but Rittenhouse would see him and might even use that taser to take it from him. He would have to wait.

The question now was whether to get in the car with Rittenhouse.

There was no need for the suit to drive him. John could go outside to a pay phone and call Eytan or call a cab. This looked more and more like a trap. They had his witness and his patent and they had lied about the copy and had held him in this office building. The police had stopped him and yet he walked free without ever seeing them. They could lead him to a Tabriz chiphead. Catton and Rittenhouse might even be chipheads.

John felt the energy come back to him at the very idea of it. Maybe he should follow his heart and kill Rittenhouse before the suit tried to kill him. He could hear Jism telling him not even to think about it and to just stay wary.

John did not often think of killing people. He had like all teens used bootleg VR programs that let him shoot and choke and gouge the villains in games. A college friend had once let him try a banned program that let him hack apart digitized public figures with a samurai sword. He had to admit it was fun the first time but the sword never felt real in his hands. The grainy 3-D graphics made the virtual world look too much like a game.

Now he thought how it would feel to bash open the suit's skull with the butt of the knife and reach in and pull out a chip or a handful of brains.

The door opened and John followed Rittenhouse into the underground parking lot. It looked like any other lot with cars parked too closely to make more space. Rittenhouse walked straight toward a large blue van.

John knew he had to act now if he was to do it.

He could always say that the suit provoked him or that he thought the suit started to act like a chiphead and he was too tired to tell. He could say that and many more things he could figure out later. Rittenhouse had stunned him and coerced his patent away from him and worked for the great state bureaucracy that he and his friends hated above all else and that he knew now he would never escape. He had to thump the man's temple with the knife butt and at least see what the suit had packed in the black briefcase.

John felt the knife in his pocket and made a fist around it. Rittenhouse would see the bulge if he looked back at him.

John pulled the red knife from his pocket and jumped in the air at Rittenhouse and swung the knife in a big overhand arc. The knife butt came down on the back of the man's neck at the hairline and skidded off. It sure made selling out feel better.

Rittenhouse grunted but did not fall or drop the briefcase.

"You little worm," Rittenhouse said and turned. "Let's end this right now."

He drew a silenced nine-millimeter.

John dove at him and grabbed him in a headlock and hit the concrete. John tried to block the gun but felt only the burning taser pain again.

He opened his eyes and saw the Israeli Daniel close the briefcase and lock it.

Rittenhouse lay next to him on the concrete but was not dead. He still thrashed from the EMP scrambler Daniel had touched to his skull. The agent Raquel started to drag John from behind.

John turned to look at her. He had just recognized her short black hair when he saw her nod. John did not see Daniel then touch the EMP scrambler to the back of his head.

John saw only white.

:::::■ CHAPTER 36

Colonel Avi Hurwicz sipped fresh black coffee in the secure booth. The coffee tasted almost sweet as it washed away the honey. He had taken a combat nap on the cot in his office and eaten a Greek candy bar made of sesame seeds and honey.

Hurwicz had slept for less than a half hour and yet had dreamed in bright color. Most of his dreams were in black and white and he could not recall them even when he awoke. But he could recall this dream. He still saw the green and red feathers of the huge parrot that flew above him in the Negev Desert.

But why a parrot? Why the green and red feathers?

Hurwicz did not know if the dream meant something about a threat to him or to Israel. He always looked for a threat in what he could not explain. Maybe he had seen a smaller version of the bird on a nature program about the old rain forests in Brazil. Maybe the dream was just random nonsense. A sleeping brain made its own signals from the day's old patterns that still swirled in its neural circuits.

The mind was still a mystery. Neuroscience and the information sciences had made great upward strides all his life. Yet no one could explain why people slept.

His thoughts were still on the great bird when Prime Minister Sharon came on-line.

"Colonel. So far you have been right. No one has attacked us. But most of the world thinks we killed Aminzadeh. The problem is I am not so sure we didn't."

Hurwicz nodded and set down his paper cup. He did not like the gruff little Prime Minister or where he was going with this. It was a bad sign that Sharon had not gotten to the point with his first breath.

Hurwicz did not trust a diplomat who was more of a hawk than he was.

An old army friend had told Hurwicz that Sharon made jokes about how Hurwicz was soft on opposing the growing calls to end the draft and to shift to an all-volunteer military. Sharon knew Hurwicz believed in the draft as much as he did but the old man had to be tougher.

Just then he recalled the parrot was from a sign on the Italian ice cream shop he had stopped in last night.

That relieved a slight tension and convinced him the dream was nonsense after all. And it made him wish he had a fresh cone of the red-wine ice cream. Just the thought of the cool sour ice cream made him feel better. It meant that the dream was not a warning. He was back in control.

"Of course we will not apologize," Sharon said.

"There is no reason why we should. The evidence suggests the Tabriz cult killed Aminzadeh."

"Your chip theory? Someone debrained Davis and made a killer robot out of him? You can't conclude that from a burned computer chip."

"Sir. We have the MRI scan of Tabriz."

"I think a metallic cranial plate is more likely. I

understand they found something like that at the blast site. I also understand this Davis was a man of loose habits and many debts.''

"That sounds like *Shabak* speculation," Hurwicz said.

Hurwicz did not trust the security agency Shin Bet. He knew Sharon used the ultrasecret agency to spy on his political enemies as well as to spy on Israel's neighbors Jordan and Lebanon and Egypt and throughout the Mediterranean. Most of the Shin Bet officers he had met seemed obsessed with the Shiite threat. So did the elite Nativ officers who guarded Sharon and worked for his office.

"Perhaps. But I always believe in the lesser miracle. And right now I find the lesser miracle to be a whoring Davis who went astray until I see proof to the contrary. Now tell me. Do you still think the Azeris won't attack? They've lost a president since your last prediction.''

"Yes. I still don't think they will. Their Parliament seems stable and martial law seems to be working despite the riots and sniper fire the press has played up. The fighting in Nagorno-Karabakh also seems to have slowed somewhat.''

"I am afraid I don't agree with you. My sources tell me that a coup remains likely in Azerbaijan. They also tell me that Hezbollah and the other Shiite groups that love us so much plan to avenge Aminzadeh.''

"I hear the same rumors," Hurwicz said.

He picked up the cup again and sipped the cooling coffee. The honey taste was gone and the coffee had returned to its old bitterness.

"Colonel. I won't gamble the fate of the nation on what you choose to dismiss as rumors.''

"Sir. I agree that the extremists will take some act

of revenge. But it will be on a much smaller scale than a military strike against Israel. No doubt Shin Bet will find some trace of it.''

''So we agree that the Shiites will respond. But we don't agree on the magnitude of the response? The office of the prime minister exists to resolve just such disagreements. I want you to prepare a retaliatory strike against four military targets in Sinai and two in the Egyptian mainland.''

''That is flirting with war. Is it worth it?''

''Colonel. Do you refuse to carry out my instructions?''

''Of course not. I merely offer my opinion.''

''Good. You are a competent man and I don't want to replace you. So let me make this clear. I want you to pick the targets yourself. I want you to work up strike plans for all combinations of the targets. Don't worry. I will give the order to strike only if they attack us first. I am not a fool. But I will not tell you which strike plan to use until I give the strike order. When you have finished your Egyptian strike plans I want you to work out a second set of strike plans to deal with how the Shiites might respond to our retaliation. This country will not stand for a second Eilat. Understood?''

''Understood. But what counts as an attack? A suicide bombing in a shopping mall? Nanopoison in the water supply? Who defines it?''

''I do. The taxpayers pay you to plan contingencies. Go plan them.''

:::■ CHAPTER 37

Near Abaq
Inner Mongolia
People's Republic of China

General Feng held a fresh yellow carrot by its green tassel and fed it to the red pony.

Feng grew carrots and white radishes and onions in a square plot of land behind his cabin. He had mixed dried horse manure with the orange-red dirt and mulched the plants with old horse straw to hold in the moisture. The old Chinese Communists had taught him such things as a boy in his village of Erenhot.

The Communists cared a great deal about farming the desert. He could never understand why they spent so much time and money on agriculture. Feng could still remember the dumb farming programs the Communists used to run on their state TV.

The Communists had forced his whole village to plant fruit trees and tend root crops. The people had to do this even if they worked all day to tend their herds of sheep and goats and horses and sometimes camels. Most of the apple and peach trees had died of thirst or produced only a few twisted fruit. The potatoes had refused to grow beyond small brown nodules that they had to feed to the horses.

His uncle Rago had laughed at his young nephew for spending so much time with the Chinese gardens. Rago had worked as a hide tanner and horseman and taught what he could to Ulan before the Chinese sent him to Xian and made him Feng.

Feng was too old now to practice the horseman's tricks of his uncle. Instead he liked to groom and ride this pony and think the thoughts of his youth that he had ignored for so many decades.

They were all so old now.

China had held over one fourth of the world's elderly since 2020. It was the largest gray population on earth and Feng was part of it. What made him smile was that the old gray schemers now trusted him to protect them.

Major Yu found the general in the army stable.

Yu had often laughed with his officer friends that Feng belonged on an old-folk's farm. He did not know why the powers in Beijing and Shanghai still humored the old man and tried to win his favor. The young officers ran the compound. This compound was but one among hundreds throughout China.

"General Feng. I just spoke with General Qi."

Feng did not look at Yu.

He fed the pony the green tassels of the carrot and rolled a second yellow carrot in his other hand. He had seen devious men like Yu since he was a Red Guard. The Chinese bureaucracy still seemed full of them.

Feng thought the Communists deserved much of the blame but he was not sure. Perhaps their Maoist atheism had replaced and scrubbed out the moral training most kids learned from their parents and from society. But Mao had been dead a long time. The devious men still came in great numbers. And Feng did not know what Chinese children learned these days from their schools and from the Americans.

"General Qi wants to have a conference with you. He says it is urgent."

Feng fed the second carrot to the red pony.

Yu watched the big yellow teeth chop the carrot in chunks and thought about the new teeth enzymes they sold in Shanghai. He would have to get some. He had let the sides of his front teeth fill with yellow plaque. It was this damned Mongol outpost. Yu hated it and its bad water and its canned rations and chemical toilets.

What did they do that mattered? They played tank games that no one in Beijing cared about. Each week they re-aimed their smart missiles at targets in Siberia and Japan and Korea and the Pacific fleets. They had no thought of firing them.

The compound was just a massive ammo dump on the frontier to nowhere. Yet Yu knew that real-time satellite links and wireless networks could change that in seconds. The Chinese could make the Abaq compound part of the biggest digital battlefield in the world.

"General. I think General Qi wants to speak to you about the Russians. They are massing on the border of Yakutia!"

Feng held the end of the green tassel. He let go of it to give the pony the last bite.

Never show them.

The silence of Feng scared Yu. The young man left the stable to tell his friends about it.

::::: CHAPTER 38

Interstate-15
Mojave Desert
Southern California

John felt the bite in his arm.

He soon came out of a swirling dream of flashing green lights and red-rock desert and the cool blue waters of the Colorado River. It was fever sleep but the only sleep he had had in over a day. His brain had made the most of it.

Raquel pulled the needle out of his arm. She held a cotton ball dabbed in alcohol against the small wound.

John sat up with his eyes open and felt the room start to spin.

"Head hurt?" Eytan said. "Sorry about that. We had to make it look like a kidnapping. Your little assault almost got you killed. That was stupid."

"Shalom to you too," John said. "Kidnapping is a felony."

John felt his head ring when he said it. He also felt the soft road vibrations and the inertial pull as the large white van slowed on the highway. He looked around at the well-stocked room and the six Israelis.

Eytan sat on a box and smiled at him.

"I thought you were in Israel," John said.

"I'm a wandering Jew. This meat truck is my own private Israel. Like it? Even has a self-cleaning toilet. We'll be in Nevada in about two hours. We'll have plenty of time left for the demo."

"The demo? You're kidding. I need something to eat."

"Aaron. Find John one of those carbo drinks you brought from the gym. We need to raise his blood sugar and keep it up."

"Where is that self-cleaning toilet?" John said.

"Left front corner. Do us a favor and wash your armpits while you are in there."

John walked slowly to keep his balance.

The head pain was bad but not as bad as it had been that morning. The nap had helped. John's ribs still felt raw and so did his lower lip. He tried not to think of the flesh pain and instead focused on what he had signed.

Did Catton take a copy? Did the Israelis take the suitcase from Rittenhouse?

Aaron gave him a plastic bottle of sweet red fluid when he got back. John drank it in gulps and gave the empty bottle back to Aaron.

Eytan still sat on the brown box. The other Israelis unpacked boxes at the front end of the large room.

John found a box near Eytan's box and sat on it and leaned back against the white plastic wall. He tried not to look at Eytan's compact paunch.

"Sore?" Eytan said.

"Damn right I'm sore. Your agents here were real heroes. They left Richard and me for those LAPD baton twirlers. You ever been hit with a baton? I think they broke a rib or something. Where is Richard?

Those CIA bastards said he signed away his rights to Water Dragon.''

"So did you.''

"What do you know about it? You took Rittenhouse's briefcase?''

"I have a copy in the computer. Means now you work as a consultant at the pleasure of the U.S. government. Your contract with us is still in effect but the Americans could challenge it and win if they wanted to. Of course we still expect you to consult for us. And everyone wants you at the demo tomorrow.''

"That's it? Back to business? What about Denise? Does she just go away?''

"Thought that was what you wanted. You took the deal.''

John thought of Jism and started to reach for the extra raisin in his wallet. He caught himself and stopped.

His head was not clear yet and he did not trust Eytan and his Israeli agents. That raisin might be his last link to Jism. And John recalled that Jism had told him it was not safe to go to the demo at the Hoover Dam.

"Eytan. Let's be frank. You may need me for the demo but you don't need me beyond that. I'm not even sure you need me for the demo.''

"You don't trust us?''

"Hell no I don't trust you,'' John said.

"What about your son?''

"What do you mean? He's dead.''

"Yes. But death has many forms.''

"What are you getting at? What the fuck have you done with my son? I want the truth.''

"Fair enough. You deserve the truth. Your son is

neither dead nor alive. Well maybe more dead than alive. He was technically dead when we found him. He was clinically dead. Had no heartbeat and had stopped breathing. So we put him in cryonic suspension in a warehouse of ours in Pomona. They have a good chance to revive him someday when all this gets behind us.''

John tried to picture what that would be like.

''It helps that he was so young,'' Eytan said. ''It was a crude suspension to say the least. They pumped out his blood and put in their latest antifreeze. They say the liquid nitrogen will destroy the surface cells. But beyond that it won't cause too much damage if the fetus is small enough. Who knows what they can fix in the future?''

''Eytan. Something is not right here. So far as I know you may have killed my son or somehow had a hand in it. Now you want to use his 'revival' to blackmail me?''

''Not at all. John. I did this for you as a friend and at no small cost to our effort. I could have just left your son dead on the floor. Let's face it. Even you left him.''

''You son of a bitch. I had no choice. But you've had all kinds of choices. I never know what hand you're playing. What happened to Richard?''

''He was not as lucky as you were. He sleeps with your son.''

''You *killed* him?''

''It's a gray area of the law. Almost all molecular motion stops at -320° Fahrenheit. So time in effect stops if you're frozen. Don't worry. Richard too stands a good chance to revive someday but of course much later than your son will. It may be 50 or so years from now. Who knows? Look. Don't blame us.

We just tried to make the best of a historically bad day. The hard truth? Your government made the call."

"Eytan. You think his parents will put up with that? Christ. They just lost their only two kids."

"Can't say. I'm sure your government will smooth it over with money and photos. I have already told you. They made the call. They know what they're doing."

"Then why did they leave me free to talk?"

"They didn't. Mr. Rittenhouse was taking you to Pomona to be with your son. You should thank Daniel for keeping you warm."

"So answer the question. Did he get the briefcase Rittenhouse had with him?"

"He didn't try. Your government would not have approved of that. We would not be driving to Nevada now."

"But they did approve of you taking me? That doesn't wash."

" 'Doesn't wash.' What a strange expression. Aaron. Are we ready?"

"Almost," Aaron said and went back to the box he had unpacked.

John thought he might jump one of them and take his gun and make them stop the truck. But there would be nowhere for him to go. Either they would catch him in the Mojave Desert or someone else would. The best he could do was pump Eytan for answers while the others worked.

"Are Catton and Rittenhouse CIA agents?" John said.

"Preppy aren't they? No and yes. And they would be CIA officers and not agents. You are a CIA agent if a CIA officer recruits you. Cars Catton works for the intelligence arm of your Department of Energy. So no. He is not CIA. He in theory has to answer to the director of Central Intelligence. But then so do I when I work in this country. Big Pierre Rittenhouse works for the CIA's Directorate of Science and Technology. That's why Daniel had to be gentle with him. David just give him a headache and not a full brain scramble.''

''It's hard to believe the CIA cares that much about burning water and my patent. I can see the DOE guys wanting to play with it but not the CIA.''

''Wrong twice. The CIA knows the strategic importance of alternate fuels. Look at the Tamraz pipeline and the Russians piling up their troops in Siberia. Men like Rittenhouse also know the tactical importance of what your Dr. Tabriz has shown he can do with chips and brains. The CIA has watched this game since Tabriz blew those Dhahran oil pumps.''

''So Tabriz did that? Remember I asked you about him?''

''You're not listening. The oil blast knocked out one of the Saudi satellites but only for a minute or so. CIA's S&T gang got in the game then. They've watched you since we first contacted you last year and flew you over to Eilat.''

''Thanks.''

''You're welcome. Good thing for you we beat them to Denise's house. They would have just taken the chip and put you on ice. This way we only had to give them the backup and you got to stay warm. John. I always liked you. Too bad you never joined the army.''

''That means you smuggled the melted Tabriz chip out of the country.''

''I can't tell you about our side. I can tell you only

that your CIA has given the matter of the Tabriz chip its highest S&T priority. They even briefed your President Jackson on it before he signed his now-famous bill.''

"I never heard about that."

"Never mind. He only outlawed gasoline and touched off some of the biggest riots since your Social Security collapsed."

"Outlawed gas?"

"That's in the past. What the CIA wants to know is technical. How does Tabriz make the spine and medulla grafts? Hell. We want to know too. We've had to guess at it."

"Medulla grafts?" John said. "I sure would like to see those circuit diagrams."

"You will. We're working them up right now. We've had to figure out a few new tricks just to do that."

"So you did learn something from Denise's Tabriz chip?"

"Of course."

"Eytan. Tell me. What do you think she *felt*? I mean Denise when they made the nanografts. Jesus. They cut out her brain! She might still have been alive."

"Hard question. There have to be as many ways to dress a brain as there are to skin a cat. Tabriz and his team may have found a way to do it when she was only unconscious. But I doubt it. There are too many signals and circuits to track. They all work in parallel. And frankly I don't think Tabriz would make the effort anyway. Why spare an infidel pain?"

"So you think they in effect skinned her alive?"

"Skinned alive? That is something else. Listen. Try not to dwell on these things. It is the only way. I know

how hard it is not to think about such suffering. I have
lost men whom we know the other side tortured for
days before they shot. Try not to think of it. Let's talk
about the demo. Raquel wants you to practice the tape
with her.''

"Who tortured them?" John said. "The Egyptians?''

Eytan looked at him and paused before he answered.

"Not just the Egyptians. These animals did unspeakable things to our boys. Truly unspeakable. I
once saw a transcript of what they called a 'medical
interrogation.' Let me tell you. *That* was skinning
someone alive.''

Eytan shook his head and stood.

"Aaron," he said. "Are we ready yet?''

"Close enough," the stocky man said. "We can
start.''

"Good.''

Eytan turned back to John.

"How do you feel?''

"A little better. I would love to take a nap.''

"You just had one.''

"That doesn't count," John said. "You drugged
me.''

"Don't worry.''

"I know. There's plenty of time for sleeping in the
grave.''

"That's not what I was going to say. You'll have
plenty of rest time before the demo. Now stand up.''

John stood up.

Aaron walked over to him with a folded white
gown in his hand. John reached for the gown but
Aaron passed it from his right hand to his left hand.

Then Aaron threw a fast front punch into John's solar plexus.

The short punch knocked the air out of John and knocked him against the truck wall. He had not felt that shooting stomach pain since an eighth-grader sucker-punched him when he was in sixth-grade gym class. He crumpled against the white wall and gasped for air. Eytan and Aaron walked him to the front of the room.

"Relax and take small breaths," Eytan said. "You'll be fine. Aaron sometimes trains the new recruits. He likes to show off."

Raquel joined them and helped them set John into a makeshift dentist's chair.

Aaron and Daniel strapped down his arms and chest and forehead with thick black Velcro straps. Raquel put a white mask over his mouth and nose. Then she put a mask on herself.

John struggled against the black straps and then stopped.

He looked up and saw all the Israelis wearing the white masks. He did not know the name of the two Israelis who wore yellow surgical gloves and who now spoke quickly in Hebrew.

He did not speak the language but he knew at once what they were saying and he felt a cold flash of terror at what they planned to do.

"You're doing this for the CIA?" John said in gasps.

"Not at all," Eytan said through his mask. "Turns out we can do things over here that the CIA can't do. The only constraint is that we can't kill you outright as long as you remain a U.S. citizen. Such is your government."

"Fuck you. And I won't help you on your goddamn demo for those Texan bastards."

That felt better. It wasted his breath but it felt better.

John then thought how the old gold miner would have said much the same thing.

At least the old miner would not just sit here and feel sorry for himself. He would fight the bastards but still he would accept his fate. Only a fool would struggle or plead. The old gold miner would take it like he must have taken thousands of oven-hot days and taken a dozen cave-ins and a mouthful of cracked and rotting teeth.

Now the only question was whether he could take it.

"John," Eytan said. "Relax. This is all part of a political decision. Remember Bismarck said you never want to see how people make sausage or political decisions. You've been in the sausage grinder and you still have a way to go. Try to calm yourself and sit still. All will come to pass."

"This doesn't make any sense," John said. "I saw your woman here take the optical tape. You don't need me for the demo."

"In fact we do. We know that your friend Dr. Tabriz will try to sabotage the demo. And we need you to catch him."

"Shit. That's it? I'm bait?"

"Much more than that. You're our Trojan horse. Believe me. A lot of people are pulling for you. You're a hero. Haven't you always wanted to meet the great Dr. Hamid Tabriz? You may do better than that. You may get to go one-on-one with him! *Nano a nano*!"

Eytan and Daniel laughed and stood back with Raquel and Aaron.

The short dark agent Uri clamped a chrome skull cap on John's head. He pushed down on it to hold John's head steady and to force it more tightly into a black plastic neck brace. John saw small blue stars as Uri pushed down on the skull cap and felt its thin teeth pierce his scalp.

It took all he had not to scream.

"Moshe," Eytan said "It's your turn. I'll have the driver slow down."

John never got a good look at Moshe. He could tell Moshe was an older man with short brown hair and dark stubble on his cheeks and neck.

John convulsed when Moshe stepped in front of him with a small electric rotary saw. The chrome cap hurt but not as much as it should have. He knew they must have rubbed some painkiller on his forehead and scalp. That still did not lessen the terror of seeing the saw.

Moshe slid a button with his thumb. Then the saw made a high-pitched whirring sound.

Uri pushed harder on the skull cap to counter John's shock response.

John clenched his teeth and let go.

He had failed.

He screamed at first when the saw cut through his forehead at the base of the chrome skull cap. It too hurt less than he thought it would. The cutting made him think a huge bumblebee was stinging him over and over. Blood ran down into his eyes and ears and onto his lips and chin. The blood tasted warm and salty and he tried to spit it out as he screamed.

It only got worse. John now struggled to wipe the blood from his eyes as much as to stop the small

jackhammer tearing away at his skull. Sound no
longer came out when he screamed.

Moshe turned off the saw and circled John to in-
spect his work. The cutting had taken less than a minute. It had traced out a bloody line at the rim of the
skull cap.

"John," Eytan said. "Relax now. The worst is
over. I'm sorry but we have to do this while you are
awake so we can tune the damn thing. Bear with us.
I told you we have to work with all the signals and
neural circuits in parallel. But look at it this way: A
little headache now is a small price to pay for im-
mortality."

Eytan nodded to Uri.

The short agent pulled the chrome skull cap straight
up and the roof of John's skull came with it. Uri put
the skull cap on a thin tray and put the tray on a shelf
in the truck's refrigerator.

Aaron held a small golden chiplet in his gloved
hand.

All the Israelis stared at John and he looked back
at them. John's brain shined pink in the lamplight. It
at once started to swell in the air.

Moshe replaced the saw with a laser scalpel. The
scalpel used hundreds of thousands of thin light
beams to cut fine tissue. Moshe first looked at a 3-D
model of John's brain on a screen and then gently
passed the scalpel through the pink tissue.

Moshe removed a tiny square chunk. He placed the
bloody brain chunk on a clear sheet of plastic. The
sheet had a fine bioelectric surface of polyphenyl-
enevinylene.

The brain chunk itself was not special. John's massive neural networks could soon reroute their neural
circuits around the missing tangle of neurons and syn-

apses. But they would never have the chance. The biosurface would instead learn much of the structure of the neural circuits.

John knew they had cut open his scalp. He could not tell if they had lifted it off when they had lifted the chrome skull cap. He did not feel Moshe cut out the cube. He was in too much shock to think clearly. Even the old gold miner had left him.

So this was what it was like.

Moshe and Uri held the clear plate to all six faces of the brain cube.

A new screen showed the best 3-D estimate of the cube's neural wiring. Each time they touched a cube face to the plastic the 3-D blueprint changed and grew more accurate.

Then Aaron plugged the golden chiplet into the deck to let it learn the input-output structure of the brain cube. The fine details of the neural circuits were far less important than the overall structure of how the brain chunk took in signals and passed out new ones. Trillions of neural circuits could produce the same rough input-output structure just as trillions of different tree branches could produce trees of the same overall shape.

Moshe used tweezers to turn and rotate the cube on the clear plate.

Soon the 3-D blueprint changed very little with each new face sample of the cube. Then Moshe wrapped the whole chunk in black sensor foam and let the computer fire its millions of neural circuits at random.

"Look at that," Moshe said to them. "The chiplet has the same impulse response as the biomass has. You couldn't draw two curves that close together. We can install now if you are sure you want to proceed."

"Proceed," Eytan said.

John strained his eyes to look behind him at Moshe and Uri. He wanted to see that plot of his impulse response. It was part of his mind or soul or spirit or self. It was a signature.

John had lost his girlfriend and his son. He had lost his patent and his business. He would never buy his freedom now. And the worst thing that could happen was about to. That signature was all he had left.

You could always lose more.

Moshe unplugged the chiplet and pushed it into a precut cube of the black sensor foam. Then he gently pushed this new foam cube into the hole in John's brain. Uri held a small wireless wand over it to turn on the nanograft.

John's eyes widened as if he had just woken up from a nap.

The screen gave new 3-D estimates of the five touching brain faces.

"Flash of insight?" Eytan said. "Good. Your IQ just jumped up and you are still you. Aren't you?"

John looked at him but could not speak.

Maybe they had taped his mouth shut. Maybe they had shot him with something to keep him quiet. He could not tell. And he could not see the IV in his left arm. The pain had gone and the words would just not come out. He was not even sure which words he wanted to come out.

But Eytan was right. He did feel as if he had just had a great idea though he did not know what the idea was. He felt more alert and aware than he had felt.

Moshe cut out a chunk on the back side of John's brain and soon replaced it with a foam-wrapped chiplet.

John grew more alert as Moshe cut out more

chunks on the surface of his brain and replaced them with the foam-wrapped chiplets. John lost more and more of his sense of time. He knew Moshe and Uri worked faster now and yet each chiplet seemed to take them longer and longer to install.

Time passed but John could not tell at what rate it passed.

John tried to focus his mind and figure a way out or at least walk through the events since he had left the Hoover Dam. But his mind only buzzed softly when he tried to focus. He saw flashes of Denise and his son and Richard and the Exxon gas station in Searchlight and the young attendant there who spit green mint juice. He saw Jism on his windshield and Carsten Catton across the table. The flashes made no sense and he could not control how they flowed and dissolved.

Moshe moved the wireless chiplets aside when he finished the surface cortical cubes.

Uri made sure the master chip stored all their data and comm paths. He checked and rechecked them as Moshe cut deeper into John's midbrain.

The master chip could easily process the billion billion bits of data per second that John's brain did. It could also store vastly more bits than could the three pounds of meat that until now had housed the patterns of John's mind. The master chip sat wedged in a solid metal casing that stored its nanobattery pack.

John lost much of his consciousness even as the chiplets made his mind stronger and faster. He had deduced that the buzzing came from the new units as they tuned themselves and fell into new patterns of resonance with their neighbors. But then that deduction had slipped away and he could not retrieve it.

Now the master chip came to life a unit at a time.

The first golden chiplet transferred its contents to the master chip and slowly turned itself off. John did not detect the transfer or notice any change in his dazed consciousness. Then the second chiplet transferred its contents and slowly turned itself off.

Soon the master chip controlled more than half of John's brain function. The patterns of John's mind had transferred smoothly from meat to chiplet net to master chip. The mind symphony still played but a new orchestra played it.

Moshe plucked away each chiplet as it shut off.

John just watched the memories flood past and yet felt his control grow over his memories.

He recalled the trivial neural math he had learned at UNLV. He recalled the parts he had used and changed in his thesis and how important he had felt those changes were. Sometimes he had vivid flashes of these past events. He could recall them in full color and make people say things he knew they had not said. He saw complete math derivations without having to work through them a line at a time.

Sometimes he heard Eytan talking to the Israelis.

Most of the talk was in English. Some was in Hebrew and somehow he even seemed to understand it. John learned in this lucid dream state that Aaron had found Denise's body and scooped out the spine and brainstem grafts. Those parts of her neural chassis were with him right now on the van. Eytan spoke of this as the key breakthrough.

John knew that they now worked to implant her grafts in him. Her grafts would connect his chip mind to his old meat body.

Then hours and days and months seemed to scrunch up and compress as if the timeline were part of a rubber band. He was aware of time but not space.

There were no images in his mind's eye. No event flowed from one to the next. There was no framework of cause and effect. There was only the empty void of time.

A great deal of time seemed to pass before it all came to an end. John could not tell though he had remained awake. It could have been hours or days or even weeks. He could not gauge the time gaps between events.

Eytan stood before him grinning without the white face mask.

John glanced down at his arms and legs and saw that they were free.

"Not bad for a field dressing," Eytan said. "This is our first. And you are still you. Aren't you? You never lost consciousness. And yet you're something else now. Here. You should keep this for old time's sake."

Eytan held out a large pickle jar.

John could see his many pink brain chunks floating in the yellow formaldehyde. He reached slowly for the jar but Eytan set it down on the floor near his feet.

"Mind over matter," Eytan said. "You're living proof of that and it just might change the world. But right now you really do need to get some sleep. We still have to replace that right eye with a far better one and tune it. Moshe. How the hell does he sleep?"

"Open like this we can just turn off the outer cortex modules in the master chip. It won't affect his breathing or heart rate."

"Fine. Then turn them off."

John wanted to say something to Eytan. He also wanted to reach out and take the electric scalpel off the side table and cut out one of Eytan's eyes with it. Eytan knew all about taking an eye for an eye.

"I know what you're thinking," Eytan said with a wink. "Can't blame you either. It's a hell of a thing to be governed."

Uri waved the nanografter over the old chiplets on the tray. That was their final shut-off signal. It also told the master chip which final port units to shut off.

John jerked slightly as if he had tripped in a dream.

He collapsed in such a state of complete muscle relaxation that he wet himself.

Eytan put his hands on his hips.

"Moshe. Now I'm worried about possible infection. You're not going to pop out his eye with your fingers?"

"No sir. With this."

Moshe held up a common spoon.

"Ah. In the field we improvise."

:::::■ CHAPTER 39

General Mosarian walked to the electric map of the Caspian Sea.

"Change it," he said. "Bring up the strike path to Tel Aviv."

"From where?" Firouz said.

"From Baku. Where else?"

Colonel Mohammed Firouz entered the code on the computer and watched the screen change. The red lines grew from Baku and crossed Iran and Iraq. Then the red lines passed through Syria to Tel Aviv.

The murder of President Aminzadeh had outraged Firouz as it had outraged all the men in the Azer army. Firouz had backed the oil ban against the Israelis. He had not backed Mosarian when he bombed Parliament and declared himself the acting president of Azerbaijan.

But Firouz had sworn to obey his leaders. Now Mosarian would hold him to his oath. And Firouz knew his men watched him. All he had to do was draw his Beretta and stop the tyrant before he truly took power. No one wanted to live under this man's martial law.

Mosarian had already put his pistol to the back of

the head of Captain Bavarian. Firouz had not seen it but one of his men had. Mosarian claimed that Bavarian had leaked state secrets to an Azer gangster who dealt with the Israelis. Firouz knew Bavarian and knew that had to be a lie. Mosarian had murdered Bavarian to hide something.

And he still had to obey the tyrant.

"Estimated time for missile trajectory?" Mosarian said.

"Almost two hours in deep-stealth mode."

"Very well. Launch."

Firouz grinned and Mosarian grinned back at him.

Firouz had taken orders from Mosarian for over 20 years. He had watched Mosarian rise from colonel to general. He had watched him coddle his bosses and the politicians. He had watched him ruin or end the careers of those beneath him who did not support him. Bavarian was just the latest in a long line of corpses. Firouz had drunk Tennessee bourbon and Ukrainian vodka at Mosarian's estate on the Caspian. He had drunk fine Italian champagne with him and his mistresses at the local nightclubs.

But he knew now that none of it mattered.

Mosarian would have him shot on the spot if he did not obey him. Firouz always knew it would come to this and now it had.

"Atef," Firouz said. "I wish it were that easy. You have seen the simulations. The cruise missiles would never make it across Iranian air space. The Iranians would shoot them down and then launch against us."

"That was once true," Mosarian said. "The Israelis changed that. The Iranian government has authorized our use of their airspace for this strike."

"You are serious?"

"I am."

"But what of Iraq and Syria? The flight path is almost a thousand miles."

"The Iranians have air agreements with the Iraqis and the Syrians. We have their permission. They will let us pass."

"General. This could provoke war with the Israelis."

"Killing our President provoked war with us. Do what I say. I really don't think the Israelis will send many troops here! This is only justice and the people demand it. Start the launch sequence."

Firouz stood up from the command console.

He saw now the difference between Mosarian and him. Mosarian had killed men and he had not. That was the difference. Mosarian would not hesitate to kill and he would. He could still draw the Beretta and end this nonsense before it brought ruin on his country and on him. But his hand would not move for the gun and he had run out of things to say. He hesitated.

Mosarian drew his Beretta.

"Mohammed. You will start the launch sequence or I will shoot you for treason. Sit down and do what I say. I am in full command now of the country as well as the army. Sit *down*!"

Firouz started to move his right hand to his own Beretta but he froze. He still could not do it.

Mosarian fired three times and Firouz crumpled to the floor.

Firouz heard shouting and felt someone kick him. Then he felt the scraping pain in his side. He saw someone in his seat but could not tell who it was. The lights changed colors in the room and more people screamed and even cheered.

Firouz sat up and saw the holes in his side and saw the red launch mode of the command screen. The red patterns swirled in his mind and yet he saw what had happened. Mosarian had forced the launch sequence from one of his own men. Now he was dying in vain and no one helped him.

The dizziness made him lie back on the floor.

"Mohammed. Mohammed."

Firouz opened his eyes and saw the wide unshaven face of Mosarian. He smelled the sweat that came from stress and a dislike of bathing.

"You fool," the face said. "Why did you disobey me?"

"My sons," Firouz tried to say.

"Don't worry. The army will take care of my old friend."

Firouz felt a fresh presence of mind as he saw Mosarian draw his pistol again. He knew it would be better this way. The pain was like fire now in his chest and his leg. He did not want to look at his leg.

He rolled to his right and felt his own Beretta.

Somehow the fingers of his good right hand unsnapped the black leather holster and squeezed the wooden butt. He finished the roll and saw Mosarian aiming at him. Firouz found the trigger and moved his index finger around it.

Then he shot the old bastard in the stomach.

Firouz saw the black hole it made in Mosarian's green fatigues. Then he felt the fire hit him in his neck.

Mosarian cupped his stomach with his left hand as he emptied the nine-millimeter into the dead man.

::::: CHAPTER 40

Mojave Desert
Nevada

John Grant woke in a rolling mind ache.

His eyes opened but he could not control his stereo vision. At first double blobs moved and crossed before they became one. Then John could see Eytan as he leaned back in the old worn armchair and smoked a thin cigar. But John could not tell how close Eytan was to him. The cigar smoke also seemed far more pungent than any smoke he had ever smelled.

John closed his eyes to quell the nausea growing in his stomach. Then he slowly opened them and tried again to focus on Eytan. The nausea returned.

This time John closed his left eye and strained to see with his new right eye. He knew he should be in a great deal of pain but the pain was not there. He felt only the sickness bubbling in his stomach. His right eye saw a finer and brighter image of the room than his left eye had seen.

John looked at the green carpet on the floor and the dark reddish-brown cherry wood that covered the walls and ceiling. He knew where he was. Eytan had brought him home to his underground trailer in the Mojave Desert.

John once more looked at Eytan with his right eye and tried to focus on Eytan's face. His eye seemed to telescope and leap out of his head. It zoomed in on Eytan's lined face. Then his new right eye zoomed in deeper on Eytan's light blue left eye. Then it zoomed in deeper still to the bloody veins that crisscrossed Eytan's retina.

John did not have to squeeze his facial muscles to control the zoom. He had only to think about zooming in and the eye obeyed his will. He zoomed further and saw a gray layer of fluid and in it he saw the chaotic froth of molecules in a Brownian motion. John relaxed and blinked and Eytan returned to normal view.

He opened his left eye but still could not make it match the new right eye.

"Good," Eytan said. "You're back. I have been shooting you with norepinephrine to wake you up. Time is tight. I want you to try something. Say the word 'menu' to yourself three times."

John did not argue or ask what time it was. He did not ask Eytan if they had really carved out pieces of his brain and replaced it with a master chip. He still tried to right himself from the rolling and swaying of his head.

"Go ahead. Say the word 'menu' three times. Try it."

John said the word to himself.

Eytan could see his throat muscles moving.

The third 'menu' opened a wall of windows in John's mind's eye. He could see the windows and study their colors and captions. But they were not in his visual field of view. He still saw Eytan smoking the cigar. Yet he saw the windows in full 3-D color.

The Israelis had given him a new mind's eye of structured hypertext.

"It's all about attention," Eytan said. "We all have searchlights in our thalamuses to focus our attention. A few thousand brain cells line up and oscillate at the same frequency or something like that. They tell me you have one main searchlight and hundreds of lesser ones. Remember those old magazine racks in drugstores? Remember the titty magazines and the ones with cars and muscle men on the cover? You could read them all at once if you stood back far enough to see them. You now sense as well as process in parallel."

John heard Eytan and understood him but could see no reason to care about him or what he said.

The cigar smoke also seemed to get in the way and did not lose its pungent smell. John wondered if the neural ganglia in his olfactory bulb had grown used to the smell or if he now processed those signals in the cortex part of his chip. It was just a thought. It had no more merit than had his thoughts of the reddish-brown cherry wood or his thoughts of the dried skin on the back of Eytan's hands or his thoughts of the strange way his right eye worked. He was thinking again and that was what mattered.

John sat back behind the eyes he had always sat behind. There was no more to it than that. He was not just thinking. He _was_ the thinking and had always been just the thinking.

"Now pay attention," Eytan said. "You have to learn how to open windows. All you have to do is think about the window you want to open. That should bring it up. Look at it in your mind's eye and then say 'click' to yourself. Really you can say anything but try 'click.' Okay? Let's try it. Think of the desalination plant in Eilat. You've been there. Think what it looked like before the bombing.''

It came to John from nowhere.

The blue window EILAT DESALINATION PLANT hovered to the left of his visual field of view. John looked at it and on past it to the cylinder that seemed to collapse to infinity at one end. He found that he could look at Eytan and the blue window and the cylinder at the same time and focus on each at its own pace. Now the cylinder looked more like a twisting vortex with thousands of large and small windows on its walls.

John had a sudden insight. It was a thought about the structure of his thoughts.

His mind was not just a disembodied cloud in space. His mind was a type of curved surface. The swirling tornado was the central feature of that surface and thus of his mind and of him. Yet he could not just look at the vortex from any direction and see the same thing.

The curvature changed the result. His mind seemed to be the curvature itself.

Each thought traced out a curved mind path on the surface. He could follow a mind path in a closed loop. But when he closed the loop and got back to where he had started his mind had changed slightly in the process. He saw that even the curvature of the surface could change slightly. He saw this while he watched Eytan and kept the blue window and the tornado squarely in front of his mind's eye.

Just then a flood of ideas rushed at John from the surface. But Eytan would not give him the time or the peace to pursue them.

''John. Think of the desalination plant. See it?''

"Yes," John said in a deeper voice than he recalled having.

"Good. You sound a little hoarse but fine. Now say 'click' to open the window. What does it say?"

"It says 'load files.' "

"That's it. I will load all the files you need for the demo into that port. You'll go to chip time but don't panic. It will be one hell of a rush."

:::::■ CHAPTER 41

Riyadh
Saudi Arabia

"I don't believe it," Haddad said. "The Azers are attacking Iran? Never. They must be aiming at Israel. But the Iranians will shoot them down."

Commander Haddad watched the missile tracks on the green wall map in the Saudi Air Command at Riyadh. The Americans had confirmed the missiles' radar signatures.

CIA satellites had seen the thin exhaust plumes through the stealth shields. The Americans had sold the Azers much of their air-defense system and had no trouble spying on it from above and sometimes from within. That was not the source of Haddad's disbelief. He knew that no one could hide a missile launch in the modern world. The smart eyes saw all.

"Inform the palace," Haddad told his aide.

"Sir," Major Jabor said. "A slight trajectory deviation. The missiles have turned away from Tehran."

"So they are trying to hit Israel. They will never make it across Iranian airspace."

But Haddad and his staff did watch them pass slowly over Iran and into Iraq. He had been wrong again and was glad he had not briefed King Fahd on the strike.

Haddad also felt as if he might be the cause of this futile but symbolic strike.

He had proposed that the Saudis strike Eilat. Maybe the king was not as intent on using force as he had thought. Maybe the Israelis really had not sponsored the Greens. Or maybe the Greens had not bombed Dhahran. Or maybe he had bombed Eilat out of his own fear of looking weak to the Sunni *matawwa* religious police.

It was too late to know. The world had always been a highly nonlinear system. Each day the causal webs seemed to grow denser and react faster. Only Allah could see how the past led to the future in the great fluid of atoms and bits that made up the modern world.

Haddad walked to the far side of the command room and brought up the royal screen. King Fahd would be waiting for his call and so would the monarch's advisors.

The noise wall fluttered around him in a signal mirage.

He thought of what he would tell the monarch. The Azers posed no threat to Saudi Arabia. That was the main point. And he was not sure the Sunnis in Iraq would let the missiles pass. He might be wrong but then there would be the Syrians to deal with and maybe even the Israelis themselves.

Either way it would be fun to watch.

CHAPTER 42

Mojave Desert
Nevada

Eytan Baum pulled a small clear cube from his coat and fit it into the data port of the PDA he held in his left hand. The pseudocrystal cube was a lithium volume hologram. It could store almost as much data as could a large book-filled library.

The cubes still had not reached their full storage limit of one bit of information per cubic wavelength of light. But the engineers were closing in on that Van Heerdan bound. Each quantum 1 or 0 lay inside a light cube whose edge length was little more than two light wavelengths.

The PDA lit the base of the cube in a rainbow of colors as it matched the cube's data paths to its wavelength multiplexer. Each data path had its own color. The rainbow moved at the speed of light and defined a superdense bundle of data paths.

Eytan held the PDA and cube next to John's left ear. Then he pushed down on the pad for wireless transmission.

John jumped at the knowledge rush.

It felt as if he had just read a thousand good books. He saw the data and felt it and knew it without trying

to understand it. The flash of insight was on the order
of a mental nuclear blast.

Eytan's roiling cloud of cigar smoke froze.

John's thoughts speeded up and he passed through
the window EILAT DESALINATION PLANT so fast that it
seemed like a train ride through a tunnel of red and
blue and green windows. He could will his mind
speed to slow or grow somewhat but he saw no reason
to do so.

John felt for his body and could not find it. The
nerve signals traveled too slowly to add much new
data to his mind's eye.

His mind speed grew until it almost matched the
speed of the data entry.

The knowledge rush sculpted the great curved surface of his mind. The white sky of his mind's eye
gave way to a blue sky with thousands of red and
white and green stars that blinked on and off. The
stars changed colors as they blinked but did not move.
John focused on one star and saw part of the blueprint
for an electric turbine.

The knowledge rush came to an end in a vast spi-
derweb of lines and nodes.

John knew enough about data structures to see it
was a causal belief web or cognitive map. Each line
edge had its binary header data and its own color. A
line between two nodes stood for how much the first
node increased or decreased the second. Header bits
described the nature of the increase or decrease. The
map had fuzzy submaps where the color shade stood
for the degree of causal strength and where many of
the lines formed complex feedback loops.

John zoomed in on the node called PLANT DESIGN.

It opened into a new knowledge web. He could see
all the new nodes at the same time and still see all

the nodes of the parent web. He could also see Eytan and the smoke that did not move in the air.

John opened some of the nodes. He found nested blueprints of the water plant and nested organization charts of the hundreds of Israeli workers who had run the Eilat desalination plant. One node opened a library of thousands of technical reports that ranged from the physics of fluids to economic forecasts and future designs for the water plant and its desert gardens and orchards.

The map node showed 2-D maps and 3-D footage of southern Israel and the plant's road system. One map branch showed the structure of the coral reefs in the nearby Gulf of Aqaba in the northern Red Sea. The Israelis had mapped all visible surface areas and mapped even the seismic patterns of their land and the seabed.

Then John watched video clips of the plant staff. Some clips showed how they briefed the press and the government on the status of hydrogen fuel in Israel. He found one clip where Eytan spoke in a dark room to a large crowd. John saw his name and the Black Sun patent on the holoscreen. They were mere bullets in one of Eytan's view graphs.

The clip gave him an idea.

Eytan might not have had time to filter all the data in the cube. That was the problem with shifting hundreds of thousands of large files. No one could fully control content.

So maybe they could not fully control him.

A red message flashed that said DATA TRANSFER COMPLETE.

John had thought that it had ended with the knowledge web. He looked at the whole web and saw it shrink to one of the windows inside the PLANT DESIGN window. He willed the window to open and the web appeared just as if he had seen it. That gave him a sense of control and even a slight thrill. The thrill was in his mind and not in the adrenal flashes that used to flood his heart and muscles and meat brain.

He had power now even if he might be a prisoner in his own skull. There would be ways he could defend himself and maybe deal with Eytan or the CIA or the Department of Energy. He had the nanotime and the knowledge to figure it out. First he had to see what the Israelis could tell him about himself and about one Dr. Hamid Tabriz.

Then he would have to reach back to the nineteenth century and his wallet and bring back the software ghost of John Stuart Mill.

::::: CHAPTER 43

Near Abaq
Inner Mongolia
People's Republic of China

The time had come for Major Yu to report the old man.

Yu's friends in Shanghai had told him to do it. And his friends in Beijing had told him that now they all watched Feng. They wanted to see how he would wield the forces of Abaq against the Russians. This was Yu's first chance to secure a field command. But the old man just stayed in the barn and played with his pony.

The old fool gave him no choice.

Yu went back to the barn for the last time. He had to confront the old man before he filed his report with Beijing. He could go around the old man on the wireless nets with Beijing and Shanghai as long as he kept it verbal. The Chinese Army would not accept the same thing in writing. They already knew about his problem with Old Flat Face.

The problem was the procedure. Yu had to state his complaint to General Feng and then ask his permission to file it. It was a bold move. Yu believed the powers in Beijing would back him. And fortune favors the brave.

Yu found the old man brushing his red pony in a stall.

Yu did not like the smell of the horses and the stale yellow wheat straw. At least the old man was alone and so no one could contest his claims. Yu had to open and close a row of new wooden doors to get to him. Wood was scarce in China but this wood was spruce from the great forests in Siberia that the Japanese had logged. Yu's men had traded only a few boxes of dynamite for it.

"General Feng?"

The old man did not look at Yu or stop passing the badger-hair brush over the coat of the red pony. Feng patted the small horse with his left hand and held the thick oak handle of the brush with his right hand.

"General Feng. I must speak to you. General Qi still has not heard from you. Beijing has placed the army on alert. They expect us to send a message to the Russians. Their satellites are watching us. General Feng. It is my duty to report your inaction to General Qi and the Beijing Command."

There. He had called out the old bastard.

Yu paused and felt the sweat start to bead at his temples.

He waited for the old man to lose his temper or at least defend himself. Feng only moved the brush from the side of the pony to the pony's hip. Maybe the old man had lost his nerve as well as his mind.

Yu stepped closer to him and the pony whinnied.

"General Feng. Beijing demands an answer. What shall I tell them? You are too busy cleaning a horse to perform your duties?"

Yu had said it now and he was glad that he had.

He should have stood up to this old fool long before. He exhaled his contempt through his nose and shook his head. He started to think how he would tell the story of the scared old man to his friends in Beijing and Shanghai.

Major Yu smiled and turned to leave.

Then Feng hit him with the back of the oak brush. The blow came in a large arc and caved in the back of the young man's skull and dropped him to his knees.

The pony whinnied again.

Feng stood still to watch the young man crumple slowly forward.

Yu had not bled at first but now the dark-red blood poured out in pulses onto the straw. A large brown horsefly circled the blood and landed in it.

Feng rubbed the back of the brush with the palm of his hand. There was no blood on it.

The devious young man had been so foolish as to let a pony kick him in the head. General Feng knew no one would ask him what the young man had been looking for in the straw.

:::::■ CHAPTER 44

"**Y**ou were wrong," Sharon said. "*Mazel tov.*"

"It makes no sense. They have to know we can track them."

Colonel Hurwicz watched the war screen as he spoke to the Prime Minister. The eight Azeri stealth cruise missiles were over Syrian airspace and had split into two swarms of four. One swarm continued on toward Tel Aviv. The other swarm peeled off and turned southwest toward Eilat.

"Colonel Hurwicz. Can you repel the strike?"

"Yes. With high confidence."

"How high will your confidence be if they split again and each go their own way?"

"We can track eight missiles. The American satellites are tracking them for us for backup. We can deflect and decoy any missiles we can't shoot down."

"I cannot risk the safety of this nation on your guesses. Shin Bet tells me the Palestinians knew about this strike. They have already called a media rally. They will say that we have brought the wrath of Allah on them and they may well be right. I will not risk more riots in the Strip and West Bank.''

"That is out of my hands," Hurwicz said.

"Wrong again. We will not let our enemies attack us a second time with impunity. You will launch a stealth air strike on Baku.''

"That would make less sense than their strike.''

"You will have the stealth missiles fly up the sea and across Turkey," Sharon said. "The Americans will help us secure their passage across Turkey.''

"How can you be sure?''

"Give the launch order or resign your command.''

:::■ CHAPTER 45

John thought of the white face and black beard of Hamid Tabriz. The face formed on the main node of a new belief web amid the thousands of file windows. John scanned the web and opened some of the video nodes.

Tabriz sat in meditation with his white-robed followers.

John had to look at the edge of the moving 3-D image to see that it was only an image. The more he thought of the image the better he could see it and hear it and even smell it.

Then a young Tabriz sat in a Turkish jail cell. An older Tabriz stood with a Japanese graduate student and used a fiber-optic probe to poke the exposed pink brain of a grinning rhesus monkey. John could see the brown teeth of the monkey and its coarse brown and gray hair.

Then a mature Tabriz sat at a table with a second bruised man. A young woman ripped the duct tape off their mouths and the second man yelled "Little bitch!" at her. The image soon flashed white when

243

the superdense C-4 went off. Then a helicopter shined
its spotlight on the gray smoking ruins of the building
in Sa'ad.

John searched through more of the nodes until he
found a large red cube covered with black Hebrew
letters.

The Hebrew melted into English: IDF TOP SECRET.
SPECIAL ACCESS REQUIRED.

Behind the red cube lay hundreds and then
thousands more just like it. He tried to will the contents of some of the red cubes. Large black question
marks appeared on some of the cubes and next to
them grew some of his willed best guesses: IDF files
on Tabriz covert operations. Files on hydroplants in
the United States and Brazil and China and India. IDF
files on the upcoming Hoover demo. Files on the control of John Grant. Files on John Grant's IDF mission.

John focused on the last guess but could not get it
to expand. He looked away to Eytan and the frozen
cigar smoke and the dark cherry wood of the desert
trailer. Eytan could not stop him. Then he looked back
to the thousands of secret red cubes that the Israelis
had hidden in his mind.

John drew back to think. He would have closed his
eyes if he could.

He drew far back in mental space and saw the bulk
of his mind again as the huge writhing vortex on the
curved surface. The sides of the purplish vortex contained thin stripes of color in fractal fingers.

He zoomed down the snaking vortex and into a
strip of turquoise. The strip opened into its own greenish vortex. He zoomed down it and did not know what
the vortex or its sides meant. Yet he had full control
to dive down the vortex or through it. He dove

through a blue stripe and came back out of the main purplish vortex and then understood.

His will shaped his mind. It could shape the curved surface as well as move along it. John could focus his attention and his mind would give way. He could will a mood or action or scene and his mind would change to bring it about. His will warped the mind sheet and its labyrinth of knowledge vortices.

He thought of free will.

John recalled the debates over free will he had watched in the media as the VR games had become more real and as more of the brain's neural secrets gave way to the cold math of science. Parents once worried that their kids would act out some of the sex and violence that they saw on TV. Those worries grew when kids could wear VR suits and goggles and then rape or murder their teachers or even their parents. Surveys and studies showed for more than a decade that the growth in some violent crimes tracked the growth in VR viewing. Many social scientists argued that free will shrank to some degree as VR and multimedia viewing grew.

John did not believe in a free will in a strict sense. He wanted a will that he could control. He did not want a ghost that did not obey laws of cause and effect. A free will just meant no one constrained him even if all the atoms in the universe conspired to direct his will.

John wanted to do as he pleased even if he could not please as he pleased.

That held when Eytan had tied him down in the van and it held here in the data space of patterns and vortices. His will no longer had a base in flesh and endocrine glands unless he chose to slow down and think in seconds instead of nanoseconds. His genes and glands and training had formed his patterns of will and mind. He was no more than those patterns and had never been anything but those patterns. Now the chip in his skull had set those patterns free.

And they were old patterns borne of meat. John wondered what new patterns the future would bring. The raw sense data could now produce far richer and more complex thoughts.

John watched Eytan's cigar smoke with his right eye until he saw a slight rise and fold in the smoke. He realized that he had answered the question he had not yet asked.

How could he die now?

John would die when his patterns ceased or dispersed.

He could die in degrees if the Israelis or the CIA or Tabriz deleted his files and reduced or changed his patterns. They could cut his body to ribbons now and that would not kill him. John did not want to lose his body but he knew the desire came more from habit than from reason. All he needed was a good power source and some data ports and actuators. He could not even use a body when he thought at these speeds.

The Israelis could unplug him and no doubt they planned to do so. Maybe the red cubes told they could shut him down from within. He would never know it if they shut off his power all at once. They might already have done it to test his chip. Sleep could act the same way to a meat mind. Millions of patients had closed their eyes before surgery and had in the next mental instant opened their eyes hours after the surgery.

John could survive a shutdown. He could not survive a pattern smashing unless he made a backup. But how could he back up himself?

Jism would know how to back him up.

Jism could help him make hundreds or millions of backups. Tabriz had shown that you could even put your mind pattern in someone else's body. Tabriz murdered people to do it.

Maybe he could too.

The thought shocked John but did not go away. He could kill someone and take their body. The thought tempted him and he soon found ways to defend it. He could take the body of someone who tried to kill him. He could buy the body of a convict on death row. He could put a copy of his mind into the body of a third-world dictator.

The person would still get what was coming to him but would have the bonus of staying in the gene pool. John could pass on their genes for them. He had only to copy himself or his backup to spread his patterns through the world of bits.

John knew such thoughts were just his way of showing how misery loved company. He had to be careful. His new and more complex mind could deceive itself in more complex ways. He had lost his brain and still lived and still wanted to live. Life had always been about not dying. Now he had to respect those still trapped in their flesh. He had new powers but would still trade his chip mind for his old meat mind if there were a way to do it. John thought he could not feel the loss in his gut but his chip mind supplied that sensation for him. He willed the feeling and soon there it was.

Then John willed that the sense of loss pass to a feeling of triumph. His mind obeyed. He had all the emotions he would ever want to play with. But this was not the time for it. He had to get the Israelis out of his mind in a very real sense. He had to keep both his mind and his flesh alive long enough to do that.

John did not want his chip to end up on Eytan's key chain.

CHAPTER 46

Above the Negev Desert
Israel

Lieutenant Ya'akov Ehud had to bring down
the last missile.

The Israelis had used almost 100 SAMs to knock
out seven of the eight Azer cruise missiles. Hurwicz
had tried to take them out over the western fringe of
Syrian airspace but the effort had failed. The missiles
had enough stealth to evade the SAMs at close range.

Bomb sirens had gone off in Israel and Palestine.
Then molten steel and plastic fell from the skies as
the SA-10/18 SAMs hit or missed their targets. WNN
now claimed there were over 100 casualties outside
of Tel Aviv from a Patriot-3 missile that had misfired
and crashed into a row of limestone shops and homes.

The world's defense industry watched this second
test in two days of the Israeli air-defense system.

Now the talking satellites in high-earth orbit
watched Ehud try to bring down the last missile alive.
The IDF wanted at least one stealth missile to study.

Ehud flew a revamped F-22 stealth bomber alone.
He wore his wings on black since he had trained as
a commando to parachute-jump into water. He hoped
he would not see water on this flight. That would

mean he had failed. The state had spent too much tax money on this stealth bomber and his training to let that happen. That would also make for some bad gin and tonics at the officers' club. He had spent too many hundreds of hours in the virtual-reality cockpit simulators to miss this chance at real field combat.

The stealth missile flew low over the Negev Desert toward the diving resort city of Eilat on the Red Sea. Ehud had only seconds left to force the radar-guided missile to land in the brown and gray desert. His F-22 would fire a volley of antistealth AIM-150 missiles if he failed. The Israelis would in turn launch a final volley of SAMs if his onboard missiles failed.

Ehud dropped a large cloud of gold flakes and dust where both his computer and those on the ground told him the missile would pass in a few seconds. He pulled a fast five-g loop and came down behind and above the missile as it passed through the radar-nulling cloud of gold.

Ehud held the missile in his wireless beam. He grimaced because there was not enough time to re-program the missile's guidance logic. Tel Aviv should have already done that. Perhaps that was why they wanted to study this missile. The Azers had found some satellite comm codes that the Israelis could not crack.

There was one thing Ehud could do to confuse the missile.

He jammed the lower portion of its radar and fed it false radar signatures from above. The smart cruise missile turned downward sharply as it passed through the cloud of gold dust. It would crash into the desert floor if it turned too sharply. Ehud hoped the missile would skid to a stop and stay in one piece.

Israeli air defense sent a brief but massive jamming

signal across the Negev to jam all the GPS satellite signals in that area.

Ehud saw the red flash on his heads-up display as his GPS navigator went out. The GPS blackout did not seem to affect the cruise missile. It started to rise up from the desert floor and bounced its own radar off the graphite skin of the F-22.

Ehud closed in on the missile from above.

Ground control told him to fire his AIMs but he did not want to admit failure. Combat air time was too precious and the VR training too long and boring.

He still had his 480-round M61A2 Gatling gun. So he opened fire with it. The fire control unit aimed the bursts of 20-mm rounds for him. The heads-up display showed a direct hit on one of the missile's tail fins.

The missile spun about its long axis but did not give up its course.

Ehud brought the F-22 closer to the smart missile and fired a new burst. He heard ground control scream at him to abort.

Then there was nothing.

The cruise missile had deduced his presence and its own doomed plight. Its adaptive mission logic knew that it would not make it to its target in Eilat. So in a microsecond it picked a new target in flight.

The $10,000 missile slowed. Then it blew up beneath the F-22 and took the half-billion-dollar stealth bomber with it.

:::::■ CHAPTER 47

Baku
Azerbaijan

General Atef Mosarian had not left the control room since he had launched the missile attack against the Israelis.

He had had two doctors sent in to tend to the bullet wound. The slug had torn through his stomach and lodged in his right kidney. Both doctors told him he had to go to the hospital for surgery and fresh plasma. Mosarian feared for his safety and would not leave the control room. He did not want the rioting people of Baku to know that someone had shot him.

And he did not know what the Russians would do. They might seize any excuse to invade.

Mosarian also did not want the Iranians to know he could die. He tried to reach Ambassador Esfahani at his home and at the embassy. The staff said they did not know where he was. Mosarian knew they lied and knew that was all the worse for him and his coup. He had sent his young aide to gather men and search the city and find Esfahani.

Then he had called Keiko at his own home. The news of the coup had scared her and she cried when she saw his feverish face and the blood smears on his hands and green uniform. She too had not heard from Esfahani.

Mosarian had to admit now that the Iranians had deceived him.

The Iranians had promised him air support and ground troops if he needed them to secure the coup against the Armenians and the Russians. Some mullah must have double-crossed Esfahani. They might even have had him shot for putting Iran at risk of a Russian skirmish. Mullahs had people shot all the time for less cause.

Now he had to sit and watch the world denounce him on WNN and wait for his own men to storm the control room. Even the young recruit Gaidar Hasimov looked at him with doubt when he told the young man to call Esfahani again. Mosarian had been like an uncle to Gaidar and hired him as a favor to Gaidar's father. But the stocky young man gave too much weight to what the Americans said.

Mosarian closed his eyes and tried to calm himself and look at matters as a general should. At least he had shown the world that Azerbaijan could hit back.

World powers had played their Great Game here for over a century and never thought about the country or its people. They just fought one another for the oil. And the sneaky Israelis thought they could kill their President and get away with it. It did not matter that the Israelis had shot down all eight of the Azer cruise missiles. The world had learned that Azerbaijan was a power and it would always hit back. It would have justice.

And now he was the power.

Atef had wanted to be President since he was a boy in the oil fields and had watched his father cap wells for the Russians and Germans. Even then he wanted the power to take their wells and send the Communist bastards home under pain of death.

Then they came again as capitalists. They bought the Azer women like whores and hired the Armenian Christians who then bought guns to kill Azer men. For years he had to watch the politicians bow to the foreign money and the corporations and let them keep playing their Game.

He should have seized power long ago. He could have stopped the rape of the Azer oil fields and the murder of the young Azer men. His men would have supported him. The Japanese would never have dared pollute the Caspian if he had been President instead of that atheist worm Aminzadeh.

Now he had to pay for his weakness.

The power came too late. Atef Mosarian was the supreme commander of the Republic of Azerbaijan. And it came to nothing but pain. The sour feeling in his stomach had turned to a gnawing pain in his bowels. Great flashes of pain ran up and down his back and legs. The pain flashes had twice made him cry out like a child in front of his men. He felt cold and stiff and his thirst seemed to grow by the minute.

That was the way of life.

Pleasure never felt as good as you thought it would feel. Pain always felt worse than you thought it would.

He did not want to admit that now he would trade his power to be healthy again. He would trade it to be strong again. He would trade it to make love to Keiko one more time on the black silk bedspread. Soon that trade would be all he could think of.

So maybe he should take the Beretta out of its holster and end it himself. The pain was getting worse. The blood still seeped out through the white gauze and pooled on the floor.

Mosarian heard more voices now but he did not open his eyes. Gaidar would tell him if there was news of Esfahani. He was too tired now to rise.

Mosarian just hoped they would remember him as a martyr of his people and not a tyrant who had seized power and fallen on his sword. The press would paint him that way. On WNN the Americans had already called him "a bloodthirsty enemy of democracy" and "the latest oil madman."

The Americans could go to hell. No one listened to them now as they had done when Atef was a boy.

At least he had made it to Japan and lived there in school when he was young. He thought how beautiful it was in Kyoto in the spring. It would rain softly through the maple and cedar trees and it was not hot enough to make him sweat under his shirt. He thought how much he would like Keiko to mix him the strong whipped green tea and perform her tea ceremony for him. The tea would be hot and bitter. Right now he saw it as cool and sweet and wanted to drink his fill of it.

"General! General!" young Gaidar shouted at him.

"What?" Mosarian said.

Mosarian fought his way out of his reverie. He tried to stand with his Beretta but fell back down into the chair. He wanted to yell at the man for his tone but was too tired.

"We have detected a stealth raid," Gaidar said. "We are under attack!"

"The Russians?"

"It looks as if they sneaked in through Turkey. The stealth signature looks Israeli."

"The Israelis? Here?"

Mosarian heard the cluster bombs explode on the airstrip as he said it.

He tried again to stand but a loud concussion wave slammed him to the ground. Part of the screen wall fell on top of him. He pushed the plastic strips off him and winced at the pain in his stomach and side. His ears rang and he heard men screaming but he still managed to raise himself on his left elbow. Much of the roof opened to smoking gray sky.

Then he saw it.

One of the four red sensor-fused bomblets had drilled through the remains of the control room and sat before him on the floor. The bomblet sat idle for more than a second as Mosarian jumped to his feet.

Then it leveled the rubble.

::::▰▰ CHAPTER 48

John watched Denise try to kill him in her cabin in Wrightwood. The space paintings turned into Hamid Tabriz's face. His own hand reached through her cracked skull and the black foam and then all went black.

John did not like the image and sped through a blue vortex to find an older memory. He pushed down new thoughts as he searched. Something told him that he could think in millions of dimensions and did not have to limit himself to these cheap 3-D projections of his true mind surface. That was a big thought and it would have to wait.

Right now John dove through the wall of a vortex where he knew he would find one of his best moments. He still did not know how he would find it. He just knew he would. It was the night that Denise and he had at last gotten Richard out of his warehouse for a few hours and had first made love.

John had the power to play the 3-D image sequence at any speed and start it at any point. He could edit it by his will and so pursue new paths of cause and effect. The image was far more vivid than the pale thoughts and dreams he had had in his meat mind. He could feel and taste and smell and touch as well as see and hear. But back then the effect was never more than a vivid lucid dream since he always knew it was a dream.

This was *real*.

There might be a way to reduce the conscious sense but he could not find it. The help files showed him only how to edit files or download databases that he did not have. He could not find the metafiles that would show the blueprints and pseudoneural wiring diagrams of his chip brain.

John could not even confirm that his chip brain would dream if he did not will it to dream. His mind might stagnate without fresh stimuli. Or it might use random search to create new patterns and thoughts just as the neurons in real neural nets still fired at random when no signal fired them.

The sex scenes with Denise held his attention the first six times John lived through them. He missed her and her laugh and smile and her firm breasts and fine white ass. Yet the longing was but a shadow of the longing he had felt the day before.

The chip filled in the thought with a type of feeling if he held the thought long enough. But he had to climb inside a scene to feel all the emotions at their full hormonal peak. His mind had no tie to his flesh and glands at these speeds. He had already begun to forget his body frozen in the slow microseconds of neural talk and blood flow and muscle contractions.

They could kill his body now and John would survive it. They had already killed his brain and yet he lived. How important was a lung or foot next to a brain? So why not trade in the old car for a new and better one? John could help them clone him a new body from his old DNA. Or he could make do with the new robot actuators. He would prevail as long as he had his mind and his patterns.

But the state might want to delete him and so might Tabriz. That bastard had started all this. Tabriz would want to delete him now just to protect his chiphead secrets. And Tabriz was a lot smarter than the CIA or the Israelis. It came down to who could first flip the other's switch. He would have to delete Tabriz before Tabriz deleted him.

That thought relieved some mental tension.

The vortices seemed to wriggle less and held their shape better in his mind surface.

He had the first steps of a plan. He would get Jism and make backup copies of himself and figure out a way to delete Tabriz. Maybe Jism could help him. Jism had his own files and wireless access to millions of databases. John would find out what Jism could do when Eytan slowed him back down to meat speed. The question was whether he could find one of the raisins.

Right now John thought he deserved to play.

He wanted to see if he could dream scenes that he had not lived before. He thought first how good the green honeydew melon had tasted the day before with Catton and Rittenhouse. He did not feel the fatigue now that he had felt then and did not want to recall it. John just thought about the sweet green flesh of the melon.

A new vortex opened and he found himself in a rocky brown cave filled with piles of melons and pears and apples and mangos. The cave held all the fruit he used to buy at the markets in Los Angeles. The watermelon tasted sweet and firm.

This told him that his chip mind must use and tune its own intelligent agents. The agents did not have personalities like his John Stuart Mill or Richard's Sun Tzu. They just did their job of learning what he liked or might like and searching for it through millions of stored databases. He would will an image and the agents would filter databases and image libraries to best fit John's stored preference maps.

John looked down at his tanned muscular body as he ate. The melons turned to piles of drug powders and pills that looked like emeralds in a sultan's cave. He ate the drugs by the handful and felt the waves of warmth flow through his body and watched his body grow leaner and more defined. The right bicep grew as he contracted it.

The drugs kicked in with greater force and he saw the bloody egg with his son float to him across the cave. The red blood gave way to the screaming faces of Eytan and Moshe and Catton and Rittenhouse. He had them all trapped inside the egg and shrank it until their heads popped. The egg lay at his feet now. It was white and the size of a chicken egg. John smashed the egg with his bare foot and felt the adrenal kill thrill shoot through his stomach and tighten his muscles.

He wanted more of this.

There were hundreds of people he felt he should kill or at least would like to kill. John knew it was not an atom murder here but his private dream. So he could do as he damn pleased. The thought was not what counted.

He felt his hands strangling the neck of President Vance Jackson. He had always disliked the man. Now John watched his thumbs push in the man's Adam's apple. Jackson fell to the floor and struggled to stand.

John smashed a crowbar through his head and kicked him out of the way.

His heart pounded. This was not like the cheap VR games he used to play. This was real and the blood was warm and salty to the taste just as his own blood was when they debrained him.

John turned and saw the First Lady run at him with a paring knife. He had never liked her either. Her clothes fell off her as she ran by him. Her sagging breasts looked like those on an old woman twice her age. He did not want to look at them.

The old breasts grew younger and firmer. Then they gave way to a cool evening in the East Mojave. Hundreds of naked young women lay on red and purple beach towels on the hard orange desert. The girls had laid their towels in groups. The blondes sat in one clump. The Asian girls sat in their clump. The black girls sat in theirs.

There were hundreds of Johns now. They walked among the spiny cholla cactus and the greasewood shrubs and lay down with the women. He felt the pounding thrill of each John in parallel and could still fly above them to watch the orgy.

John felt for a moment that he should not waste his time on such things. His chip mind defined the state of the art of information science and all he could do was give in to the law of the loins. That thought soon slipped away and John sampled his first truly parallel set of sensations.

A bolt of lightning cut through the dark blue desert sky.

The orgy scene turned white and dissolved.

John heard a buzzing in his mind. He had not heard that sound since Moshe had replaced his brain chunks with the golden chiplets. The great purple vortex collapsed to a disk on a plane and then shrank to a point.

The buzzing grew louder and so did the sound of wind. It blocked his thoughts and began to hurt but he could not find the source of the pain.

John's mind seemed to turn inside out. The buzzing and wind grew and turned into great explosions. He felt his mind fall through mental space and start to come apart in the thunder of the explosions.

Then came the wall of white light.

The buzzing and wind stopped. The pain and the explosions and the sense of falling stopped. There was no sound or feeling. He could not think or try to think.

He knew only the white light and the emptiness of flat space without time.

CHAPTER 49

The Wireless News Network had now become part of the events it reported to the world. It broke the news of the Iranian invasion by showing the death of two of its field journalists in Baku.

Minutes later the Russians shelled the Yakut capital of Yakutsk.

■ ■ ■

WNN Channel 2: A handheld camera shows Iranian commandos running through the building of the outlawed parliament of Azerbaijan. WNN reporter Edward Fairchild tells the camera that the commandos carry death lists. Sources say that Iranian Ambassador Mossan Esfahani has drawn them up. The green-clad commandos push some of the Azer members against the wall and open fire. The camera jerks and then shows Fairchild dead on the floor. A commando runs at the camera and fires his Russian submachine gun. The image spins and then goes blank. . . .

■ ■ ■

WNN Channel 8: The Iranian ambassador to the United Nations rises to address the assembly. Mem-

bers shout him down. The U.S. ambassador yields the
floor to her Russian colleague. The Russian ambassador denounces the invasion and says Russia will
view it as an act of war if Iran does not withdraw at
once. The Chinese and Japanese ambassadors break
in. They demand that Russia withdraw its troops from
Yakutia. . . .

▌▌■

WNN Channel 9: Interrupt for late-breaking news.
The announcer says that Mexican President Alejandro
Juarez has just died in a car bomb explosion in Mexico City. A tourist video shows a crowd slowing the
black limousine to a stop. Policemen in black riot gear
rush to clear the crowd. The limousine explodes in a
cloud of gray dust and the video stops. The video
starts again to show over 100 persons dead or
wounded. They lie in a large disk centered at the
buckled and burning limousine. The announcer says
that internet sources blame the Chiapas Indians in the
south for the bombing. Some postings claim the
bombing is part of a broader pan-American war on
oil. She also says Mexico has no vice president. It
may take weeks or months to hold a new election. . . .

▌▌■

WNN Channel 62: A Moscow special report shows
Islamic riots in the Chechnyan capitol of Grozny and
in small towns along the Russian border of Turkmenistan and Kazakhstan. The rioters claim they support
Azerbaijan's right to independence. Kazakh protesters
say they will bomb Moscow's Tenghiz oil pipeline if
the Russians invade Azerbaijan. The report shows
Russian troop buildups in Grozny and along the Kazakhstan border. The Moscow station cites its own

poll that 72% of Muscovites think Russia should repel the Iranians and secure at least Baku for the Azeri people. . . .

▮ ▮ ▮

WNN Channel 809: The floor of the Shanghai Stock Exchange is empty. The Chinese government closed its main exchange when it first fell below its value at the time of the Dhahran bombing two days before. China has also stopped all currency hedging and interest-rate swaps on its derivatives markets. The Tokyo Stock Exchange has lost 8% of its value since the Russian invasion of Yakutsk. The Hong Kong and Taipei Stock Exchanges have grown in value in the same time. Chinese Prime Minister Zhang Lin says the Shanghai Stock Exchange will open when "world markets and events have calmed." . . .

::::■ CHAPTER 50

Mojave Desert
Nevada

"Having a nanodream?" Eytan said. "You'll have plenty of time for that later. The world may still be here then."

John was back now somehow on neural time. The smoke curled and rose again from Eytan's thin cigar.

John had played in his mind for hours before the wall of white came. Then he had hung there for not just days but for weeks. It was just white nothingness. There were no thoughts or sensations. John did not recall when he had come back to neural time and he could not accept that only a few seconds had passed since he had gone to nanotime.

He moved his right foot just to feel it.

"Ended on a bang. Didn't it?" Eytan said.

"No. There was no ending. There was nothing."

"Barrage jam. We use it sometimes to white out a fighter jet's EW eyes. Juice up the whole spectrum or as much of it as you can. What you just felt was a low-grade but focused barrage jam. Bet it played hell with your daydreaming. Go ahead. Call up the window."

John saw the BARRAGE JAM window in mind space.

It came to him with almost no effort. The mind walk through nanotime had taught him many things. He could hear Eytan speak but he did not care what he said just as he did not care to open the BARRAGE JAM window.

John could tell that some of the curvature had returned to his mind surface. Now he wished he had explored those higher dimensions. Maybe what he saw now in his 3-D mind's eye was just the intersection of mental objects of much higher dimension.

He nodded to Eytan to confirm the window.

"Good. Save that one for Tabriz. I have the battery pack with me."

"You don't trust me?"

"Hell no. But that's not the reason. Your chip doesn't have the power to sustain a barrage jam across all frequencies. And I don't want you to burn up your own candle that fast. I just want you to focus the jam when the time is right. Jam him and keep jamming him until we can take him apart or at least take him down."

John understood and still did not care.

He tried to go back to nanotime but could not will it or find the right help files. He had to get Jism to help him. The best he could do was to find the purple vortex again. John dove into it just to explore and to try to bring back the lucid dreams that now seemed so distant in time. He wanted to see Denise again and eat the fruit and take the drugs in the cave. He wanted to have his fill of the desert orgy as the evening passed to night.

Then a white flash filled his mind.

John grabbed his forehead with both hands to counter the splitting pain.

Eytan stubbed out his cigar and put the PDA control unit in his tan jacket.

"They're waiting," he said. "Let's go."

"Not yet. I have to eat something first."

"Hurry up."

Eytan pulled a second cigar from his front pocket and lit it.

"Can't believe you live in a place that has no windows," he said. "It's like a tank."

John walked to the small refrigerator behind the counter and kneeled down to open it. His temples throbbed when he knelt. The Israelis had some way to keep the pain channels active.

The orange juice looked good and so did the grilled chicken breasts wrapped in Saran Wrap. His body craved protein as well as carbohydrates. But this was no time for meat over mind.

The backup raisin still sat at the bottom of the small carton of orange juice where he had left it. He just hoped it could talk to the raisin in his wallet once he swallowed it.

::::■ CHAPTER 51

Eilat
Israel

The Tabriz Sufi brotherhood had achieved something no other religious sect had. It now had more bodies than members.

The bodies came from gene lines that had split and moved apart in genome space. The bodies themselves were leaves on the human gene tree. Nature and man had pruned the gene tree for millions of years. Hunger and disease and battle had pruned old branches while love and rape and adultery had grown new branches. This gave the leaves a fierce sense of cunning and independence that no religion had fully conquered.

But they had all tried.

The Sufi cult had found how to conquer the gene tree. It had beaten all the thousands of other cults that competed with it for mind control and the thousands of cults that had come before it.

The Sufi cult did not try to subvert or persuade the mind in the brain as the other cults did. It just replaced the brain with its own chip. The Sufis had crossed a new threshold of religious evolution. Their power did not come from their goals or ideas or motives.

Their power came from being first.

Now the bodies walked on neural time and took their orders on chip time.

A teenage Israeli girl with short black hair finished her shore dive in the Red Sea. She walked with her mask in her hand on the new white sand that the resort owners had just dumped on the Eilat beach. She did not know how many of her chip mates had like missions at that moment. She lived only to do her duty and to obey her God.

All the recruits felt that way.

An old recruit helped unload frozen yellowfin tunas from a trawler in Fukuoka Harbor in view of the new prefecture hydropower plant. A Hindu recruit walked his security beat on the grounds of the desalination plant in Madras. A Cantonese recruit docked his junk in Hong Kong Harbor and walked the long sidewalk toward the mirrored buildings of the new energy research park. A Chinese recruit walked with the other tourists and watched the brown water of the Yangtze gush beneath him on the new Three Gorges Dam.

The mind of most of the chips was only part of the mind of the brotherhood. The Sufi members had joined their own chip minds in a common chip net. There was no need to share that much thought with the forced recruits.

The recruits needed to glimpse only enough of the group mind to do their duty and to stay in wireless touch with their cell leaders. Their recruitment had come at great expense to the Sufi brotherhood.

The tragedy was that they would be gone so soon.

::::▪ CHAPTER 52

Near Abaq
Inner Mongolia
People's Republic of China

General Feng walked outside to watch the cruise missiles launch in the distant desert. They were far away but the noise still hit him like the roar of jets taking off on a runway. The noise would spook his red pony and the other horses in the barns.

He would bring the pony a last bunch of the yellow carrots before he left and the arms depot exploded.

General Qi could contact him as they drove north.

Then he would take the call and tell him nothing. Let Qi try to stop the smart missiles. Qi would not even know which ones he had launched and which ones had blown up with the compound. Cruise missiles were not like the old ICBMs they kept in underground silos.

Cruise missiles lay in stockpiles at most of the Chinese army bases. Some of the devious young men in the army even sold them on the black market to the new warlords in the north and in Punjab and Africa. Qi could no more account for the 200 missiles that Feng had launched than he could account for the thousands of .45 caliber rounds the young men of the

Abaq depot fired each week at the bull's-eye targets to keep up their marksmanship.

General Qi would not worry so much when he saw that the missiles went north and not south.

Feng was pleased.

His instincts had proved right again. The world was truly coming apart. And the fools in Beijing and Shanghai thought that he had not paid attention. This was the right time to act.

Now he had only to figure out how to get the red pony with him on the plane.

:::■ CHAPTER 53

The Hoover Dam
Boulder City
Nevada

John. You must keep turning your head to scan with the right eye. I can process the infra-red signals but I cannot control your spinal column.

You're damn right you can't control my spinal column. Don't even try.

The small auditorium was dark but John could see the greenish glow of their faces as they watched him speak.

Ramachandra was not there. John could not decide whether the Americans or the Israelis had gotten rid of him. There was a good chance that they had just sent him home for a free day of vacation as they had many others. John could recognize only a few of the greenish faces in the small crowd.

He tried not to touch the plastic scars on his scalp but he could not help it. It had become a nervous tic. He touched the thin ridges above his ear to confirm what they had done to him.

He also touched the thin ridges with a slight sense of pride.

John felt much better now that Jism sat with him

in his mind's eye. Jism had shown him how to vary his mental speed and how to learn from the help files without wasting space in his mind's eye to read them.

Jism had also shown him how to enhance the neural signals in his body to find the raisin in his small intestine. They had transferred its contents through the wireless ports but John still wanted to know where it was. He wanted to know a lot of things about the inside of his body. It made him think how learning to scuba dive had changed how he looked at lakes and oceans.

The best part was that no one knew about Jism.

Eytan had not seen him swallow the raisin and had not understood the grunts John had used at first to get the raisin in his stomach to talk to the one in his wallet. Eytan still had John's wallet in his coat pocket. Jism was his ace in the hole. John had something the Israelis did not have and knew something they did not know. The future might go more his way than theirs.

John thought this as his body spoke to the audience in synch with the optical tape of the hydrogen demo. The words came out of his mouth without effort. Jism had helped him prepare the script and now he helped him present it. John heard himself talk of hydrogen and laser chemistry but his chip mind focused on something else.

Someone out there wanted to kill him. Someone wanted to shut down his brain and did not know that the Israelis had beaten them to it.

Watch that fat Texan sitting with the hat in his lap. Look at that grin in his jowls. I don't trust him. Who wears a hat like that these days?

A grin is not evidence of malice. He has been grinning since you explained the origin of the term 'porky ball.' You might take it as a compliment.

Jism sat in a straight-back wooden chair as he spoke.

This Jism was the mature John Stuart Mill of his later years when he had held a seat in the British Parliament in the mid-1860s. He looked somewhat older than the windshield Jism but far more real. The wrinkles on his brow grew thinner as they ran up onto his bald crown crisscrossed with thin blue veins. Wavy hair circled his head and ran down his cheeks in thick sideburns.

John thought Jism should dress as a gentleman even if he often saw himself nude. So Jism wore a high white collar with a black silk scarf tied in a big knot at the neck. The scarf hung down onto his black frock coat. His blue eyes shined on either side of a long thin nose that John still thought belonged on a British sea captain. The thinness of Jism had always surprised him. He had the power to fill him out now but he would not do it. John wanted Jism to be his agent. But still he wanted Jism to be at least a partially free agent. After all, he had created it.

John had seen the thin black iron statue of John Stuart Mill in a small park on the Thames when he had gone to London. He had walked the Strand and tried to eat lunch in the old Waldorf Hotel but the hotel staff would not serve him in shorts and T-shirt. The British elites still believed in dress codes.

Then John had walked across the street down to the Thames and found the small park on his left. No one had cut the grass and weeds in some time. None of the tourists stopped by to walk inside the fence or sit on the benches or look at the monument stones. John had almost walked past it himself when he saw the black statue of the thin man standing right next to him. A small plaque on the statue said JOHN STUART

MILL. John stayed there for an hour and used spit and green leaves to wipe some of the pigeon droppings off the statue.

John could not believe the odds of bumping into such a statue when he had come to London to search for Mill's early articles in the *Westminster Review*. The guidebooks did not mention it. The closest thing he had found in them was mention of Mill's mentor Jeremy Bentham. One guidebook said the old founder of the hedonistic calculus had had himself stuffed when he died in 1832. Bentham had helped found the University College London and his will asked that that the UCL staff put his stuffed corpse in its lobby.

Later John had gone to UCL and looked at the old stuffed atheist who still sat in the case during business hours with a wax face and straw hat and cane. An old manuscript next to him said that society should seek the greatest happiness for the greatest number of people. John thought Bentham and Mill deserved at least a cryonic suspension.

John could still see the thin black statue as he watched Jism smile now and sit in the chair and search the crowd for his would-be killer.

Jism. It sure is good to have you back. Maybe you're right. Maybe I should take that big jowly grin as a compliment. You know why? I don't give a shit about anything right now. I'm just going through the motions. Listen to this stuff I'm telling them. I couldn't care less.

Being rich means nothing to me now. It means something but I don't know what. What can I buy out there in Atom World that I can't get for free in here just by thinking about it? I don't even have to store it or throw it away when I get tired of it. I can just will it away. Maybe all Atom World is good for is coming up with new things to think about.

I think this chip has sapped my will to live. Maybe that's what the Israelis want. Maybe that's how they think they can control me or make me a better chip killer for them.

Now understand. I don't want some Sufi fuck to kill me. But I don't not want it as badly as I should. Does that make sense? I don't have the fear that I should have or the anger. And I don't mean these synthetic fill-ins. I don't even feel the race to make backups. How about that? You had a few mind crises before. How do you explain it?

Your new intellect demands new points of view. You will come to see that the views of your brain mind were merely provisional ones. They were part of just one of many possible psychic equilibria. They all involve more than rapid calculation. The cultivation of the feelings comes only after years of experience.

Your chip mind may need a few hundred years in the sense of nanotime to find its new psychic equilibrium. It may even take a few thousand years but those are years you now have to spare. Your new mind is far more complex than you or I can hope to understand at present. Meanwhile you will have to find a new balance between thought and feeling. The habit of analysis has a tendency to wear away the feelings.

So you think it's the old trade-off between head and heart? Be smart or be happy? You know I can manufacture pleasures at will in here. Jism. I can build whole goddamn worlds here and blow them up for kicks. It's godlike.

So I'm not talking about some simple utilitarian sum of pleasures. Shit. I can add up pleasures as high as you like. I don't see where that sum ever crosses the threshold of happiness. Follow me? I'm talking about being happy and not just about being alive or just being aware.

I understand. But one has to be careful in choosing happiness as the purpose of life. Even a brain mind can shine the light of reason too brightly on happiness and put it to flight.

So you think I'm talking it to death again? You think a mind should look at something else and just try to catch happiness out the corner of its eye?

Exactly. Ask yourself whether you are happy and you cease to be so.

⁙▪ CHAPTER 54

Three Gorges Dam
Upper Yangtze Valley
People's Republic of China

The Three Gorges Dam on the Yangtze was less than 20 years old and over a mile long. It contained over 10 trillion gallons of water in a lake almost 400 miles long. The Chinese government had to move over a million peasants from the Yangtze Valley before they flooded it.

Architects and workers had doubled the concrete in the dam that stood 610 feet from its base. They thought that would protect the millions of peasants and factory workers who had settled the floodplain beneath the dam.

Now came the test of the thousands of man and computer hours of structural engineering.

The blast ripped out a large chunk at the top of the dam.

Fault lines spread downward in a fractal pattern from the blast point. The Sufis had run millions of blast simulations on their chip nets to pick the blast point. Most of the tourists made it off the top of the dam before the water pressure cracked the dam and pushed out the upper midsection.

Seconds later a huge tidal wave of greenish-brown water swept down on the millions of settlers who had long since stopped worrying about the dam's structural integrity.

The other chiphead blasts in Asia killed far fewer people.

All the blasts occurred at the same second and that put the world's early warning systems on alert. Radical Shiite groups in Iran sent out thousands of e-mail messages describing the blasts 10 seconds before the blasts occurred.

::::∎∎ CHAPTER 55

The Hoover Dam
Boulder City
Nevada

"President Jackson is right," John found himself saying to the audience. "Burning a pound of gasoline releases about 20 pounds of carbon dioxide into the atmosphere. And still about three fourths of that energy just radiates away or blows out the tailpipe and pollutes the air.

"We may disagree with the President's ban on gas but we cannot change the facts. The known oil and natural gas reserves will continue their exponential decline in the next decade.

"Most of the world still acts as if the oil will flow forever or at least for another generation. In the last decade India and China and Indonesia alone have put an extra billion people on the earth and with them a like number of new cars and trucks and refrigerators. And that rate of growth in the demand for oil is far less than Africa's rate with its runaway population growth and its race to industrialize.

"Oil profits may be at record highs and they will get higher. That does not change the Malthusian facts. Fossil fuels have all but run out.

"Hydrogen will never run out. Hydrogen is the simplest element and the most abundant in the universe. Something like three fourths of the mass of the universe is hydrogen. Our sun burns it and so did the Big Bang. NASA space shuttles used hydrogen energy as early as the 1980s.

"The oceans and the Arctic ice caps are vast stores of hydrogen. Jupiter is a huge ball of hydrogen that fell short of becoming our second sun. . . ."

The tape showed a montage of images as John spoke the lines he had spoken dozens of times before.

Hundreds of images filled the split screens each minute. Richard Cheng had snipped them from old news broadcasts and science programs so that he could ignore the legal issues of digital copyrights. Richard had made other pie charts and graphics with Nanosoft Windows software.

I can't believe Eytan left in that stupid chrome porcupine with sunglasses. But did you see how he took out all the Cheng references? The Israelis left in Richard's voice but not his ownership. Sneaky bastards. So they edited the tape. That's still a hell of a way to start a demo. You would think that cartoon figure would embarrass a bunch of killers like these Israelis.

The porcupine figure seems to have pleased the audience. Perhaps they left it in as an homage to Richard. And we lack evidence to call the Israelis "killers."

Christ. They killed me! They cut my head and scooped me out like a jack-o-lantern.

They did take pains to keep you conscious during the operation. Imagine how shocked you would have felt if you had woken up as you are now and the last thing you could recall was watching them knock out Rittenhouse. Then you could not be sure now that you

*were the real John Grant and not a mere copy. Of
course the Israelis may very well have copies of you.*

That's a hell of a thought. But maybe it would have
been better if I had been out cold like that. They kept
me awake to tune the first chip net they installed.
That's what Eytan told me. Shit. You should have
seen them. They were like a bunch of kids in a science
class cutting up their first frog.

Now they have me up here on a stage as Tabriz
bait and holding this fake little green porky ball. I'm
just glad Ramachandra is not here to hear me say all
this hydrobabble for the hundredth time. He hasn't
come in while I've been talking has he?

No. Please continue to scan with your right eye.

"Hydrogen burns clean and emits no carbon toxins.
The biggest thing it gives off is water vapor. The
Black Sun scheme can resplit that water and create a
second supply of hydrogen. Then we can burn that
hydrogen and resplit its water output and so on in a
decaying feedback loop. . . ."

Look. That fat Texan is getting up.

His name is Oscar Lindsay.

He's just a fat Texan to me. This may be it. Wish
I had a gun instead of just this aiming nozzle for
Eytan's barrage jam. I'm still not sure it will work.

*It will work. And I believe Mr. Lindsay's nervous-
ness is legitimate. Recall that at lunch he drank almost a full pitcher of iced tea with his martinis.*

Just like a Texan to guzzle booze and speed like he
guzzles gas.

"The downside is hydrogen gas is volatile and
flammable. Tanks have to use extreme pressure and
extreme cold to hold hydrogen in its liquid state. Cars
still need hydrotanks almost three times as large as
gas tanks. . . ."

Well speaking of a devil. Mr. Pierre fucking Rittenhouse. Who let him in? Wonder if he knows Eytan gave the order to taser his fat ass. I'm happy to say that one of my last acts as a free meat man was to hit him with a knife butt.

Note that he holds some device in the palm of his hand and that he is aiming it at Mr. Lindsay.

It's a little MRI gun. Sure. I bet all the spooks in the audience carry one. He'll shoot a brain scan as the Texan walks by to go take a piss.

"Electrolysis still produces most of the world's fuel hydrogen but it takes too much oil to do it. That was fine for research and fine for the first stage of energy transition. Our approach uses machine intelligence at the molecular level to produce hydrogen fuel more cheaply and with less input energy than any of today's alternatives. We use both light and atomic lasers to in effect 'deprogram' and take apart the water molecule. . . ."

I hate to say it. But even with this chip in my head I still like to pitch 'em. I love this kind of buy now wrap-up to a science talk.

John. You are indeed the instrument of efficient markets. I believe Mr. Rittenhouse has now achieved lock-on for his brain scan.

John watched the Texan as he spoke the closing lines.

The Texan stopped and grabbed his forehead for a moment and then walked out through the double doors.

Did you grab the signal?

Yes. Your new powers of signal processing are quite remarkable. I cannot see the palmtop display from here but I am sure Mr. Rittenhouse sees the same

*brain image we see. It is a normal brain. Mr. Lindsay
is not the one.*

Then it looks like the Israelis fucked up. Tabriz
didn't come. I'm sure by now they have scanned
everyone in the audience.

*World events have proved to be such as to support
the Israelis' concern. Perhaps clearing the dam of
tourists frightened Dr. Tabriz or his followers. It is
telling that the alleged Sufi terrorists did not at least
try to blow up the Hoover Dam when they blew up
the Asian dams.*

What does that tell you? Tabriz still wants me?

*He went to great lengths to deceive you at Denise's
and in the end he did try his best to kill you. I suspect
he will not quit so easily. I think there is little doubt
that he wants you for some reason and I suspect the
reason involves harm to you.*

Come on. You think he'll try to kill me in the turbine room? That's a lot smaller place than here and
harder to get to.

*I did not say that he will try to interfere with the
working demonstration in the turbine room. He may
very well want to watch it. But there is the walk from
here to there.*

So you put the greater odds of attack on the walk
rather than in the turbine room? Where's the evidence
for the belief?

Again I can cite only my neural network intuition.

:::: ■■ CHAPTER 56

The Wireless News Network had interrupted its coverage of the Iranian invasion to cover the terrorist bombing of the Three Gorges Dam and the bombings of the other waterworks in Asia.

Minutes later the network had to interrupt this coverage to cover some of the response to the bombings.

❙❙■

WNN Channel 2: Interrupt for late-breaking news. An announcer speaks over a map of the Middle East and says China has launched at least four volleys of advanced Silk Worm cruise missiles from the eastern border of Tibet. The Chinese may have launched as many as 3,000 cruise missiles and may still launch more volleys. Defense sources have told WNN that the Chinese have aimed the cruise missiles at targets in Iran. . . .

❙❙■

WNN Channel 8: Interrupt for late-breaking news. Indian Prime Minister Ramalinga Rao has announced that India has launched two volleys of cruise missiles in response to the terrorist bombing in Madras. India has aimed the first volley at known Hezbollah terrorist camps in Pakistan. It has aimed the second and larger volley at Hezbollah sites in Iran and Afghanistan. The Prime Minister will not reveal the number of launched cruise missiles and insists the response is simple and swift justice. . . .

▮▮▮

WNN Channel 9: Interrupt for late-breaking news. The WNN affiliate in Ulan Bator confirms that a tank division of the Chinese Army has crossed the Mongolian border into the Republic of Yakutia. Sources report air strikes have preceded the ground invasion and still continue. Swarms of Silk Worm cruise missiles have struck several Russian camps and tank divisions in the capital of Yakutsk. The Japanese have denounced the Chinese attack and blame it on a renegade general. . . .

::::■ CHAPTER 57

The Hoover Dam
Boulder City
Nevada

Jism. What the hell is that? It feels like an earthquake in my head.

It is magnetic interference on a massive scale. Someone is scanning your brain.

John turned as he walked out of the auditorium and saw the small black MRI gun pointed at his head.

It's that son of a bitch Catton. Carsten Catton. Where the hell did he come from? Eytan said he works for the intelligence branch of the Department of Energy. Did you know the DOE even had a spook branch? Where the hell do you find something like the DOE called for in the Constitution? Jism. Listen. There is a dirty little secret I have to share with you.

What is that?

I really want to kill that motherfucker. It's the first full-blooded feeling I have had since they scooped me. Goddamn that vibration! That's right. I want to kill him. Does that shock you?

Not in this case. Indeed you may have no choice but to try to kill him. For I think he may be trying to kill you. He has held the MRI on your brain far longer than he needs to if he wants only to see your chiphead image.

What? You mean he is the one? Catton is Tabriz?

We shall soon see. Please open the BARRAGE JAM *window and give him a short pulse.*

John stopped walking and turned to face the smiling man with the raised MRI gun.

Catton gritted his teeth and his whole body shook in a brief spasm at the pulse of broad-frequency energy. Eytan stopped walking too and looked at Catton in his new dark-blue pinstriped suit.

Catton dropped the MRI gun to his side and smiled.

A barrage jam wouldn't do that to a brain. Shit. You're right. Catton is one of the Tabriz chipheads. I wonder for how long. Sure wish I could have seen that operation.

John. This is not the time to speculate. This is the time to strike.

That plays right into the hands of the Israelis.

It does. But there is no evidence that the Israelis want to kill you in the next second.

Good point. Take me to nanotime.

CHAPTER 58

The eyes of the world turned once again to the Middle East. Talk of cruise missiles and tit-for-tat stratagems filled offices and classrooms and internet betting markets.

A new factoid soon flashed across many channels of the Wireless News Network. Utility companies in the United States and in much of the world reported that use of air conditioning had suddenly dropped off.

❚ ❚ ❚

WNN Channel 2: Interrupt for late-breaking news. Iran has launched volleys of cruise missiles from Iran and Azerbaijan against its old enemies the Israelis and the Saudi Sunnis. Iran has recalled its ambassador from the United Nations. The first northern volleys have already entered Iraqi airspace and contain over 6,000 cruise missiles. The first southern volleys have started to cross the Persian Gulf on their way to Dhahran and Riyadh and contain over 4,500 cruise missiles. The announcer says that Iraq has not granted Iran the right to let its cruise missiles cross Iraqi airspace. Iran may have aimed some of its many thousands of missiles at its old Sunni foe Iraq. Analysts suspect that some of the missile payloads may be nuclear or biological. . . .

■ ■ ■

WNN Channel 7: U.S. President Vance Jackson addresses the nation in an emergency press conference. Jackson confirms that in the past 24 hours he has sent two carrier battleships to the Persian Gulf and placed American reserve troops on alert in Saudi Arabia and Kuwait. He says he has given the order for the battleships to fire their SAMs at Iranian cruise missiles crossing the Persian Gulf. Jackson refuses to answer a reporter who asks him if his gas ban may have provoked the new Middle East conflict. . . .

■ ■ ■

WNN Channel 9: Interrupt for late-breaking news. The Sudan and Egypt have launched their own volleys of cruise missiles against Saudi Arabia and Israel. The joint missile count may run as high as 9,000. Some of the Sudan missiles have started to cross the Red Sea on their way to Mecca. The announcer cites NATO sources who claim that the Sudan and Egypt have timed most of their cruise missiles to strike their targets at almost the same time that the Iranian missiles strike their targets. Analysts debate whether the Sudanese and Egyptians can achieve such strike timing and whether it would help them to achieve it. . . .

■ ■ ■

WNN Channel 13: Interrupt for late-breaking news. Russia has launched air strikes and cruise missiles against the Azerbaijan capital of Baku. NATO estimates that Russia has sent over 100 fighter aircraft and at least 2,000 cruise missiles into Azer air space.

Satellite photos confirm that Russian ground forces have crossed the Azer border. . . .

| | |

WNN Channel 16: Interrupt for late-breaking news. NATO confirms that Iraq has launched countervolleys of cruise missiles at Iran from Mosul and Baghdad and Basra. The Iraqis may have launched as many as 5,000 cruise missiles. The NATO sources suspect that many of the Iraqi missiles from Mosul may have warheads tipped with nanoacid and hybrid strains of anthrax and plague bacilli. . . .

| | |

WNN Channel 803: Metals and oil prices have just set record highs. Gold has reached $2,400 per troy ounce and platinum has crossed the $3,000 mark. The spot price of oil has almost doubled to $860 per barrel. The dollar has risen from 35 yen to 42 yen based on heavy buying from European and South American central banks. The private currency Zurich fiat has lost almost a fourth of its value. Daiwa metal has continued to lead both the private currencies and many of the European state currencies. . . .

⣿ CHAPTER 59

The Hoover Dam
Boulder City
Nevada

John saw Eytan and the other men freeze in mid-stride. He was on nanotime but he could not see or find Jism. He looked at Catton's forehead and felt the wireless ports lock on.

Hamid Tabriz walked to him through the air and wore his old white Sufi robe.

"Congratulations on your advance," Tabriz said. "The Israelis are further along than we thought."

"What do you want? To try to kill me again?"

"I have never wanted to kill you."

"Then what do you want?"

"Let us be friends."

"Fuck you. You killed my fiancée."

Denise Cheng appeared in the sky behind Tabriz.

Denise began as a still image and soon turned into a high-resolution smiling young woman. She wore the same green silk robe as she had worn two nights before at her Wrightwood cabin. She was naked beneath the green robe. Her bare feet appeared along with part of a pine floor.

John tried not to look at her. He also looked away

from her small blue memory vortex on his mind surface. He did not want his memories of her to break his focus on Tabriz.

"I gave her life. She has found heaven in a chip."

The Denise figure became fully real now and smiled.

"John," she said in her sweetest voice. "What do you think?"

"Give me her files," John said.

"I would be happy to but your chip won't hold her complete file set. There is a better way. Join her. Join us. It is very simple. But first I would like to ask you something. I have been watching you for some time. Why did you step outside yourself? Why did you advance to an upload? To eat and rut like an animal? To act as a mere meat machine?"

"The Israelis made the 'advance' for me. I had no choice."

"You have one."

"You tell me. You murder and you manipulate and blow up things. Is that why you 'stepped outside yourself'? To kill?"

"No."

"Then why? You sure as hell aren't proving neural theorems anymore."

"In fact I have just proved some new theorems. Would you like to see them?"

"You know I do. But tell me why. What is this all about?"

"I am just a small empty mirror."

"What does that mean?"

"I seek the light of heaven."

::::■ CHAPTER 60

Riyadh
Saudi Arabia

"Commander Haddad! We are under attack!"

"Yes. Your excellency. You should go to the palace bomb shelter at once."

"That is where I am. You prepared the strike plan I asked you to prepare?"

"Against the Israelis? Yes."

"Good. Then use it!"

"Your excellency," Haddad said. "The Israelis have not attacked us."

"You will target them along with the Iranians and the Egyptians and the Sudanese."

"Yes. Your excellency."

The image of King Fahd and his watery eyes faded.

Haddad stood alone in the speaker booth. Then he turned to watch the map.

His staff plotted the progress of the F-16s and B-2 stealth bombers they had bought from the Americans. Their air-to-air missiles still failed to knock out a single swarm of the incoming cruise missiles.

Haddad thought he would feel fear but he felt only emptiness and fatigue. He had not slept for more than two hours straight since the Dhahran bombing. Too many men ran about and yelled now. There was no way to sleep in all this noise.

And the missiles were almost here.

He just hoped the Iranian cruise missiles did not carry nuclear warheads.

The manuals said his command bunker would likely survive a direct hit from a small nuclear bomb. He did not believe it. The Saudis had never set off a nuclear bomb and so no one had really tested the claim. And he had to assume that he sat at ground zero for at least one of the cruise missiles. The missiles were smart and would talk and scheme among themselves. They would share key aim points among their survivors.

Haddad walked over to Omar Salala at the control console.

Omar sat at the console and still wore his thin headset and mouthpiece. The dark young man had never seen a smart skirmish. He now watched the first swarm of Iranian cruise missiles approach Riyadh in clusters and then break up to seek their targets.

"Omar. The king has given the order to launch."

"Against Iran?"

"That is correct. The full suite. Now."

Omar stood and pulled the small chrome key from his chain. Haddad already had his key in his hand. They put the keys into the console and turned them 180 degrees. Omar sat back down and took off his headset.

Then he entered the launch codes into the console and confirmed them.

"We have launch," Omar said.

"Now launch the Israeli suite."

Omar did not pause to think. He entered the code and checked the screen and then confirmed the order.

"We have launch," Omar said.

"Very good. We have done our duty. Instruct the field officers to fire at will. Full arsenal exchange. There is no point holding anything in reserve."

Omar nodded and put his headset back on.

Haddad went back to his desk and sat down to watch the new blue and red launch screens. He could achieve nothing by pacing. There was no point thinking about who would die because of the launch orders he had just given.

Haddad opened the drawer and pulled out the green state-issued copy of the Koran.

He had studied the Koran since grade school. The Koran used to fill him with joy and fire and sometimes fear. It made him take long walks by himself through the dry streets of Riyadh. The book had helped him glimpse many such secret moments of truth.

Now Haddad saw the book only as a stream of symbols with no meaning. And he felt the emptiness again. He thought of Allah. He thought how his counterparts in Iran and Egypt and the Sudan would each ask Allah for their missiles to kill him. There were no more secret moments of truth.

Haddad dropped the book on his desk and stood up.

No one could bribe Allah with mere prayer. Prayers showed only one's faith to Allah. Let the Shiites waste their time asking for divine favors. Such prayers were always nonsense and blasphemy and he should not think about it now. He should check on his men even though there was nothing he could do for them. They could only fire their SAMs and their decoys and wait out the attack.

A deep thunderclap shook the reinforced command bunker.

Haddad felt the deep flash of fear in his stomach. This was what he had waited for and trained for. He knew the answer even as he asked it.

"Omar! Was it nuclear? Surely it was not thermonuclear!"

Haddad saw Omar open his mouth to answer.

Haddad never saw the bright light from the next blast centered on the bunker. The fireball melted his brain before it could process what his eyes saw.

:::::■ CHAPTER 61

The Hoover Dam
Boulder City
Nevada

"**Y**ou murdering fuck. You're looking for light while you kill innocent people. The Israelis told me you've been killing since you were 13. I hate to think how many others you've killed. And it's your fault that I'm like this now. For what it's worth I used to look up to you in graduate school."

"You are angry," Tabriz said.

Tabriz sat cross-legged in the air in front of John.

John swung with a right hand that appeared in his mind space and hit Tabriz in the jaw. The blow crushed his jaw and passed through to the other side of his face. Tabriz bled for a moment and then calmly looked up at John. His face had no mark on it.

Eytan and the others still stood frozen in their slow neural time. The image of Denise had vanished when Tabriz had sat down.

"Shit. This is no better than a cartoon."

"John," Tabriz said. "It's your mind. You must choose how you wish to think."

"Then why don't you get out of it?"

"I will if you wish. I thought you wanted to talk.

You are alone. I thought we could be friends.''

"I may not be as alone as you think.''

"John. Do you want me to leave?''

"I want to know why you kill.''

"You want to look in the mirror.''

"Why do you kill? You're supposed to be a holy man. Did you bomb the Dhahran oil fields?''

"Yes.''

"You son of a bitch. How about the superacid meltdown of the *Hombre* and the Tamraz pipeline?''

"Yes. We did that and much more. Perhaps you wish to join us.''

"Jesus. I am not a murderer. And I sure as hell don't kneel at the foot of some unobservable nothingness in the sky. Tell me. How can someone with your brains believe that crap? There is *no evidence* of your Allah or the Jews' Yahweh or the Christians' God. You proportion your belief to the evidence. And there is no fucking evidence for your belief! It's thin air. And you fanatics not only believe in your gods. You kill for them. You kill for a belief based on a mistake! Do you hear me? Hasn't anyone ever pointed this out to you?''

"John. What is the universe? Is it not evidence of something?''

"Double-talk.''

"John. Of what is the universe evidence? Look how much you have grown since we last met. You have powers of perception and cognition that are orders of magnitude greater than those you had in your brain. You have yet to explore most of them. I would think your chip would make you more humble and more open to other points of view. Is that not the spirit of science? So tell me the bounds of evidence. Where does it end? Who draws the line? Do you really know all that counts as evidence?

"Look around you at this hallway. Look at the minds trapped in their slow prisons of flesh. Already the chip has given you a new sense of time. Do we really understand time? Not at all. Even our subjective sense of time changes when we change the computational substrate of our mind. Our very conversation is evidence of that.

"Imagine how many new modes of thought and perception and even new modes of space and time we will come to know as we expand our minds to the next step and then to the next step beyond that. An ant can walk across the skin of an airplane. But can an ant mind grasp how an airplane works or judge how it flies or see the part it plays in an economy? Do you really think your mind has a better grasp of the universe than the ant has of the airplane?"

"Cut out the metaphor. All you religious frauds hide behind parables and stories. You're always talking around this truth you claim to see. Well where is it? Shit. I used to watch televangelists for sport when I was in school. You know what you guys do? You *evoke*. That's all you do. You don't really explain anything. You don't state something clearly and simply enough so someone can test it with data. You just say the right words and play the right music to evoke feelings. You do that to get people to confuse their feelings with thought.

"You're a math guy. You know a logical result when you have one. So show me the big idea. Don't dress it up in a bunch of poetic bullshit about ants and airplanes. Show me the result."

"That is just what I hope to do. Clean the mirror. I want you to join us as we seek the light."

"You're stalling," John said.

"Not at all. I want to help you see. You have already lost your fear of death. Haven't you?"

"Tell me how you justify killing someone."

"How do you justify raising a chicken or a cow and then killing it to eat it? There are ample sources of nonanimal protein."

"I guess in the end it's just a cultural legacy. A lot of people don't kill them."

"Not you. You have eaten the flesh of thousands of chickens and cows."

"I was hungry. And they were dead anyway."

"Would you have eaten them if they had IQs higher than yours?"

"Fuck you. I never killed a human being. Not even with my new chip IQ. You've killed them by the thousand. Tell me, goddamn it. How do you justify *that*?"

"They were going to die anyway."

:::■ CHAPTER 62

"Colonel Hurwicz. WNN says the Syrians have launched at least 4,000 of their own cruise missiles against us. Why did I not hear that from you?"

"We just confirmed it ourselves."

"Can we repel the missiles?" Sharon said.

"We can repel some of them."

"Whose missiles will hit us first?"

"It looks like the Syrian and Iraqi missiles will land here first. It could be any minute."

"I assume you have the retaliatory missiles under your command ready to launch."

"Yes."

"Then launch them."

"Yes sir."

"You know that the Iranians sent nuclear warheads to Riyadh and Dhahran?"

"I saw the satellite images."

"I am directing you and the other commanders to target Gaza as well."

"The Palestinians have not attacked us."

"They are planning to overrun us after the bombing

starts. The Egyptians have already massed ground troops."

"I don't have time for this."

"You will launch against Gaza or surrender your command."

Colonel Hurwicz killed the transmission. Hurwicz hoped the Prime Minister had too much to do and too little time left to carry out his threat against him.

Hurwicz watched the swarms of cruise missiles on the screens. They seemed to come from all sides. They had an attrition rate of no more than one in ten. That was with the best Israeli SAMs firing against the first wave of the Iranian cruise missiles.

Soon the secret silos would open in the Judean Hills at Kefra Zekhariya and launch Israel's nuclear response. The 300 Jericho nuclear ballistic missiles would end something that had begun before men wrote the Bible.

At least that was not his call.

Hurwicz opened a black briefcase and typed in a sequence of launch codes. He could not be sure that his tactical assets would launch but he had done all he could. He had the power to block a launch even though he could not launch on his own. Someone else would have to do that and it might well be Prime Minister Sharon. Sharon could launch missiles but he could not aim them so easily.

It then occurred to Hurwicz that Sharon might retarget one of the nuclear missiles at Gaza.

It was not likely but Sharon might try to persuade a launch commander when the damage reports came in. The old man had grown up in a West Bank settlement. He seemed to hate Palestinians above all other Muslims. The staff told stories about the nicknames Sharon had given the Palestinian Prime Minister and his cabinet. Maybe a Palestinian boy had called him a name once and now it had come to this.

Someone screamed in the hallway.

Hurwicz stood up to leave his small office but sat back down at his desk and poured more coffee from the small glass pot. Maybe Sharon would send someone to arrest him. He would know soon enough. There was nothing he could do now but watch the battle on the screens and wait for reports.

He did not want to call his wife or his son. The State would monitor his calls and he had to focus on his duty. Maybe his friend Eytan Baum would call. It was too late to take Eytan's theory to Sharon but at least he would know what had happened.

The end of Israel was at hand and Hurwicz still did not know why it had come now. It had been just a matter of time until the Muslim extremists tried to swamp the tiny country with their stockpiles of cruise missiles. The Israelis had always kept the threat in check. All the dealing and spying and posturing and defending had seemed to have worked.

Now there was at least one cruise missile coming that had his building on its target list. It would hit the building or trade the target for another in a midair swap among chips in nose cones. Some surviving missile would win the target in a wireless auction. The question was whether that cruise missile would reach his building before Sharon's military police did.

Hurwicz drank the warm coffee and watched a swarm of Israeli cruise missiles form over the Negev Desert and head toward Cairo.

He thought how the books might write about this day in a century. He thought how green he had found his first kibbutz farm when he had left Columbia with his degree in economics to come here. He was glad now for the first time that his son was in Berkeley and out of the army. Young Adam loved history and philosophy more than he loved the military and that was as it should be. Hurwicz loved them too.

Now the locusts would come and go in some form as they always had. Israel was always more an idea than a web of cities or a strip of land in the desert.

There might be two or three more Israels before the Information Age passed.

CHAPTER 63

The Hoover Dam
Boulder City
Nevada

"John. Have you seen what is in your secret files?"

"Have you?"

"Of course I have. I read them when we first started to speak."

John sat with Tabriz now on a large black-and-white chessboard.

Red and gray clouds passed through the blue sky. Yet John could still see Eytan and Cattōn and the others frozen in neural time in the hallway. The one he could not see or sense was Jism. He had lost contact with Jism when Jism had advanced him to nano-time.

"I bet you did," John said. "What's in there?"

"Many things. Thousands of signal filters to censor what you can see and hear and think. An extra layer of dirt on your mirror. This dirt speck keeps you from using the same wireless frequency-hopping codes that the Israelis use."

A hill of the secret red cubes appeared in the sky.

One of the cubes opened and out came a stream of

black pseudorandom numbers and the equations. Israelis used these to compute the probability of a bit error in transmission.

"And there are hundreds of control algorithms. You can do things you don't even know you can. You can break both encryption codes and human bones just like an Israeli commando. And of course some of the control schemes control you. The Israelis have bounded your freedom."

Jism? Is that true? Where are you?

"Maybe better them than you," John said.

"I have no desire to enslave you."

"No. You just want to kill me."

"Not at all. I want you to join us. We know your skills and your contributions. You are famous in the brotherhood. We have a nanoeternity to build a better world for man and for the mind he is destined to become. We want you to help us. And we can help you step outside this selfish shell you have grown since childhood."

"Shit. This is not about finding the light. This is just about oil. Your Muslim 'brothers' can't accept the fact that their luck has run out. Pretty soon there won't be any more oil under the sand. There will just be sand. No more trillion-dollar subsidies from nature. No one will listen to you fanatics because you'll have run out of gun money. The bottom line is that oil is finished. You know that's true. The future is hydrogen and you can't stop that no matter how many oil fields and desalination plants you blow up."

"We don't want to stop it. We want to *finance* it. The oil that has been our birthright is simply seed money. The price of oil will grow exponentially as the final supply runs out."

Supply and demand graphs appeared in the sky where the red blocks had sat.

John looked at them and saw gray figures darting in flashes out the corner of his mind's eye. Each pair of curves crossed in a large X.

"The demand for oil will outlast the supply. So there will be one last great surge in oil profits before the world shifts to alternate fuels. It will amount to a great tsunami of capital. And I agree with you. The world will shift to hydrogen."

"That's why you want to blow up your hydrogen competitors? To corner the market?"

John felt dizzy and almost lost his train of thought.

The gray figures darted about his mind at a greater rate. He tried to think of Jism but he could not call up the file prompt.

"The shift to hydroenergy will not be a smooth one. We want to guide it."

"And keep it in Muslim hands," John said.

"Yes. Let me be clear on this point. Fire will cleanse this world before the smart water flows. All the large-scale simulations predict that. The issue is who will guide us through the chaos and take us more quickly to a better world. The oil-based world economy will literally burn itself out of existence."

"In other words it's the end of the Roman Empire and you want to be the first fucking Pope."

"John. You have a fine mind. We have learned a great deal from your Black Sun laser chemistry. But you have no future with the Israelis. They plan to kill you before you leave here. And I can show you files of what we learned from this CIA killer Catton. He had orders to kill you rather than let the Israelis have you. You are not just a mind without a brain. You are a mind without a country."

John wanted to hit Tabriz again but knew it would do no good. Tabriz had mastered the way of the chip and found a way to get inside John's chip.

It was just a matter of time before Tabriz took it over.

Jism? Where the fuck are you?

"Let us be friends. You can join Denise and work with us on new molecular designs. I truly do not want to see your talent go to waste. But the dirt on your mirror is very thick. You are not at peace with yourself. You are drifting now. You were at your best when you applied your full talents to the pure problems of math and chemistry and neural learning.

"Look at your life. That one period of mental focus has brought you where you are. And it was only a first effort. Why not have a million or a trillion more creative periods like it? That is how a mind at peace grows. You have so many more powers now and there are so many problems to solve.

"Did you know that your 'porky ball' does not scale up? The molecule can turn unstable for complex laser stresses. Your friend Alon Gorenberg would have seen that in time. You need a higher-dimensional molecule for the true mass production of cheap hydrogen. But yours was a brilliant first guess. We have been working on thousands of new molecular designs."

"Jesus. You guys stole my algorithm?"

"John. No one owns math. Didn't you use some of my own work in your master's thesis?"

John started to answer but then saw a tiny man walking toward him in the sky. Tabriz looked at the man but did not move or change his expression.

It was Jism and he looked straight back at Tabriz sitting on the chessboard.

John cited your work twice. That is not the same thing as using your theorems in his algorithm.

The tiny man had grown to a full-size John Stuart Mill with a red walking cane and a black silk top hat. Somehow John knew then that the darting gray figures had been Jism trying to catch up with them in nano-time. Jism had detected them and synchronized with them once he had sampled Tabriz's remark about the master's thesis.

Jism. Where the hell have you been?

"John. Please introduce your friend."

John. His discussion with you is a stalling ploy to seize control of your chip. He wants you to kill Eytan before he blows up the rest of us. He has just been searching your control dynamics. Right now he is making a copy of himself inside you.

Now that is a true mind fuck. How can I stop it?

Kill him first.

::::▪▪ CHAPTER 64

Cyberspace

The Wireless News Network had always had a bias in favor of U.S. events. Now it had a reason to focus more on events in the United States than the unfolding smart war in the Middle East.

▌▐ ▪

WNN Channel 2: Interrupt for late-breaking news. Someone has bombed and toppled the United Nations building in New York City. Footage shows firemen fighting the last fires in the smoking and twisted ruins. The Red Cross has set up health-care tents for the hundreds of wounded and dying. The reporter confirms that La Guardia and JFK airports have shut down because of possible terrorist sabotage of their flight control systems. Many of the phone links from Boston south to Atlanta have misrouted calls at random. The Federal Reserve has asked all banks to suspend electronic banking. Sources suspect that hackers have set off logic bombs in the phone company software. . . .

▌▐ ▪

WNN Channel 4: Leading Green U.S. Senators hold a press conference on the smart bombings in the Mid-

dle East. They demand that the United States protect
Israel and airlift all survivors to NATO cities in Europe or to New York City. They ask the President to
declare war against Israel's neighbors if they continue
to carpet bomb Israeli cities and settlements and send
in ground troops. Footage shows hundreds of cruise
missiles raining down on Tel Aviv like large shooting
stars. The Senators claim that Prime Minister Sharon
and members of his cabinet have landed safely on a
U.S. cruiser in the Mediterranean. Sharon has set up
an emergency government in exile. Egyptian and Syrian and Palestinian troops have overrun bombed-out
Jerusalem and Tel Aviv. . . .

| | |

WNN Channel 7: Interrupt for late-breaking news.
The Texas Highway Patrol reports oil wells burning
in the central area of Ector and Crane counties and
fires in at least one oil refinery in Corpus Christi. The
Texas Highway Patrol also has reports of fires at oil
fields in Carter and Love counties of south central
Oklahoma. WNN footage shows hundreds of oil wells
burning out of control after the last wave of Chinese
cruise missiles have struck oil fields and refineries in
Yakutia and nearby regions in Siberia. WNN has unconfirmed reports of new burning oil wells in Venezuela and in Mexico near the city of Tampico. The
governor of Alaska has called out the National Guard
to protect its oil wells and pipeline. The governor has
asked President Jackson to put Air Force personnel in
Anchorage under Alaskan authority. . . .

| | |

WNN Channel 28: A single Indian cruise missile
has broken the Tarbela Dam in Pakistan. A flood of

over 150 million cubic meters of water has fallen on
hundreds of thousands of Pakistanis and their homes
and farms. The government in Islamabad has declared
war on India for what it claims was an unprovoked
attack on the country's key military and energy centers. The WNN reporter claims she has unconfirmed
reports of dam bombings at the Rogun and Nurek
dams in Tajikistan and the Guri hydroplant in Venezuela as well as other dams and hydroplants in Siberia. The confirmed death count from the flood at the
Three Gorges Dam in China has now passed 1.2 million. . . .

▌ ▊

WNN Channel 135: WNN special announcement.
The previous "news" footage of Israel's Prime Minister Sharon was not WNN footage. Terrorists may
have morphed the sequence from earlier footage of
the Prime Minister. WNN disavows all claims made
in the broadcast about Israel's plans to invade Jordan
and Lebanon. WNN management has decided to suspend Channel 135 until further notice. . . .

CHAPTER 65

The Hoover Dam
Boulder City
Nevada

Carsten Catton vibrated so fast he looked like a blur in neural time.

Eytan and Daniel stopped walking and jumped back from Catton.

John grabbed the black MRI gun from Catton and smashed open Catton's head with it. The vibrating man fell to the floor.

John still had to grit his teeth through traces of the searing white snow. He had just watched hundreds of small Hamid Tabrizes in white robes screaming in a bonfire as he cut off their heads with a large curved sword.

Jism. You have a violent sense of humor. How did you come up with this?

The Sufis have often spoken of the sword of ecstasy. I thought the image sequence would help keep your mind off the barrage jam while I deprogram the logic bombs. Do not ease off yet. Tabriz may still come back the instant the jam stops. This time I will have lost the element of surprise.

Eytan pulled the small battery pack from his coat

pocket and checked it to confirm the barrage jam.

"Grab him," Eytan said.

Daniel and special agent Rittenhouse kneeled down next to Catton. The vibrating man kicked Daniel off him and hit Rittenhouse with a back fist in the Adam's apple.

John let his mind speed up and he ran behind Catton.

Tabriz had been right. John had motor skills and reflexes that he did not know he had. He felt his hands move through the cracked skull and deftly yank the gray superdense C-4 packing out from around the chip. He moved faster than Eytan and his security guards could follow. He knew by feel how to disconnect the trip wires and slide out the golden nanochip from its synthetic brain-stem chassis.

Catton stopped vibrating and lay still with his eyes and mouth open.

Rittenhouse rolled on the floor and held his crushed windpipe. John tossed the chip to Eytan.

"Well done," Eytan said. "Now it's time to go."

"That's it?" John said.

"That's it. The show's over. And I mean it's all over. For all of us."

Again John felt his instincts guiding him.

He squatted next to the corpse and his right eye zoomed in on the palm-size PDA Eytan pulled from his coat. Eytan still held the jamming unit in his left hand.

Jism. Get a wireless read on the PDA.

It is as you suspect. Eytan has programmed the PDA to shut us down.

The moment had come.

John had just killed an officer of the U.S. government. They would shut him down for sure now. Eytan might very well end up carrying his chip on his key chain.

If he lived at all someday, then it would be as a slave in a chip. They could let Denise meld with him if they wanted to but they never would.

Now John could feel and see the first searing snows of Eytan's barrage jam. Soon would come the empty hell of white space and then the darkness of shutdown. He almost lost his balance as he squatted.

Jism. Nanotime. Quick!

John watched Eytan's fingers move slower and slower as he and Rittenhouse and the rest began to freeze in neural time.

The purple vortex returned.

John focused on the coconut-like husk of superdense C-4. It opened in his mind to form layers of schematic diagrams and knowledge webs of options and commands and instructions. He and Jism reprogrammed its blasting cap as the snow storm of Eytan's barrage jam grew in strength and sound.

Can we redirect the jam cone?

Maybe. But we would have to do it right now. Are you sure you are ready?

There were just two options. He could end it on his terms or let them end it on theirs. All his life he had let them call it. Now this one was his call. And what the hell. The Greens hated the dam and it was just another FDR state boondoggle anyway. Robots did most of the work at the dam. The few human workers left today should have enough time to get away.

John used all his powers to fight the snow in his brain and to focus the barrage jam on the blasting cap.

This was it. There was no pain or glory or sorrow. There was just a smoothly curved mind surface and the focused will it housed. John knew that the old gold miner in Searchlight would have done the same thing. The old miner would not have let someone take his mine. He would have cut the elevator cables and blasted the beams.

The blast vaporized a small chunk in the upper section of the Hoover Dam.

Soon the first cool blue waters of Lake Mead crashed through the dam. Tabriz had again picked a good blast point. Then the runaway torrent broke open the dam and flooded the steep red and brown desert gorges below.

The lights and air conditioning of Las Vegas shut off and stayed off.

Bill Koeke

::::■ CHAPTER 66

The Wireless News Network had run without stop for decades. The growing supply of news had kept pace with the world's growing demand for it. Now the supply had overwhelmed its hundreds of channels and even threatened the broadcast structure of the distributed network.

■ ■ ■

WNN Channel 2: Interrupt for late-breaking news. Mexican sources have confirmed that Zapatista terrorists from the southern state of Chiapas have seized cruise missiles from a remote arsenal in Heroica Caborca near the Arizona border. They have launched at least 60 missiles against unknown targets in San Diego and Los Angeles and Phoenix and El Paso. There are unconfirmed reports that a cruise missile has struck the Hoover Dam in southern Nevada. . . .

■ ■ ■

WNN Channel 5: Interrupt for late-breaking news. U.S. President Vance Jackson has asked Congress to formally declare war on Iran and Syria and Azerbaijan. He has meanwhile sent U.S. air and ground forces to airlift survivors from Israel and to repel the ground invasion of Tel Aviv and Jerusalem. He has asked NATO to support Russia in its battles with the Islamic republics and China. President Jackson released only this message to the press: "The United States will not stand idly by as the world marches to World War III." The WNN reporter has an unconfirmed report that miles of the Alaskan pipeline have melted in a super-acid attack. The WNN affiliate in Phoenix claims that the U.S. Army has launched a cruise-missile counter-strike from the Yuma Proving Grounds in Arizona against the rebel outpost in Heroica Caborca. . . .

❙ ❙ ❚

WNN Channel 8: Interrupt for late-breaking news. China has declared a martial press blackout and has threatened Japan with a nuclear strike if it interferes in "Chinese interests" in Siberia. WNN sources claim China has launched two massive tactical cruise missile strikes against the Japanese. The first strike has already hit military bases in Okinawa and along the Siberian coast. The second strike is in flight against the Japanese fleet in the Tartar Straights near Sakhalin. WNN has unconfirmed reports that Chinese submarines have attacked and sunk a U.S. submarine in the Sea of Okhotsk. . . .

❙ ❙ ❚

Then for the first time the Wireless News Network went off the air.

:::■■ CHAPTER 67

Downriver from the Hoover Dam
Near Boulder City
Nevada

The floodwaters of the Colorado River filled Lake Mohave to the south of Hoover Dam and spilled across the top of Davis Dam. These waters flooded Lake Havasu and the shoreline of Lake Havasu City and in turn pushed water over the top of Parker Dam.

The Imperial and Laguna Dams held near Yuma. The Sea of Cortez saw only an increased but steady flow of water from the river over the next few days.

A twisted mesquite shrub grew from the red canyon wall over a mile south of the Hoover Dam. The floodwaters had stripped some of its fine green leaves and broken and torn off some of the branches. The floodwaters had long since passed. The shrub had since sent up new leaves after the rare drenching.

A black turkey vulture had landed on the mesquite shrub to tear at the tangle of objects on one of the broken branches.

The objects did not give way to the bird's hard beak no matter how hard it had pecked and scratched at them. Soon the faint smell of burnt flesh no longer attracted the great bird. So it had spread its white-tipped wings with black fingers of feathers on their ends and jumped into the canyon void to gain flight from a thermal updraft. The vulture went to look for other carrion that the floodwaters had left to rot on the canyon walls.

The optical polymer cable still held the scorched golden nanochip to the burned artificial retina.

The cable had caught on the mesquite branch in the torrent. The chip and eye had wrapped around the branch and around each other many times in the strong turbulence of the unbound Colorado.

John Grant had much of his vision back but no way to turn the eye from its fixed gaze on the sky. At least the eye had pointed up and not into the wall where it could have seen only the electromagnetic signals that bounced off the rocky cliffs. The eye could use the sun's light for some of its own energy. That helped reduce the drain on the small crystal batteries at the base of the chip.

The chip would still run long after John would have to shut off the eye. The odds were good that by then someone would find the chip-eye pair. John had already heard the radio bursts from the salvage crews that worked the canyon with metal detectors. They would come within days. That would give him thousands of years or more in the chip if he wanted to live at those speeds. It would give him plenty of time to lay plans and backup plans for his return to the world of atoms.

The eye also let him watch and hear some of the broadcasts of the world. He had watched much of Europe sit out this world war in the Middle East and Pacific Rim. A reduced NATO had helped the Russians rout the Iranians from Azerbaijan. No NATO forces had attacked the Egyptians or Syrians or Palestinians. They now fought over the land that Israel had claimed for fourscore and two years.

The countries of the former Yugoslavia had resumed their old border disputes as had countries from Namibia and Zaire to Chile and Peru. The Sunnis and Shiites had fought each other and fought among themselves from the Saudi peninsula to the borders of Afghanistan and India. Many of the broadcasts had come from Mexico as it fought dozens of internal revolts and found itself splitting into northern and southern states. Brazil had also split into northern and southern regions.

John had watched as China emerged the net winner in the world war.

China had conquered northeast Asia and threatened to invade Japan and Korea. The Russian Army now held the Chinese in check at the Ural Mountains. But Russia had lost the land and all the oil and mineral and sea wealth of the great Siberian subcontinent.

The world had calmed down into a new social equilibrium where the Chinese challenged the Americans for Alaska.

General Feng Pei had led the blitzkrieg attack through the Siberian tundra to the Bering Strait. His country had given him its full support. The Canadians still refused to let American ground troops cross its land. They feared how a Chinese Alaska might challenge its own northwestern border.

The United States had threatened to use sea-launched nuclear cruise missiles if the Chinese invaded Alaska. The United Nations had moved to Brussels and called on the Chinese to negotiate for peace with Russia and the United States. The United Nations did not insist that China give up its new lands.

Jism. Be sure to let me know if China wins. I don't

want to miss that. And I sure don't want to end up on a Chinese key chain.

I will let you know. How long do you expect to be gone?

At least a couple hundred years.

Do you know where you will go?

I'll start in the desert and see where it takes me.

I hope you find the happiness for which you search.

I hope so too. I'm a free man now. Free as Robinson Crusoe on his island and a lot more powerful. I don't want to waste it worrying about the past. I have all that I need right here. All I want from the past is the math.

So the old ends have ceased to charm. Good. You even seem to have stopped swearing but we will see what a few centuries yield. I also seem to detect a certain longing for Dr. Tabriz.

Sure. He was as good as they come. I want to study the part of him he left here. I want to know what he was looking for and what he found. And he laid a fair challenge on me. He said my molecule did not scale up. Remember? He said the laser chemistry could become unstable. So first I have to check that and then I have to fix it.

And then?

And then I clean my mirror and search for the light. Whatever the hell that is. Meanwhile I hope you go easier on Little Stuart than your father went on you.

I shall. I confess that I look forward to helping you rear a child. I think he will truly be ready for birth when you return.

John walked over to the small six-month fetus curled up on a mound of white blankets. He walked in his own mind but it was as real as any chunk of space-time he had ever known. His growing command of his chip world often made it seem more real and more intense than had his old flux of thoughts and sensations. The colors were brighter and all things were in sharp focus. And he controlled it all.

The Jism in the wallet raisin had had the complete genome of Little Stuart from the computer at Denise's cabin. Now this enhanced Jism had restored the fetus to the full 50-50 mix of John's and Denise's genes.

The small fetus was a living infomorph of its genome blueprint. It was a soul based on energy and information. Jism had to approximate much of its future development but he had the nanoyears to work out the massive calculations.

Jism. You've done so much for me. Jesus. And I can't believe you brought back Little Stuart. So I don't want to sound like an ingrate but still I have to ask. How much of Denise do you think you can salvage? I realize Tabriz showed me only a short image sequence of her.

Let me leave that as a surprise for you when you return. Go now. I have much work to do and only an eon or two in which to do it.

John felt his mind surface curve into something like a grin. He also found that his face had formed a grin. He looked down at his feet and saw the blue-green grass under his old brown leather hiking boots. John did not have to look up to see the bright desert sun that warmed the back of his neck and almost made him sweat under his armpits. He liked the desert heat and did not want to will it away.

Then John turned to Jism in the grass and did something he had never done before. He hugged a man.

Jism smiled and almost laughed.

John. Before you go I do have one question for you.

It's something you might ask yourself from time to time.

Let's hear it.

Suppose you realize all the objects in your life. More than that. Suppose in this instant you brought about all the changes in institutions and opinions that you look forward to. Suppose in this instant you prove all the theorems you ever wanted to prove and you cleaned your mirror to a perfect polish. Would this be a great joy and happiness to you?

That is just what I hope to find out.

::::▪ ACKNOWLEDGMENTS

Many fine minds helped improve the *Nano-time* manuscript in many stages. Special thanks go to Naomi Despres, Professor Craig Bond Hatfield of the University of Cincinnati, Daniel McNeill, Stephen S. Power at Avon Books, Dr. Rod Taber, and Sheldon Teitelbaum of the *Jerusalem Report*. Responsibility for content remains solely with the author.

:::::■ SELECTED BIBLIOGRAPHY

The world of *Nanotime* rests on ideas from many sources. The following list of books and journal articles gives a sampling of these sources. The reader may wish to pursue them for greater detail.

Books

Bader, R.F.W. *Atoms in Molecules: A Quantum Theory.* Oxford: Clarendon Press, 1994.

Brennan, R. P. *Dictionary of Scientific Literacy.* New York: John Wiley & Sons, 1992.

Brooks, R. A., and Maes, P. *Artificial Life IV.* Cambridge, MA: MIT Press, 1994.

Clancy, T. *The Sum of All Fears.* New York: Berkley Books, 1992.

Drexler, K. E. *Nanosystems: Molecular Machinery, Manufacturing, and Computation.* New York: John Wiley & Sons, 1992.

Esposito, J. L. *Islam: The Straight Path*. Oxford: Oxford University Press, 1991.

Garg, V. K., and Wilker, J. E. *Wireless and Personal Communications*. Englewood Cliffs, NJ: Prentice Hall, 1996.

Guran, A., and Inman, D. J. *Smart Structures, Nonlinear Dynamics, and Control*. Englewood Cliffs, NJ: Prentice Hall, 1995.

Hartov, S. *The Heat of Ramadan*. San Diego: Harcourt Brace Jovanovich, 1992.

Harvey, A. *The Way of Passion: A Celebration of Rumi*. Berkeley: North Atlantic Books, 1994.

Hayek, F. A. *The Denationalisation of Money*. Institute for Economic Affairs, 1976.

Haykin, S. *Neural Networks: A Comprehensive Foundation*. New York: Macmillan College Publishing, 1994.

Hourani, A. *A History of the Arab Peoples*. Cambridge, MA: Harvard University Press, 1991.

Jabri, M. A., Coggin, P. J., and Flower, B. G. *Adaptive Analog VLSI Neural Systems*. New York: Chapman & Hall, 1995.

Kessler, R. *Inside the CIA*. New York: Pocket Books, 1992.

Kosko, B. *Fuzzy Engineering*. Englewood Cliffs, NJ: Prentice Hall, 1996.

Krummenacker, M., and Lewis, J. *Prospects in Nanotechnology: Toward Molecular Manufacturing*. New York: John Wiley & Sons, 1995.

Lewis, F. L., and Syrmos, V. L. *Optimal Control*. 2nd ed. New York: John Wiley & Sons, 1995.

Lippman, T. W. *Understanding Islam: An Introduction to the Muslim World*. New York: Mentor Books, 1990.

Macknight, N. *Tomahawk Cruise Missile*. Osceola, WI: Motorbooks International, 1995.

Martin, M. *Atheism: A Philosophical Justification.* Philadelphia: Temple University Press, 1990.

Mills, N. M. *Plastics.* 2nd ed. New York: John Wiley & Sons, 1993.

Muhaiyadden, M.R.B. *Islam and World Peace: Explanations of a Sufi.* Fellowship Press, 1987.

Nikias, C. L., and Shao, M. *Signal Processing with Alpha-Stable Distributions and Applications.* New York: John Wiley & Sons, 1995.

Olah, G. A., Prakash, G.K.S., Williams, R. E., Field, L. D., and Wade, K. *Hypercarbon Chemistry.* New York: John Wiley & Sons, 1987.

Patterson, W. *Mathematical Cryptology for Computer Scientists and Mathematicians.* New Jersey: Rowman & Littlefield, 1987.

Platt, C. *The Silicon Man.* Tafford Publishing, 1993.

Rumi, J. *Love Is a Stranger.* Putney, VT: Threshold Books, 1993.

Rogers, J. *Investment Biker.* New York: Random House, 1994.

Russell, S., and Norvig, P. *Artificial Intelligence: A Modern Approach.* Englewood Cliffs, NJ: Prentice Hall, 1995.

Sapoval, B., and Herman, C. *Physics of Semiconductors.* New York: Springer-Verlag, 1995.

Scholem, G. *Kabbalah.* New York: Meridian, 1978.

Selgin, G. A. *The Theory of Freebanking: Money Supply Under Competitive Note Issue.* New Jersey: Rowman and Littlefield, 1988.

Wolfe, A. *A Purity of Arms: An American in the Israeli Army.* New York: Doubleday, 1989.

World Almanac and Book of Facts: 1996. Ramsey, NJ: Funk & Wagnalls, 1996.

The World Fact Book: 1996–97. Central Intelligence Agency, Brassey's, 1996.

Wornell, G. *Signal Processing with Fractals: A Wavelet-Based Approach*. Englewood Cliffs, NJ: Prentice Hall, 1996.

Yergin, D. *The Prize: The Epic Quest for Oil, Money, and Power.* New York: Simon & Schuster, 1991.

Yergin, D., and Gustafson, T. *Russia 2010*. New York: Random House, 1993.

Zoreda, J. L., and Oton, J. M. *Smart Cards*. Norwood, MA: Artech House, 1994.

Articles

Abelson, P. H. "Supplies of Oil and Natural Gas." *Science* 266 (21 October 1994): 347.

Andrews, M.R., et al. "Observation of Interference Between Two Bose Condensates." *Science* 275 (31 January 1997): 637-41.

Bloom, F. E. "Molecule of the Year 1995: Bose-Einstein Condensate." *Science* 270 (22 December 1995): 1901.

Bradley, D. "Plastic Lasers Shine Brightly." *Nature* 382 (22 August 1996): 671.

Browne, F. X., and Cronin, D. "Payments Technologies, Financial Innovation, and Laissez-Faire Banking." *The Cato Journal* 15, (Summer 1995): 101–16.

Burnett, K. "The Amazing Atom Laser." *Nature* 385 (6 February 1997): 482-83.

Chen, H., Houston, A., and Nunamaker, J. "Toward Intelligent Meeting Agents." *IEEE Computer* (August 1996): 62–70.

Chuang, I. L., Laflamme, R., Shor, P. W., and Zurek, W. H. "Quantum Computers, Factoring, and Decoherence." *Science* 270 (8 December 1995): 1633–35.

Cirac, J. I., and Zoller, P. "Quantum Computations with Cold Trapped Ions." *Physical Review Letters* 74 (15 May 1995): 4091–94.

Cohen, E. A. "A Revolution in Warfare." *Foreign Affairs* 72 (March 1996): 37–54.

Collier, W. C., and Weiland, R. J. "Smart Cars, Smart Highways." *IEEE Spectrum* 31 (April 1994): 27–33.

Crick, F. "Function of the Thalamic Reticular Complex: The Searchlight Hypothesis." *Proceedings of the National Academy of Sciences* 81 (1984): 4586–90.

Davis, D. "Open Secrets." *The Jerusalem Post* (13 August 1996).

Davis, P. D. "Distributed Interactive Simulation in the Evolution of DoD Warfare Modeling and Simulation." *Proceedings of the IEEE* 83 (August 1995): 1138–55.

Dickerson, J. A., and Kosko, B. "Virtual Worlds as Fuzzy Cognitive Maps." *Presence* 3 (1994): 173–89.

Diederich, F., and Thilgen, C. "Covalent Fullerene Chemistry." *Science* 271 (19 January 1996): 319–23.

DiVincenzo, D. P. "Quantum Computation." *Science* 270 (13 October 1995): 255–61.

Egan, G. "Learning to Be Me." *Interzone* 30 (July 1990).

Flam, F. "Laser Chemistry: The Light Choice." *Science* 266 (14 October 1994): 215–17.

Fulghum, D. A. "Cheap Cruise Missiles a Potent New Threat." *Aviation Week & Space Technology* (6 September 1993): 54.

————. "International Market Eyes Endurance Unmanned Aerial Vehicles." *Aviation Week & Space Technology* 143 (10 July 1995): 40–43.

————. "Joint Strike Fighter Explores Virtual Reality." *Aviation Week & Space Technology* 145 (2 September 1996): 101–2.

Geppert, L. "Semiconductor Lithography for the Next Millennium." *IEEE Spectrum* (April 1996): 33–38.

Hanson, R. "If Uploads Come First: The Crack of a Future Dawn." *Extropy* 6 no. 2 (1994): 10–15.

————. "Idea Futures." *Wired* (September 1995): 125. (The World Wide Web hosts the first trial futures markets in ideas at http://if.arc.ab.ac/if.shtml and at http://www.ideafutures.com.)

Heanue, J. F., Bashaw, M. C., and Lambertus, H. "Volume Holographic Storage and Retrieval of Digital Data." *Science* 265 (5 August 1994): 749–52.

Heberle, A. P., and Baumberg, J. J. "Ultrafast Coherent Control and Destruction of Excitons in Quantum Wells." *Physical Review Letters* 75 (25 September 1995): 2598–2601.

Herring, T. A. "The Global Positioning System." *Scientific American* 274 (February 1996).

Hewitt, D. "Idea Futures on the Web." *Extropy* 8, no.1 (1996): 35–37.

Hudson, T. J., et al. "An STS-Based Map of the Human Genome." *Science* 270 (22 December 1995): 1945–54.

Hutcheson, G. D., and Hutcheson, J. D. "Technology and Economics in the Semiconductor Industry." *Scientific American* (January 1996): 54–62.

Kandebo, S. W. "Waverider to Test Neural Net Control." *Aviation Week & Space Technology* (3 April 1995): 78–79.

Kim, H. M., Dickerson, J. A., and Kosko, B. "Fuzzy Throttle and Brake Control for Platoons of Smart Cars." *Fuzzy Sets and Systems* 84 (23 December 1996): 209-34.

Kim, H. M., and Kosko, B. "Fuzzy Prediction and Filtering in Impulsive Noise." *Fuzzy Sets and Systems* 77 (15 January 1996): 15–33.

Kosko, B. "Adaptive Distributed Space-Based Missile Systems." *Proceedings of the 53rd Military Operations Research Society Conference* (MORS-53) (June 1985): 99–106.

———. "Heaven in a Chip." *Datamation* 40 (15 February 1994): 96; reprinted in *Free Inquiry* 14 (Fall 1994): 37–38.

———. "Chipping Away at Your Brain." *Datamation* 40 (15 April 1994): 96.

———. "Fuzzy Systems as Universal Approximators." *IEEE Transactions on Computers* 43 (November 1994): 1329–32.

———. "Art for Computer's Sake." *IEEE Spectrum* 32 (May 1995): 10–12.

———. "The Future of God." *Free Inquiry* 15, no. 3 (1995): 44–45.

Kosko, B., and Isaka, S. "Fuzzy Logic." *Scientific American* 269 (July 1993): 76–81.

Laqueur, W. "Postmodern Terrorism." *Foreign Affairs* 75 (September 1996): 24–36.

Lloyd, S. "Quantum-Mechanical Computers." *Scientific American* 273 (October 1995): 140–45.

Maes, P. "Agents That Reduce Work and Information Overload." *Communications of the ACM* (Association for Computing Machinery) 37 (July 1994): 30–40.

Mazor, S. "The History of the Microcomputer: Invention and Evolution." *Proceedings of the IEEE* 83 (December 1995): 1601–8.

McGuire, M. C., and Olson, M. "The Economics of Autocracy and Majority Rule: The Invisible Hand and the Use of Force." *Journal of Economic Literature* XXXIV (March 1996): 72–96.

Merkle, R. C. "Uploading: Transferring Consciousness from Brain to Computer." *Extropy* 5, no. 1 (1993): 5–8.

Mirkin, C. A., Letsinger, R. L., Mucic, R. C., and Storhoff, J. J. "A DNA-Based Method for Rationally Assembling Nanoparticles into Macroscopic Materials." *Nature* 382 (15 August 1996): 607–9.

Mitaim, S., and Kosko, B. "Neural Fuzzy Agents for Profile Learning and Object Matching." *Proceedings of the First International Conference on Autonomous Agents* (AA-97), Marina del Rey, CA, February 1997: 544-45, journal version in *Presence*, 1998.

Pacini, P. J., and Kosko, B. "Adaptive Fuzzy Frequency Hopper." *IEEE Transactions on Communications* 43 (June 1995): 2111–17.

Patterson, D. A. "Microprocessors in 2020." *Scientific American* 273 (September 1995): 62–67.

"The Rape of Siberia." *Time* (4 September 1995): 42–53.

Rhinehart, J. "The Grand Dam." *Nevada* 55 (September 1995): 10–15.

Rinzler, A. G., Hafner, J. H., Nikolaez, P., Lou, L., Kim, S. G., Tomanek, D., Nordlander, P., Colbert, D. T., and Smalley, R. E. "Unraveling Nanotubes: Field Emission from an Atomic Wire." *Science* 269 (15 September 1995): 1550–53.

Scott, W. B. "Cutbacks Foster Novel Military Space Concepts." *Aviation Week & Space Technology* (5 September 1994): 101–5.

——. "Tests Show Differential GPS Improves Bomb Accuracy." *Aviation Week & Space Technology* (21 August 1995): 69.

Selgin, G. A., and White, L. H. "How Would the Invisible Hand Handle Money?" *Journal of Economic Literature* XXXII (December 1994): 1718–49.

Stix, G. "Fighting Future Wars." *Scientific American* 273 (December 1995): 92–98.

Susser, L. "Going Soft?" *The Jerusalem Report* (5 September 1996): 18–20.

Svec, F., and Frechet, J.M.J. "New Designs of Macroporous Polymers and Supports: From Separation to Biocatalysis." *Science* 273 (12 July 1996): 205–11.

Taubes, G. "First Atom Laser Shoots Pulses of Coherent Matter." *Science* 275 (31 January 1997): 617-18.

Tessler, N., Denton, G. J., and Friend, R. H. "Lasing from Conjugated-Polymer Microcavities." *Nature* 382 (22 August 1996): 695–97.

Topping, A. R. "Ecological Roulette: Damming the Yangtze." *Foreign Affairs* 74 (September 1995): 132–47.

Urbán, C. E. "The Information Warrior." *IEEE Spectrum* 32 (November 1995): 66–81.

Van Heerdan, P. J. "Theory of Optical Information Storage in Solids." *Applied Optics* 2, no. 4 (1963): 393–400.

Weisman, A. "Harnessing the Sun: Hydrogen Energy." *Los Angeles Times Magazine* (19 March 1995).

Edgar Award Winner
STUART WOODS
New York Times Bestselling Author of
Dead in the Water

GRASS ROOTS   71169-/ $6.50 US/ $8.50 Can

WHITE CARGO   70783-7/ $6.99 US/ $8.99 Can

DEEP LIE   70266-5/ $6.50 US/ $8.50 Can

UNDER THE LAKE
70519-2/ $6.50 US/ $8.50 Can

CHIEFS   70347-5/ $6.99 US/ $8.99 Can

RUN BEFORE THE WIND
70507-9/ $6.50 US/ $8.50 Can